GW01326521

LOUISE VA

Into
Thin
A Robyn Walters
Mystery
Air

Dear Andrea

Happy Reading!

from Louise

xx

Twynham Press
Copyright © Louise van Wingerden 2019
Louise van Wingerden has asserted her right to be
identified as author of this Work in accordance with
the Copyrights, Designs and Patents Act 1988

ISBN 978-0-9566-9379-2

1

It's Monday morning, I'm at work early, and for once my editor seems to notice that I'm making an effort. Jack calls me into his office before I have a chance to take off my coat. I sit down in the chair opposite his and he pushes something across the desk towards me.

'Robyn,' he says, 'I've got a job for you. It's a week-long assignment. Not even that, in fact. You get to stay in Netley College for Psychic Skills – for five days. You're enrolled as a student on a course called 'Channelling the Spirit'. You take part in the course and then you write up the story. That's all. And of course, it's all a load of crap. But you should go with an open mind.'

My head is spinning. What is this Jack's saying? A college for psychic skills? And – it's a load of crap, but I should keep an open mind? I glance at the glossy college brochure on the desk. It's decorated with some sort of New Age symbols and coloured in pastels and gold. It looks like the art project of a highly-strung child. 'A college for clairvoyants?' I really shouldn't interrupt my boss, or laugh when he's not joining in, but I can't help it. 'Channelling the Spirit? Honestly?'

Jack might be middle-aged and balding, but he has a commanding presence. When he looks at me over the top of his glasses, I feel his disapproval and start digging fast.

'What I mean is,' I say, 'surely they don't actually teach you how to read tea leaves or, um, look into crystal balls or whatever? It must be just learning techniques to kind of…intuit, or guess….' Even to my own ears, I don't sound convincing, so I take a different tack. 'It sounds… um…interesting.'

In fact, it sounds annoying. I'm supposed to be a reporter on a national broadsheet newspaper, which means that my job should consist of writing real stories about events that have actually happened. Not swanning off to spend a week studying mystical skills with a bunch of deluded crackpots, then writing up my experience of what happened. For a split second, I consider refusing to go.

That's not an option though. If Jack wants a story about a supernatural college, that's what he'll get. After thirty years working at The Globe, twenty of them as Editor of Features, my boss knows what sells papers. People want entertainment these days, not news, he's fond of saying. And I have to take any assignment he gives me, if I want to keep my job. Which I do. I love my work. I love living in London. I've dreamed of being a journalist for as long as I can remember, and the Globe is the top broadsheet in the country.

My career isn't going entirely smoothly, I admit. I always wanted to report hard news, but somehow, over the three years I've worked here, I've been well and truly side-lined into features. I decide on the spot that I won't give up though. I'll take this job and run with it and maybe it'll be just the break I need. In any case, it'll be good for me to get away from the newspaper for a few days. I'll have the time to think properly about what happened last Friday night with Rick and what, if anything, I want to do about it. At the thought of Rick my stomach flutters, as if it belongs to the vacant heroine of a Victorian romance novel. Traitor, I tell it silently.

Jack is still scanning me. 'It will be more than interesting,' he says. 'You're lucky to get this job, Robyn. This Netley College is like a boutique hotel.'

I begin to flick through the brochure as my boss continues. 'You stay at the place, get fed and watered, and all you have to do is listen and take notes. What I want to know is basically, what sort of a college is this? Who are the staff, what do they teach, what are the other students like? – And when I say what are they like, what I want is their motivation. Do they really believe they have magical powers? What's led them to the point in their lives where they're ready to part with their hard-earned cash to study the sort of things that are supposed to be taught on this course? If you can work some humour in, all the better.'

I slip the glossy pages into the back of my A4 notebook. Humour, I write carefully, then underline it. I pause before speaking. 'Um... I was just wondering whether there is anything else. I mean, any other reason why you want me to go to this particular college.'

Jack continues to examine my face closely. Maybe he's intending to pick up a pencil and draw my portrait from memory once I leave his office. 'You're not as silly as you look,' he says at last. 'Okay, Robyn. It's like this. I've had a tip-off from a member of the public who thinks Netley Hall Psychic College is not entirely above board. Normally I'd ignore it, because it's pretty obvious that any place which claims to teach people to develop their paranormal powers is not going to be kosher. On the other hand, it's occurred to me that there might be a story in this. Call it instinct, if you want.'

'Jack, instinct, story,' I say aloud, writing the words carefully in my notebook as I do so. He's looking at me hard, wondering if I'm taking the mickey, but I keep my face stony straight and he lets it go.

'In any case, we can't lose,' he goes on. 'Psychics are all the rage at the moment. The middle classes are having tarot readings after their dinner parties, the office workers are talking about their horoscopes over the water coolers. Whatever happens, this piece can't fail to engage the public interest, providing you make it fun to read. And now you know everything.'

Somehow, I don't think that's the case. What is it that Jack's not telling me? He's keeping it deliberately vague. Who, I wonder, has tipped him off, and about what in particular? But if he knows more, he's obviously chosen not to share the information with me. I don't ask any more questions and when he says, 'Got it?' I take my cue.

'Got it,' I say, standing up. I'm still wearing my coat

and I'm swelteringly hot. 'And thanks for the job,' I add, trying to sound grateful. 'I'll go and get started on some research. When do I leave?'

2

I take the coat off and hang it on the back of my chair in the open-plan news room. Stretching expansively, I let out an exaggerated sigh as I fire up my laptop.

Jack has caught me on the hop. He's booked me onto a course starting tomorrow, which means that I have to be at Netley College in less than twenty-four hours. And it isn't as if the place is just down the road. It's in Sussex, near a village I've never even heard of before, Micklehurst. On the bright side, the search engine tells me that Micklehurst is only ten miles from Brighton, which means I can drop in to see my parents on the way back to London on the Saturday. As my mum keeps reminding me, they're overdue a visit. –

Jack must have signed me up for 'Channelling the Spirit' before he even asked whether I'd go on the course. Did he ask me or tell me? I'm not actually sure. But then, that's normal, I know. When you work for someone, they make the plans and you carry them out. I'm basically a wage slave.

I hear a cough and look up to see Rick just a few feet away, sitting at his desk and grinning across at me. I smile back, warily. It's unusual to see him in the office these days. He's far more likely to be out on a news story – the sort of story I'd like to get my own teeth into.

I'm more than a little jealous of how Rick's career has taken off, in fact. We started on the Globe as trainees together, straight from Uni, and somehow he's flying and I'm not. It feels unfair. I work as hard as he does. But I can't keep a grudge against Rick for long – he's good fun and we've shared a fair few laughs in the time we've been colleagues. What I'm not sure about is whether we should have taken it any further. This is the first time I've seen him since he woke up in my bed on Saturday morning and I don't know quite how to behave, so I'm glad when he speaks first.

'Thought you were going to huff all the papers off my desk with your dramatic sighing. You've got a face like thunder,' he says. 'I gather it wasn't a great meeting?'

How does he even know I've been in with Jack? I have to give Rick credit; he's a born journalist, nosey to a fault. He's also pretty fit. I realise I'm lusting over him instead of answering his question, and pull myself together.

'It wasn't,' I say, holding up the Netley College leaflet. Rick swivels in his wheeled chair to look over then glides on it, over the coffee-stained carpet, towards my desk. He leans in close to read over my shoulder and I take the opportunity to breathe in the scent of him. Cologne mixed with eau-de-Rick. Heady.

He reads intently, lifting the glossy paper from my hands to turn the pages. 'Intriguing,' he says. 'A college for clairvoyants. So, what's the story?'

'That's what Jack wants me to find out. He's sending me there for a spot of 'Channelling the Spirit'. I may be gone for some time. But just you wait until I get back, because I'll be able to see into your soul…'

Rick grins again. 'Can't wait.' He rolls away on his chair, leaving me to mull over the Netley brochure and the week ahead.

I'd better get on with the job. My laptop has timed out, so I type the password in again and begin to write in the search engine: Netley College for Psychics. Not for the first time, I wonder how on earth journalists managed to do their research pre-internet.

I spend the rest of the morning trying to find out about the college. I find a slick website, from which I gather that Netley College seems to be a successful business. Courses run for five days each week, from Tuesday to Saturday. Each course has a maximum of six students, who pay two thousand pounds each. It sounds like a money-spinner. I gaze at a photo of the owners and course directors, Laura Barker and Danny Collins, who between them apparently do all the teaching at Netley Hall. They look like a glamourous couple, standing close and smiling broadly, and I wonder whether their relationship is personal, but there's nothing about the two of them anywhere online except the college website.

In fact, apart from the official website, I hit a total block in my Netley College research. There's no online information about the place from any other source. Most institutions thrive on publicity but in this case there aren't even any reviews from past students. Which is unusual, considering that according to the website the college has been established for almost a hundred years, and run by Laura and Danny for the last eight. I am getting increasingly bored and frustrated as Rick appears by my side. 'Hey Robyn,' he says. 'Hate to interrupt, but you've had your face glued to that screen all morning. Coming for lunch?'

I smile and nod. I check that I have my phone, then pick up my bag, ready to go. I suddenly feel embarrassed of the bag, which is brown leather, battered and many years old, one of my mother's hand-me-downs. I'm awkwardly aware, too, that my clothes are similarly old and scruffy. It doesn't seem to matter most of the time because none of the other journalists at The Globe bother much about what they wear – except, of course, the style and fashion writers, who are a completely different breed. Right now though, I wish I'd made more of an effort.

'Any luck?' says Rick, as we walk out of the Globe building. I look up at him blankly, straining my neck to do so because he is stupidly tall. 'I assume you're still doing the research for your holiday,' he says.

'Oh that. I was lost in thought. And it's hardly a holiday. Although Jack did compare it to a stay in a boutique hotel.'

'Maybe there'll be a spa,' Rick says. 'You can go for a swim. Get your nails done.' I glare at him. 'Joking aside, it sounds like fun. I'm a bit put out that he didn't offer it to me, actually. Why don't you want to go?'

'It just doesn't interest me. I'd rather be doing whatever it is you've been assigned this week. Which is what? Interviewing the PM? Or reporting on some massive fraud case?'

'If you want to know what I'm up to, you'll have to work your wiles on me.'

An image flashes into my head. Friday night, late. Rick in my bed, lying back, his deep blue eyes fixed on me. I push it to the back of my mind. 'The thing is, if I wanted to go away, I'd go somewhere sunny,' I say, 'and get right away from freezing February in miserable England.'

'Count yourself lucky. This is a cushy number for The Globe. You're getting a week off, in effect, and you'll probably end up with a large spread in the Saturday magazine with your by-line attached. Just go for it – enjoy yourself.' Yeah, right. Easy for him to say.

Rick and I have lunched together regularly over the years since we met as trainee journalists. We soon find ourselves at our usual café near Borough Market, sitting at the same small table we always choose, by the window. When the waiter arrives, I ask for coffee and Rick orders a cheese and tomato baguette.

'Tell me more about this college,' says Rick. He's genuinely interested, which is good because I want his perspective.

'It's odd,' I begin. The waiter brings Rick's food, and he starts to shovel in one huge mouthful after another. He's always teetering on the edge of starvation, a trait which I find strangely endearing. 'I haven't been able to find much at all about the place online,' I say. 'Everything I've got has come from the official Netley Hall website. The College was established in the village of Micklehurst, in Sussex, back in 1923. It's housed in a grand old building which used to be the home of the de Vere family. When it was inherited by two sisters, instead of selling the place or just living there, they set up the college. Spiritualism was all the rage at the time. When the last of the sisters died eight years ago, the new owners continued to run the College. It appears to be well-established and reputable. And yet it's hard to know for sure. There are no student reviews on the website or anywhere else online. It's not mentioned on any blogs either. There are various forums for clairvoyants, but whenever Netley Hall comes up, there's a tag underneath that says, "Post removed." I can't get a personal angle at all.'

I pause for breath. In the short time it's taken me to say my piece, Rick has already finished wolfing down the huge baguette. 'That does sound odd,' he says, wiping his mouth with his napkin. 'But surely that's why Jack's sending you. To find out more about the place.'

'I realise that, but usually when you search for something you get thousands of hits, and there's literally nothing on this.'

'Perhaps they've asked for information to be deleted. You know, when you search against somebody's name and it says at the bottom of the webpage that some results may have been removed due to data protection law. If they're...' He screws up his face to think and I experience an unexpected surge of tenderness – how sweet he looks. 'Inadequate, irrelevant or excessive,' he says, looking pleased with himself.

'Yes, the right to be forgotten. But that applies to people. Individuals, not institutions.' I know my stuff as well as he does.

'Well then, maybe that couple who run the place – Laura Barker and Danny Collins – have asked for their names to be removed from internet searches, for whatever reason. And that might be the bulk of what's been written about Netley College in recent years.'

I'm surprised, and despite myself impressed, that Rick noticed and remembered the full names of both college directors from his quick look at the brochure, back at the Globe this morning. 'Oh well,' I shrug. 'I suppose I can look into it later this afternoon. Make a few calls to people who might know something.' I don't actually have a huge number of contacts, but Rick doesn't need to know that. 'Or I can find out when I get there. I'm leaving first thing tomorrow morning.'

Now Rick looks surprised. 'That's quick. It'll be fine though, you'll see. And when you get back I'll cross your palm with silver, then you can look deep into my soul like you promised and tell me what you see.'

'Mmm. Thing is, it's not actually your soul I'm interested in,' I say, and his blue eyes crinkle in response.

3

I'm soon back at my desk, ready to find out as much as I can in the brief time available. I'd hit a brick wall with my research on Netley Hall but I soon discover that there are a number of clairvoyant colleges in the UK, and there's no shortage of information about most of them. After browsing various webpages and the links they lead me to, I settle on the Emily Shoreham School of Psychic Studies, which is based somewhere in Devon and looks pretty similar to Netley Hall.

I scroll through the Emily Shoreham website, looking at the list of courses offered. It must be a tricky balancing act trying to pretend to others, and perhaps even convince yourself, that you have a paranormal gift whilst simultaneously learning techniques to con the public. The course titles themselves don't give much away. They're couched in general terms like 'The Path to Natural Healing' or 'The Power of Spirit' and the accompanying blurb consists of phrases such as 'the theory of mindfulness', 'spiritual meditation' or 'the interpretation of body language'. Basically, these are subjects that anyone could teach, as long as they possessed a bit of general knowledge and the gift of the gab.

Interestingly, the courses are priced a lot more cheaply than the ones at Netley Hall. £650 would buy a week's stay, tuition included, for any one of the Emily Shoreham courses. And there are a lot more tutors there than at Netley Hall – one for each subject, it seems. Jack got ripped off when he paid two grand for my course. Not that I have any intention of pointing that out to him.

If I'm posing as a psychic student, I'm going to need to think up a backstory. Have I been aware of my clair-voyant powers since I was young, or did they just sneak up on me unexpectedly? Should I make out I'm just curious to learn more about clairvoyance, pretend I've had a vision of some kind, or say I believe I'm gifted with second sight? I could invent a mind-reading grandmother, or a friend who's noticed that I have a strange, totally accurate, ability to see into the future. I shrug and knuckle back down to my online studies. I can think about all that later.

Several hours on it's dark outside the Globe building, and I've learned a few things about the world of the average psychic. It seems to be a surprisingly ordinary sort of life, consisting largely of paid readings at coffee mornings, cafes, community centres and small village halls across the country. Many so-called mediums must earn virtually nothing. But then, of course, there is the phenomenon of the showbiz psychic. Nationwide, there are just a few of these, but they can draw huge audiences, packing out large public venues for up to thirty or forty dates each year.

None of it is as mystical and weird as I'd first imagined. In fact, the profession is starting to look like a cross between simple entertainment and a sort of spiritual counselling service. A business which mostly attracts the vulnerable as clients, as I'd thought. What I hadn't realised until now though, is that the clairvoyants themselves, with their poorly designed websites and over-sharing biographies, appear to be just as needy – and to genuinely believe in their ability to help others.

As usual, the web throws up a tangled heap of information. I read about Uri Geller, who once managed to convince the CIA that he had a genuine psychic gift, and about The Amazing Randi, who has devoted his life to proving that, on the contrary, Geller was nothing but a fellow-magician and a con-man. I learn of Doris Stokes, an extraordinarily ordinary-looking little woman from the North of England born in 1920, who billed herself as a professional medium and boasted a huge fan base by the time of her death in 1987. I discover the difference between psychics, who apparently possess powers of extra sensory perception, and mediums, or clairvoyants, who use spirit energy to communicate with the deceased – although in practice, these terms seem to be interchangeable.

The more I learn, the less overwhelming my assignment feels. In fact, I'm starting to look forward to it. There's a whole world out there that I didn't know existed until this morning, and I'm getting the opportunity to investigate it first-hand.

I realise, too late, that I haven't made any calls to try to find out more about Netley College. It's already past six o'clock though and I need to get home, packed and organised. Rick didn't return to the office after lunch. At the end of the meal he announced that he needed to be somewhere else and simply disappeared. Now I feel irritated, more with myself than him. Maybe I shouldn't have confided my feelings about being sent on this job. After all, Rick is my rival at work, whatever he might turn out to be outside it.

My phone pings and I pick it up to see a message from Rick. 'Have a fun trip. Missing you already.' Just when I was thinking of him. Maybe he's psychic. Although, of course, he has been on my mind about a hundred times today. I wonder for a moment what to text him back, scroll through the options for inspiration, and settle on a blushing emoji. A picture speaks a thousand words. Although the beauty of emojis is that the exact nature of those words is open to interpretation.

I take the stairs instead of the lift, nodding to the young, male receptionist on my way out into Bridge Street. It's drizzling, although that's hardly a problem because the entrance to the underground is just a few seconds' dash from the doors to the Globe building. I head into the depths. The tube is one of my favourite things about London. I like the anonymity of travel and the fact that nobody ever makes eye contact, meaning that I can observe other people closely. I enjoy riding the rackety, high speed trains, the sensation of being completely lost in the underworld and at the same time able to pinpoint exactly where I am on the multi-coloured maps. It reminds me of being on a roller coaster, this feeling of impending disaster co-existing with the knowledge that I am entirely safe. Almost, I remind myself as the train hurtles along.

I am almost entirely safe.

4

I count the stops on the Jubilee line automatically. Southwark, Waterloo, Westminster, Green Park – that's mine. I walk for about ten minutes in the company of a horde of other tired-looking, silent commuters through a poorly-lit concrete tunnel, then change to the Piccadilly Line for the second leg of my journey. – Comfortably seated again, I let my mind drift back to where it wants to dwell, on the events of last Friday evening.

A hard core of Globe journos, including Rick and Jack, head to the pub at the end of every working week. I don't usually join them but last Friday I decided to go for it. – I'd recently started to wonder whether schmoozing up to the boss over a few beers once a week was giving Rick the edge at work. If that was the case, then two could play at that game.

The Horse and Cart is a quaint old pub just a couple of minutes' walk from the Globe. Considering how close it is to central London, it's refreshingly tourist-free. That evening I arrived slightly later than the other journalists. I got a small vodka from the bar and made my way through a warren of small, dark rooms to where they were gathered. Jack was holding court with stories about old times at the paper, the days of worldwide scoops and wild adventures, when lunches were long and boozy and journalists were never held accountable. Everyone hung onto his words, but after an hour or so he said he had to get home before his wife sent out a search party. The rest of the group filtered out slowly, either back to their families like Jack or on to meet friends or for Tinder assignations.

Only me and Rick had no other plans and since he was hungry as usual, we decided to stay and eat. I followed Rick up the twisting staircase to the restaurant, noting how he had to fold his tall frame to fit under the low beams. We found a corner table, and from there the evening flew by.

Rick was always good company. We gossiped about fellow workers and he told me the juicy details of a story he was working on, involving a well-known politician and her private aide. The vodka must have helped me lose track of time, because I had no idea it was so late until the shout of the bartender calling 'Closing!' echoed up the stairs.

'We've got a long walk home,' Rick said.

'Have we?' I asked, emphasising the 'we'.

'Well, you need to sober up.'

'You have a point.'

'And I could do with a walk.'

'Right,' I agreed, with a curious mixture of relief and disappointment.

I don't walk much in London. I'm always in too much

of a hurry to feel comfortable taking the slow and scenic option, and anyway I like the Tube. That evening with Rick was a departure, and an eye opener. He led me away from the pub, down the Thames path. 'Butler's Wharf,' he said, looking around at the looming warehouses. 'It's where Dickens set Oliver Twist.'

'It's amazing,' I said, 'That a century ago, this place must have looked almost the same, and yet it was such a different world back then. I can almost see poor Nancy, running for her life from Bill Sykes. It sounds corny, but I feel as though we are a part of history, standing here in the place that inspired such great literature...'

I started to feel a bit self-conscious for waxing so melodramatic, but just at that moment Rick's hand found mine. I wasn't sure how it had happened, but I didn't pull away. I couldn't. It might have been the romance of the surroundings, or the effect of the moonlit, constant river set against that ancient, still flourishing, backdrop and our breath frosting into one mass in the cold, dark air, but all I could think about were the small but potent electric pulses urgently flooding my body. There was a nagging worry somewhere at the edge of my mind, but I refused to let it flit in any further. It's fine, I told myself. It's fine, for now. We're just holding hands. Meanwhile, another part of my brain was working out how I was going to get Rick through the door of my flat at the end of our long walk home, and dwelling on exactly what I hoped was going to happen once I had him in there.

Our hands stayed entwined all the way back. I sobered

up during the walk but my body remained on high alert from the contact of Rick's skin against mine. Rick was clearly impressed by the address of my apartment block. 'Kensington, no less!' he exclaimed when I told him where I lived, and when we arrived he didn't wait to be invited in, just followed me through the main entrance of the building, to the hall and up the stairs. My hands were numb with the cold. I finally managed to get my key into the front door and let us both into the flat. He stood speechlessly in the hall, staring in mock awe at the large crystal chandelier dangling from the high ceiling. It had been there when I moved in and I didn't even notice it anymore, but it made a definite impression on Rick. 'You must be loaded,' he said finally.

'It's not mine. The flat belongs to Katie, I rent a room from her.' I've always thought of myself as an honest person and was mildly shocked that the lie seemed to come so easily.

'Katie?'

'She's a lawyer. A barrister. My flatmate. My friend now, although I only met her when I moved in here.'

I didn't know why I lied. Maybe I was embarrassed by his reaction to the decor. Anyway, there was no time to dwell on it because I'd barely shut the door behind us before Rick's arms encircled my body. In response, I reached up and locked my hands behind his neck, pressing myself against him. The effect was incredible. I couldn't believe that I'd known Rick for three years and never experienced this before. What a waste.

We practically fell into the nearest room – the living room – and onto the sofa. His hand moved to my leg, which he began to stroke as he kissed me. I reached out and drew him closer, lost in the moment and the passion. I started stroking his leg too, then my hand ventured further...to my surprise he pulled back and began to sing, in a low, deep voice. 'Anything you can do, I can do better'. I collapsed, laughing so much that by the time I caught my breath again I felt like a new person. And I couldn't wait to get more of the man that I was clinging to so hysterically.

I woke the next morning feeling safe, rested and happy. Rick was just beginning to stir as I got out of bed and dressed, and he sat up and watched me lazily, smiling.

'Are you going to make the coffee, or shall I?' he said.

'Help yourself,' I told him, but the sarcasm was wasted. He stalked from the bedroom into the kitchen wearing my dressing-gown, of all things. I followed, feeling a bit annoyed at his presumption but also amused at how incongruous he looked striding confidently down the corridor with a bright pink towelling robe barely covering his bum.

I sat at the kitchen table, watching as Rick tried to figure out where the mugs were and how to use the kettle. I was smiling inside, calmer and happier than I remembered feeling for some time. Then I heard Katie's voice, low and mellow with a knowing inflection. 'Good morning Robyn...ooh. Good morning to both of you.'

I didn't reply. For the first time in a year, I found myself wishing I didn't have a flatmate.

Katie was leaning on the worktop, waiting to be introduced. 'Rick, this is Katie,' I said, and he glanced over his shoulder, smiling politely. Then he turned around properly and took a long look at her. I felt a spark of irritation. I knew Katie was attractive, but Rick had just spent the night with me. Did he have to stand staring at my flatmate like a hungry dog eyeing a bone?

'I've just remembered somewhere I have to be this morning,' I told Rick abruptly. 'I think you'd better go.' He didn't object as I ushered him out of the room, which annoyed me further. Katie was still smirking, and apart from how I felt about the fact that Rick wasn't bothering to hide his attraction towards her, I didn't want the two of them to get talking. I couldn't risk him catching me out in my fib about the flat ownership.

I didn't follow Rick to the bedroom to say goodbye properly while he got his things together. Instead, I stayed in the kitchen and when Rick popped his head around the door after a few minutes, I just said, 'Bye then!' and carried on chatting to Katie. If I felt a little guilty when I heard the front door closing behind him, I certainly didn't let on.

5

In any case, I reflect, things were perfectly normal between us at work today, which goes to show that Rick isn't harbouring any hard feelings about being kicked out on Saturday morning. I'm so deeply lost in thought that I don't notice the train passing through Knightsbridge station, the stop before mine, but luckily I've forced my mind back to the present moment as it halts at South Kensington.

When I leave the tube station, the roads are still slick with damp but the rain itself is only a faint memory hanging in the air. There's just a hint of back-blown drizzle as I walk rapidly along the familiar path home, turning into Queensberry Place after just a few minutes.

'Hi, Joe,' I greet the doorman at the Gainsborough, who touches the edge of his cap with an ironic wink. I like living opposite the hotel. Watching the comings and goings of the guests from my windows is a welcome distraction from the daily routine and I appreciate the presence of the security guys, Joe in particular. The crime rate along our short road is almost non-existent and I'm sure that's because they act as a deterrent to any trouble. I'm glad, though, that Joe wasn't on duty last Friday night. His eagle eyes definitely would have clocked my overnight visitor, and he wouldn't have hesitated to ask me about Rick the next day. Nosiness might be a part of Joe's job description, but I don't want to get involved in any discussions about my private life.

Crossing the road, I enter the building where I live, taking the stairs at a run. Home is a handsome Georgian townhouse, which my grandmother bequeathed to me several years ago. My grandparents bought the place when they married, scraping together all they could to finance the purchase and then dividing the building into flats and letting out two of them to help pay the bills. I now live in the third flat, on the top floor, which used to be theirs.

The original tenants still occupy the other flats – they've brought up their own families in this building just as my grandparents did. They pay only nominal amounts to live there – a peppercorn rent, it's called – but once they move out, which won't be long considering their ages, I can re-let their flats at proper London prices. I feel bad even thinking about this, but it means that, thanks to my grand-parents, I'll have an additional income as well as a home.

I spend most days commuting between home and work, practically a door-to-door journey. Because of this, during the week the only workout I get is incidental; the stairs at the Globe and at home, the short walk through the under-ground tunnel between Green Park and Hyde Park Corner. I make sure I put my back into the exercise. By the time I reach the second floor and turn my key in the lock, I can smell a heady mixture of garlic and turmeric. 'It's nearly ready,' Katie calls out as I enter the flat. 'I hope you're hungry.'

'It's better than having a wife. Separate bedrooms, my own space, but also great companionship and meals on tap.'

'Watch your step,' she retorts. 'Anyway, you're not my type.' I stand at the kitchen doorway watching as Katie stirs the pot. She's so pretty with her blonde bob and curvy figure, squeezed into one of many designer suits. When we're out together heads turn, and none of them look in my direction. Jeans, straight brown hair and a long, skinny body just don't produce the same effect.

We agreed to share the domestic budget after just a few months together in the flat, side-stepping the usual squabbles about who's drunk all the milk or gobbled the butter. Katie does the shopping and she likes to cook. She says it's a chance to relax after the strains of work. My part of the deal is to keep the flat looking nice. Actually, I pay a cleaning lady to do it, which amounts to the same thing. Life is too short to play at being a domestic goddess.

Katie really is the perfect flatmate, as I'd told Rick. We've shared for almost a year and never had a serious falling-out. Although we're both single we don't socialise together a lot, but around a year ago when she first moved in, Katie took me out to for dinner at Lincoln's Inn. As she explained it, there are four Inns of Court and every barrister has to belong to one of them. While they're training, the students have to eat a certain number of formal dinners there every year, even if they're based outside London. Once the student barristers are accepted to the bar they only attend dinners on a voluntary basis.

Katie has continued dining at her Inn regularly though. She finds the traditions comforting, she says, and apparently the opportunities to network are useful. And when she took me there, I understood immediately why Katie liked the place. The dining hall was amazingly grand and ornate, like something out of the Harry Potter books. Also, it was packed with intelligent, good-looking lawyers. If I'd been looking for a partner it would have been the perfect hunting ground.

Katie introduced me to a couple of her work colleagues, although I didn't join in much with the conversation. They were talking shop and the legal terminology seemed like a different language. After a while, one of the older barristers sitting nearby asked who I had come with, and looked surprised when I said it was Katie. 'Really?' she asked and was about to continue speaking when Katie interrupted. 'I don't think my friend feels comfortable being interrogated, Sarah,' she said crisply. I was about to assure her that I was fine, but Katie took my hand and pulled me up from the table. 'There's someone I want you to meet,' she said.

It was obviously an excuse to get away. 'Let's get a drink,' she said, leading me to the bar area. I followed, confused. She ordered the drinks – vodka and bitter lemon for me, and just bitter lemon for herself. Katie rarely drank alcohol. 'Sorry to drag you away, Robyn. That woman doesn't like me. She's always trying to nose into my business.'

'She seems so nice,' I said, glancing over my shoulder at the well-dressed, perfectly groomed Sarah, now making polite conversation with the person sitting to her left. Katie looked annoyed at my comment. 'I'm sorry she's giving you a hard time,' I added. 'Do you have to work closely with her?'

'Never mind,' Katie said. 'I probably over-reacted.'

We stayed at Lincoln's Inn late into the evening and I enjoyed myself a lot, but Katie didn't invite me to any of her work events again. Which doesn't bother me – it makes perfect sense to keep my home and social lives separate. It does mean, though, that since I rarely go out with my workmates either, I end up at home either alone or with Katie a lot of the time. A few of my friends from school and University used to visit when I first moved to London, but contact has gradually tailed off. I still miss them a bit, but as time goes on, life seems to close up around the gaps.

Perhaps that's why I got together with Rick. Maybe I'm just lonely... My thoughts have come full circle, and I chide myself for fixating on Rick. I should probably just put him out of my mind. An entanglement with him would not be good for my career, or my self-esteem. That flutter in my stomach is back though, and it's telling a different story.

6

I feel lucky to have met Katie. When I first moved into the flat three years ago, straight down from Newcastle after my finals, it made sense to look for a flatmate. But when I raised the subject, my parents both insisted that they didn't want me to share the space with anyone else.

'We just want to know that you're safe,' my mother said. 'And comfortable. Maybe we can come up and stay with you, now and again.'

They never had come to stay, which was a relief. I love my parents but once I left home to go to Uni I didn't want to live with them again. Two's company but three's a crowd, as the saying goes, and in my opinion that applies to family situations as much as any others.

I lived alone for a couple of years before I decided to go ahead and look for a flatmate. It was my home and my choice to make, after all. I put a flat-share advert in the local supermarket. It was just one of those slips of paper that slot into a board and I wasn't even sure that anyone would see it. Later, I decided it must have been fate that Katie spotted the advert so quickly and that she turned out to be the perfect candidate – female, close to my own age, and with a professional job.

The timing, in fact, was immaculate. I'd literally just placed the ad on the noticeboard, and in the general super-market bustle and noise I was barely conscious of someone at my shoulder until Katie spoke. 'I can't believe it! Here I am, looking on the board to see if there's a room to rent, and then you arrive and put a card on asking for a flatmate. My name's Katie, and...' I was staring at her, confused. 'Er...it is for you?' she asked. 'The advert? The flatmate?'

I took in Katie's appearance, noting the eager puppy behaviour, slightly at odds with her smartly tailored suit. 'I am looking for someone to share with, yes,' I said. 'So...let's go for a coffee and talk it through.'

We hit it off instantly over coffee, and it was an easy decision to let Katie move in. I didn't tell my parents about it for a few weeks though. It was Katie's idea that I should. I'd been saying that they hadn't been keen on me looking for a flatmate and Katie suggested that I should just bite the bullet. 'Get your dad over for dinner one night. On his own. Men love me. Especially older ones. And especially when I wear something revealing.'

'I don't think Dad is going to be bothered by any of that.' I laughed and she blushed endearingly.

'Oh no, of course', she stammered, 'I didn't mean anything...I was just being silly.'

I was pleased that Katie didn't dress too provocatively on the appointed evening. I'd invited my father over on his own, as she'd suggested. He came to London for work regularly anyway. It would have been more of an effort for my mum to travel up from Brighton mid-week and there wasn't really any need. Dad could tell her about Katie. It was the coward's way out for me, but so what?

The evening went well. Katie cooked up a storm – Chinese beef noodles and stir fried veg, which just happened to be my father's favourite – and entertained us both with her tales of court and various clients. She was a skilled storyteller and my dad thawed considerably as the evening went on. It was late when he announced that he was leaving in time to catch the last train home.

'Bye, Toby!' Katie called out cheerfully as I walked him to the front door.

'Sorry I didn't tell you that I have a flatmate, Dad,' I said to him quietly. 'I just wanted you to meet her and make your own judgement. She's such a good friend to me already.'

My father smiled and for a moment I thought he was going to say something, but he simply kissed me on the cheek. 'I'll see you soon,' I assured him. 'Give my love to Mum.'

Katie turned to me triumphantly as soon as I shut the door behind my dad.

'Told you I'd win him over!' she gloated.

'I acknowledge your superior sucking-up skills,' I said, and Katie took a mock bow.

7

The delicious aroma wafting from the copper pot that Katie is tending has made me hungry, and I breathe out in relief when my friend places two bowls heaped with food on the kitchen table. 'How's work?' I ask as we tuck in. 'Have you been in court today?'

'Same old,' Katie smiles ruefully. 'Too much pressure. It's as though they are trying to break the junior barristers before we have even got properly started. Survival of the fittest, I suppose.'

The stew is distracting. It's heaped with generous chunks of chicken and chorizo sausage, bulked out with rice and vegetables. The combination of flavours is delicious and I wonder fleetingly whether I should learn to cook. How will I manage if Katie ever moves out?

I try to focus back on the conversation. 'Like trainee doctors,' I say.

'I wouldn't mind, but I spent a long time training on virtually no income, and I've been fully qualified for four years now.' says Katie. She's a little older than me, twenty-seven to my twenty-four. 'I'm starting to wonder if things are ever going to change.' She continues to speak, tearing small pieces from a baguette as she does so, and dropping them lightly into her dish. 'I really would like to see some of the more interesting jobs. And the more lucrative ones. But you need connections in this line of work and if you're not part of the old-boy network...' She stops mid-sentence. 'What's up with you anyway? How was your day?'

'I thought you'd never ask,' I smile. 'There's something I'd like to run by you, actually. I have to go away for work for a few days.' I tell Katie about Netley College, the misgivings I'd felt about the assignment earlier in the day and the fact that I'm now looking forward to it. 'I feel the same as you do about wanting more interesting work,' I say. 'And this job beginning to seem promising, although I'm still miffed about how I have been pigeon-holed into features. I'm not sure how it happened, and I have no idea how to move on.'

'Is the paper sexist?' Katie asks. 'Or journalism gener-ally? It does seem to be mostly the women who write the features in the broadsheet papers, but I always thought that was because they preferred it.'

'It does feel like sexism, sometimes.' It's a relief to say it aloud. 'The Globe have only ever given me beauty, fashion and now features. I don't want this...this fluff in my life.'

'What is it you don't like about writing features?' Cross-examination is Katie's forte at work, she's told me. I can believe it – her gift lies in asking the right questions and always seeming to be genuinely interested in my answers.

'It's just so – frothy,' I say. 'Pointless.'

'I don't agree. It's entertaining, but there's no shame in that. People need to be distracted from the harsh realities of life. I can't wait to read your piece about the psychic college.'

I smile. Katie spends hours every weekend reading the magazines and supplements from all of the newspapers, which I buy for work purposes. It always surprises me that she never even glances at the proper news, given that she works in the law. I suppose she needs a break from the serious stuff, at the end of a gruelling day in court.

'I had lunch with Rick today,' I say, by way of a subject change.

Katie looks at me in a way that reminds me of Jack, in his office this morning, glaring at me over the top of his glasses. 'Isn't he the one who stayed over on Friday night? And then you turfed him out the next morning, unfed and unwashed. You didn't even make him a coffee.'

'I don't think he was bothered.' I laugh. 'He didn't mention it today. He's good fun and we've been mates for a while, that's all. It's just a fling.'

Katie's holding the Netley College brochure and studying the picture of Danny with Laura. 'This guy's fit, I have to say. Positively George Clooney-esque. Definitely my type. Do you think they're a couple?'

'I was wondering that myself,' I say. 'I can't seem to find out anything much about this Netley place. I was going to phone around a few people, try to find out whether Danny and Laura had somehow managed to get the college records taken offline, but I ran out of time – or rather, I got side-tracked by all the stories about psychics.' I take another forkful of stew. 'I can't believe Jack is sending me off in such a hurry. I'll just have to do my research on the job. It would be so much easier if the paper just sent me to interview them.'

'Right. Not as much fun though. Didn't you just say you were looking forward to the experience?'

'I like the thought of undercover journalism. It will certainly be more interesting than the average week at work. But the psychic thing seems…laughable. Even a tiny bit spooky. I mean, isn't this the occult?'

'Plenty of people do believe in that stuff though. And some find comfort in it.'

'I know. I'm just not one of them. But it is a step forward for my career, in a way. A proper assignment. Rick even claims to be a bit jealous that Jack is sending me and not him.'

'Does Rick know you're pissed off?' Katie asks. 'About him getting proper news stories to report on, and you being dumped with writing features?'

'Rick?' I splutter. 'He's the last person I can talk to about that. He started on the paper the same week as I did, and was given proper news jobs from the beginning. Now he's well on the way to promotion. But I don't want him to know I'm jealous. It's not his fault, after all, that I'm not happy with my career. And I can't tell him I think the paper is sexist…he's a man. It will just come across as sour grapes.'

'You don't think you can trust him? Either personally or professionally?'

'It's not that I don't trust him. I'm just being cautious.'

'Do you think he's a gold-digger?' Katie's never been one to beat around the bush, and I'm surprised by the strength of my reaction to her words.

'No!' I exclaim. 'I really don't,' I repeat, more calmly. 'He's got a good job and he's not that sort of a person. Anyway, I told him the flat was yours.'

'Did you?' Katie says. She sounds fascinated. 'So,' she muses, 'it must have been at the back of your mind that he could be after your money. I diagnose guilt at your own good fortune. Perhaps mixed with a little natural suspicion.'

I digest this for a moment. 'Whatever,' I say. 'Anyway, I'll stop boring on.'

I've stacked the bowls and am taking them to the dishwasher when Katie says, 'Why don't you ask your mother?'

'Ask her what?'

'About the psychic college place. You said it's at Micklehurst and your parents live in Brighton, right? Isn't that nearby?'

'It is,' I say. 'It's just a few miles away, I was thinking of popping in to see them on my way back on Saturday. You're right, one of them might well have some local knowledge of the place. I should have thought of that. I'll call them.'

I say goodnight to Katie and go to my bedroom, but I don't phone home after all. A call to my mother is never a short one, it's getting late and I need to get on with packing. I cast an eye over my wardrobe, trying to decide what a psychic, or a student psychic, might wear. I don't own anything tie-dye, embellished with sequins or tassels or otherwise hippy-ish in nature, so decide to attempt a vaguely Gothic look. I pack one blue and two black pairs of jeans and the darkest coloured tops and sweaters I can find. Then I organise the slim folder of notes I've assembled on Netley College and similar institutions and pack that too.

I hesitate over whether to bring my laptop. Somehow, I don't think many people will be working on their computers at a college for clairvoyants. I can't bear to leave it at home though. It would feel as though an integral part of me was missing. And it might come in useful. I could make a start on writing the piece up while I'm away. Eventually, I slide the machine into its slim leather sleeve and wedge it safely into the side of my suitcase.

8

I take a while to drop off and sleep only fitfully. I'd set the alarm for 5.15am but I wake even earlier and switch it off before it rings. I'm tired but that doesn't worry me. I'll get plenty of rest at the College.

Katie's lucky that she never needs to get up early. The courts don't get started much before ten in the morning, she's often told me. I do my best not to wake her, padding softly around the flat, showering as quietly as I can. Before going to sleep last night, I'd placed my case ready by the front door and now I scoop it up and open the door softly. I won't bother with breakfast. I can always grab something to eat on the train later.

It's six am when I leave the building. Joe is on duty at the door of the Gainsborough and I cross over to tell him that I'm going away for a few days. 'Have fun!' he says. 'Are you leaving that flatmate of yours home alone, then? I'll make sure she doesn't head off with the family silver, shall I?'

I laugh, but feel slightly uncomfortable. Joe doesn't like Katie. He never has and he's never said why, he just makes sly digs about her now and again. I don't question his attitude – Katie's my friend after all, and I don't want to hear bad things about her. Then again, I think of Joe as my friend too, although I usually only nod to him on my way home, or sometimes stop for a quick chat and a gossip about the goings-on in the hotel. Maybe I should get out more, if I've reached the point where I'm starting to count the doorman who works at the hotel across the road as my buddy.

I've travelled between London and Brighton enough times to know the train schedule by heart. A tube, then an over ground train, takes me to Clapham junction, where I buy a latte in a cardboard beaker and settle down to people-watch. There aren't many people travelling in my direction at this time of the day – most of the Brighton commuters are heading into London, not out.

My father used to commute to the City daily, but over the last few years since his parents died he's come into London less frequently. He used to run a management consultancy, but he's semi-retired now and just spends two or three days at work here. Which must suit my mum, since she basically retired twenty-four years ago, when I was born. I often wonder why she never went back to work. She's got a degree in marketing and before she met my father, she used to travel all over the world promoting a luggage firm. It sounds like fun. And yet for as long as I can remember she's had practically no life outside the home. She meets the odd friend occasionally for coffee or lunch, but she's still young, not quite fifty, so most of the people she knows have busy working lives, which means that she's alone an awful lot of the time.

The Brighton train arrives like clockwork at 6.40 am, and I find a double seat in a half-empty carriage. Just under an hour later, we pull in at Brighton station. I get off the train and breathe a sigh of relief as I look around. I can feel the Brighton vibe already. It's so relaxed compared to London I think, as I inhale the tang of the sea air drifting up the hill.

There are no taxis waiting at the rank so I call one. Being a local girl, I have the number on my phone – and although the man who answers my call isn't impressed when I say where I'm heading – 'Micklehurst? That's almost ten miles – this early in the morning!' – he agrees to send a car.

I'm a little taken aback when the taxi driver gets out of his cab to help with my bag. He's built like the Hulk, covered with tattoos and is wearing just a thin T-shirt, although there's a heavy frost in the air. I usually sit next to the driver when I take a taxi on my own, but now I climb into the back of the cab, although this feels a little rude. It soon becomes obvious that I've misjudged the guy, who navigates slowly and carefully along the city streets, holding my eye in the mirror as he makes polite conversation. When I say, 'I can't believe the number of homeless people on the streets since I was last here. There seem to be whole settlements of them,' he launches into a long story about how the London councils give these people one-way tickets to the seaside towns, usually Brighton or Portsmouth, so they're no longer the problem of our capital city. It leaves me open-mouthed. 'How is that possible?' I ask.

'The councils do what they want. They're the law, innit?' he says, shrugging.

If this is true, it's a scandal, something that people should know about. I make a note on my phone, 'One-way tickets for the homeless?' I'll look into writing a piece on it, as soon as I get back to London. It must be bad enough being homeless, dispossessed. To be moved from place to place like unwanted human garbage can only add to the indignity. It's inhumane behaviour and my blood's boiling at the thought of it.

The car leaves Brighton and heads out into the surrounding Sussex countryside of winding lanes and tall hedgerows. We arrive at Netley Hall just before eight o'clock and I ask to be dropped at the top of the driveway, so I can walk up to the entrance. The course isn't due to start until nine-thirty, but arriving early is part of my plan. It's a technique I picked up long ago, before I started at the paper. Get to an appointment early, and there's every possibility you'll find out something that somebody doesn't want you to know.

'Twenty-six quid. Are you sure you don't want a lift up to the Hall? It's quite a walk, love.' I smile and pay the driver with three ten pound notes, telling him to keep the change as I hand over Jane Austen's portrait immortalised in plastic triplicate. I dismiss his warning about the walk. It will be invigorating. The February morning is cold but bright and the air, although crisp, has no bite to it.

The taxi-driver is right, though. It's quite a distance up

to the main house. The driveway seems to go on endlessly, and I follow tailored hedges curving past count-less outbuildings for what feels like miles before I finally see the grand Georgian façade of the Hall rising up before me. I'm shocked. The course brochure, glossy and alluring as it is, did not imply quite this degree of opulence. Netley Hall, College for Psychic Studies, is practically a stately home.

9

I follow the driveway around, past lushly cultivated lawns, to where several cars are parked at the back of the building, near what must once have been the tradesman's entrance, and press the doorbell. I'm not kept waiting long. I smile brightly and innocently at the woman who opens the door, who I recognise immediately from her photo. Laura Barker is a suitable chatelaine for Netley Hall, elegant and immaculately groomed with mid-length hair that looks expensively cut and highlighted. It's hard to tell her age, even at close quarters, but I'm guessing she's in her mid- to late-fifties. She resembles an exclusive divorce lawyer, the sort who works in central London and only accepts Russian billionaires' wives or members of the English aristocracy as clients.

She speaks clearly, in a measured tone. 'I'm Laura,' she says. 'Pleased to meet you. You must be Robyn Bennett.'

I can't help wondering how Laura knows it's me, rather than one of the other five students signed up for this course. I must be the first to arrive, since I'm more than an hour early, and I'm operating under a pseudonym assigned to me by Jack for the purposes of this job, so she couldn't have looked me up anywhere. The course application form, which Jack emailed me before I left, didn't include any information on my age or any photographic ID. So how has she worked it out?

It must be an educated guess. I feel a flicker of resentment as the realisation strikes that Laura is trying to impress me with her supposed other-worldly powers. I respond calmly, as though I haven't noticed anything in what she's said. 'Yes, I'm Robyn.' I extend my hand, aware that I'm being appraised in turn, that Laura is making her own judgements based on my jeans and long, loose hair. 'Pleased to meet you, too.'

'Of course,' she says. 'And this,' Laura inclines her head and a man emerges from the shadows, 'is Danny. My partner.'

Danny Collins looks as though he's stepped straight out of the glossy pages of the Netley College brochure. He has even features and thick, fair hair flecked with grey, a thoroughly fit body, and is dressed in a shirt and trousers combo that fit so perfectly I'm sure he can't have bought them off the rack. He's a similar age to Laura and although I don't usually find older men attractive, Danny's case, I decide as he takes my hand in a firm, smooth grip, is an exception. I remember laughing with Katie last night about whether he and Laura are partners in business, pleasure, or both.

'You're very early,' Laura says coolly. 'You'll have to wait in there.' She gestures towards a room down the hallway.

'Can I just quickly take my things upstairs?' I'm eager

to get a look around before the other students arrive.

Danny's voice is deep and cultured, and in contrast to Laura he smiles charmingly. 'The bedrooms are still being serviced.' I don't try to argue further as Laura ushers me down the corridor, past a few closed doors and into a space which she refers to rather grandly as the 'drawing room'. It looks to me more like the bar of a shabby seaside hotel. So far, the inside of the building is nowhere near as impressive as the outside.

Laura leaves the room and I position myself on a high-backed, slightly tired-looking brocade chair near the tall window, from where I can see lush green lawns spread invitingly before me. I know from my online searches that the college – which means, essentially, Laura and Danny – owns the freehold of this huge property. They'll have running costs to meet, but if the courses are regularly full – at two grand a pop – they must be making a fortune. Plus, the building itself is an amazing asset. I take my notebook from my bag. 'How much did L and D pay for Netley Hall?' I write. I can look it up when I'm back in London.

I decide to send a brief text to Jack to let him know I've arrived at the college, but the phone screen doesn't respond to my taps. It takes several seconds before I realise that I have no mobile reception. I'll have to communicate online through one of the message services. I'm left with only my thoughts for company for now though, and quickly make up my mind to explore after all.

Leaving the room as noiselessly as possible I stand in

the corridor, waiting to get my bearings. Black and white reproductions of old photographs line the walls. My eye is drawn to an octagonal table, with stacks of various magazines balanced on it haphazardly. They boast a variety of titles – Fortune, Spirit and Destiny, Psychic World. I'll have a proper look at those later.

The hallway is long and wide, and it leads off in two directions. One staircase curves down to what must be a basement of some sort and the other, which is grander with beautifully carved banisters, leads upwards. Down, I decide, might be more instructive, but as I take a step towards the stairs, Laura materialises from one of the nearby rooms. She turns to lock the door behind her, then fixes her gaze on me. She's blocking my path.

I stand stock still, like a guilty child expecting to be scolded, but Laura doesn't say a word. The silence is stifling until I speak. 'Er, hello. I was just looking around and…because, you see, I can't get a phone connection. I was just looking for you, to ask whether you know why?'

'There isn't one,' Laura says.

'No phone connection?'

'That's correct. And no internet either. It's a deliberate choice. We want our students to use this place as a haven from worldly distractions, just as we do ourselves. It makes it much easier to learn, too.'

I'm feeling slightly panicked. No mobile or internet access – is the woman unhinged? 'But – how do you manage?'

Laura smiles. 'Danny and I can remember the world as

it was pre-internet. We're not a million miles from anywhere. And we do have a landline. Would you like to use it?'

'Um, thanks, but I won't bother right now. It's not urgent.' I wonder how Laura and Danny manage to keep the College website updated, or indeed how they keep in touch with the world in general. It wouldn't be clever to question her too much right now, though, so I stay quiet. We continue to stand together in the hall for a long, awkward moment, then I hear footsteps.

A small nervous-looking woman is coming down the stairs. I put her age at around forty. When she sees us both watching her the newcomer looks startled, but Laura moves forward and extends a hand graciously. 'Hello. I'm Laura Barker. Director of studies. And this is Robyn Bennett, who will be studying with you this week. Did Danny let you in? Did he send you to find me? I'm assuming you are a new student too?'

'Er...yes. I'm Sophie,' the other woman says. She's staring like a rabbit caught in headlights.

'Well,' says Laura. 'You two can wait together in the drawing room. I still have a few things to prepare for this morning.' She walks Sophie and I to the room I've just vacated. The two of us sit down obediently, while Laura heads off back into the depths of the house.

Silence rules for a minute or more. Sophie is so fidgety that just being in her presence makes me uneasy, and it's a relief when she asks the time. I check my watch and groan. 'Only eight thirty. I arrived at eight and have been shut up in here ever since. Laura caught me trying to escape just now.'

Sophie's eyes widen before she realises I'm joking, then she forces out a small, unconvincing laugh.

'What time did you get here?' I ask.

'Just now,' she says.

'So, how come you were allowed to put your bag upstairs already?'

She looks around the room, then down at my bag, confused. 'Um…I don't know. I just was.' She's agitated, clearly at a loss for words.

'What's your story, Sophie?' I ask gently. 'What brings you here?'

'Oh, you know…'. I obviously don't, but decide not to push the issue. Sophie is visibly panicked and continuing to interrogate her would make me feel cruel. Instead, I make small talk about the weather and the beauty of the surrounding landscape until she seems to relax a little. My mind is still racing though. How come I didn't hear the doorbell or voices in the hall when Sophie arrived? And why had Sophie been allowed to put her bag away upstairs, when I wasn't? I find my notebook and write a single word. 'Sophie'. I put a question mark next to it for good measure.

Gradually, the other students filter in. I introduce myself to Hilary, who looks to be in her late forties, with thick, curly auburn hair, gaudy clothes and too much make-up, and Charlotte, who's not much older than me and a lot more smartly dressed than I am. It's only when two male students appear in quick succession that I realise I'd assumed the group would be all female.

There are now six of us – the full complement. I don't introduce myself to either of the two men, who seem in any case to be quite intent on speaking to one another. The room feels crowded and it's noisy with the buzz of conversation as nine o'clock comes and goes and we're all still waiting. Finally, Laura enters and tells us that we can take our bags to our rooms, although we'll have to come back downstairs as soon as possible for the start of the day's classes.

'I have a schedule for each of you,' Laura says, 'which gives your timetable for the week ahead. I hope you are all looking forward to it as much as Danny and I are.' She hands a sheaf of papers to Charlotte, who quickly passes them around. Then all of us, clearly relieved to escape the confines of the drawing room, head as one up the stairs.

On the first floor, the air of faded gentility is even stronger. The carpets are old and threadbare, although everything seems clean enough. I see a small framed notice fixed to the landing wall and stop to read the handwritten lettering. 'The cats are trusted and valued members of college staff. Please do not pet them or take them to your rooms.' I can barely suppress a snigger at this, and make a mental note to feed it back to Katie at the earliest opportunity.

I nudge Hilary, who's standing beside me, and smirk knowingly at the sign. She glances at it, then returns my look with a disapproving stare. 'You'll get nothing out of this experience if you have the wrong attitude,' she says sternly. I feel a stab of irritation, then remember that I'm supposed to be gullible enough to have paid a lot of money to study at this college. I should be grateful to Hilary for reminding me of my student status.

Our schedules have our names and room numbers on the front pages, and I find my room easily. A metal number 4 is fixed onto the door, which is slightly ajar, and a key protrudes from the lock. I remove the key and pocket it, then enter the room and shut the door firmly behind me. The space is better than I expected from the rest of the college décor. It's clean, large and comfortable, with a double bed and an en-suite bathroom. I have a sense that it will be my refuge in the days ahead.

I glance at my timetable. Today is Tuesday and the session is called 'Channelling the Spirit'. Wednesday's tutorial will be on 'The Art of Reading'. On Thursday, we will receive instruction in 'Use of the Tarot'. On Friday we're going to be 'Feeling the Flow' and on Saturday morning we're just down for a short tutorial called 'Until we Meet Again.' Jack said he wants me to work some humour into the piece and I don't think that's going to be difficult. There should be some comedic value in the tutorial titles alone.

Netley Hall's website hadn't included course details, but the set-up of the timetable, tutorials in the morning and free time in the afternoon, is exactly the same as the information I read on the Emily Shoreham College website about their courses, although the Emily Shoreham courses were rather more imaginatively titled. There's an uncomfortable creeping sensation of worry in the back of my head. How am I going to cope for almost a week in this alien environment, in the company of people I have nothing in common with, and without any phone or internet to connect me to the rest of the world? I take my notebook out again. 'Why would anybody block access to mobile phone signals? And the internet. And how?' I write angrily.

It occurs to me that I don't have a clue how a person is actually supposed to go about undercover journalism. Is what I'm doing here – essentially, spying – even ethical? I try to think back to the ethics module on my journalism degree up at Newcastle. I only graduated a few years ago but it already feels like a different lifetime. Think, think. Oh yes. Journalists should obtain material openly, I'd learned, unless it is in the public interest to act differently. Well, exposing the con-artists operating at Netley Hall can definitely be described as being in the public interest. Anyway, I reason, it's not really my concern. Jack sent me here, so the ethics of the situation are his problem, not mine.

Ah well. Time to get to class. I grab my notebook and pen, pick up the timetable and take a deep breath before I head back downstairs, leaving the contents of my suitcase strewn over the bed.

10

My fellow students are also hurrying downstairs. We're directed to a room in the basement which, we're told, will be our classroom for the days ahead. The space is airy, with a high ceiling and classical proportions. Light floods in from a set of glass doors which open onto a sunken garden. Money has clearly been spent on this area of the house.

I haven't got my bearings properly yet; Netley Hall seems huge and unknowable. I am sure there must be space for more than six students to stay at a time and wonder why the courses are restricted to this number, and what all the other rooms are used for.

When Laura and Danny arrive, we're told that we're going to arrange our chairs in a circle. Laura then asks each of us to introduce ourselves and tell the others our reasons for attending the course. An ice-breaker – so far so normal I think, as the sound of eight sets of chair legs scraping on slate tiles assaults my ears.

The first person to speak, in the newly formed circle, is one of the male students. He's only a boy really, in his late teens or possibly early twenties, and he's skinny, with greasy mid-brown hair. His clothes are baggy and unkempt, and he looks like a victim of severe self-neglect.

'My name is Justin,' he says. 'And I want to understand what we are all doing here. I know I have magical abilities, as all of you do.' He's looking around the room intently, 'I can hear voices when people are not speaking. I can hear people thinking. I am tuned into the spirit world.' His voice is rising in both volume and pitch, and I intercept several uneasy glances from the other students. I'm feeling a little unsettled myself.

Laura and Danny, however, remain calm as Justin's monologue becomes increasingly animated and convoluted. When he finally stops speaking, Laura smiles kindly, as though she completely understands what he's trying to communicate. 'Thank you, Justin, for sharing with the group,' she says. 'Danny here is particularly knowledgeable in the field of spiritual attunement.'

She turns towards Danny, who nods sagely. 'Would you like to discuss this further on a one to one basis?' he says to Justin. 'Right now? We can grab a coffee in the canteen while we chat.'

Justin looks as happy and excited as a young child who's finally gained the undivided attention of a beloved parent. He's beaming as he leaves the room in the company of Danny. I'm impressed with the way his outburst has been dealt with so effectively. Perhaps Laura and Danny have a strategy ready for dealing with these issues. But how will Justin manage to study, when his ability to concentrate is clearly so impaired? And how can somebody whose personal life is clearly in such turmoil find the money for course fees in the first place? I have so many questions, but for now I only write one word in my notebook; 'Justin' with a question mark, just as I'd done for Sophie.

Laura speaks to Hilary. 'Would you introduce yourself next? Just say who you are, and why you're here. Then we'll continue around the circle in an anti-clockwise direction.' This will make me the last to speak, which can only be a good thing as I still don't have the faintest idea what I'm going to say.

I try to concentrate on Hilary's introduction, making brief notes in case I need them later. Hilary, whose dangling earrings and brightly coloured, loose-fitting clothing clash with her bright auburn hair, tells the group that she used to be a drama teacher. 'I had a wake-up call recently,' she says, 'and decided it was time to follow my true path.' I wonder idly what Hilary's enlightening experience consisted of. She might have told me off for laughing about the cat notice, but it's pretty obvious to me that Hilary's not for real. She's clearly signed up for the course with the intention of using her acting experience to play the part of a medium. She looks as though she's even dressed for the role.

Charlotte is next to speak. She unlike Hilary, does not fit in with my expectations of what an up-and-coming clairvoyant might look like. She's trim, smartly dressed, very pretty and young. She could be a successful sales executive, or even a lawyer like Katie. 'I've already had some experience of reading the Tarot cards professionally,' she says. 'But I would like to increase my clientele, so I enrolled on this course to learn to be more consistent in my predictions.'

'That's very interesting,' Laura says. 'I'm sure you'll find what you need here.' She glances around the circle. 'There are many different sorts of Tarot cards,' she continues, 'and as you will have seen from your timetables, we will cover this in the class tomorrow. The cards are very useful in many ways, especially as tools for starting conversations.' Conversation starters are a surprisingly rational way to describe the Tarot. I approve.

I continue to listen whilst taking notes. It's Sophie turn to introduce herself next and she starts by announcing, 'I am a psychic medium.' She's painfully nervous, trembling as she speaks. 'I've only recently begun to experience the other side breaking through.'

'It comes to us all in different ways, my dear,' says Laura. 'When we are needed, we are called.' I feel sorry for Sophie, who I think is in urgent need of counselling, and perhaps a course of calming sedatives. Encouraging her delusions is certainly not going to help.

The final student to speak (apart from me) is dark-skinned and very good-looking. I judge him to be somewhere in his mid-thirties. He tells the group that his name is Chris. 'I've recently been made redundant,' he says, 'from my job in sales, which means I have some time to explore my hobbies. I've always been fascinated by spiritualism and by the unseen and unexplained.' This seems a bit odd to me. You'd need a stronger reason than curiosity to stump up for a course like this, I'm sure. Something doesn't ring true, but Laura doesn't seem to notice or care.

'Thank you, Chris,' she says. 'I do hope that you will find this course to be of use to you.' Her gaze moves around the circle and comes to rest on me. I panic slightly as I mentally consider my options. I should have thought this through already. I sit up straight and take a long, deep breath.

11

'My name is Robyn Bennett,' I say firmly. The false surname was a sensible precaution on Jack's part. Some of the journalists at the Globe are celebrities in their own right but I don't get enough high-profile work on the paper for that to be the case. The by-line 'Robyn Walters' is rarely seen and never accompanied by a picture. I do have an online presence though, like everybody who works in the media, and an internet search under my real name might well uncover some personal information.

'I'm employed as a legal secretary,' I say, 'but I've been wanting to find out more about the spiritual world for some time. And,' I pause for effect, 'I have reason to believe that I might have some supernatural ability.'

'Indeed.' Laura raises one elegant eyebrow. 'Explain.'

'Well. There are a few things. My friend was expecting a baby and I told her – before the twelve-week scan – that I thought it might be twins. And it was. Another friend had just split from her partner and I told her that she would meet someone else really soon – and she did. You know…that sort of thing. It's eerie, sometimes. I even guessed that the new royal prince was going to be called Louis…'

I'm warming to my theme, but Laura cuts me off. 'Thank you, Robyn. That's very interesting.' The way she says it sounds as though I have failed to engage her interest at all and I feel, irrationally, disappointed. It doesn't matter, I know. I'm here to write an exposé of the college, not to impress the con-woman who runs it.

'Now,' says Laura, 'I will introduce myself. You all know my name, but what you don't know is that I have been communing with the spirit world since I was six years old. My experiences intensified following the death of both my parents in an accident, when I was just twenty-eight.'

She stops speaking for a moment as Danny and Justin re-enter the room. Justin goes to his place in the circle quietly, but Danny moves to stand next to Laura and takes her hand tenderly. Ah, I think, so they are a couple. Laura's eyes are dark pools, threatening to overflow with what look like real tears, as she continues. 'So I came to my vocation early in life. At first I worked as part of a team, but before long I set up on my own, working from a small office in London. I rented this tiny space in the centre of the city and people came from far and wide, from all over the world, to consult me. My name became known quickly and I was called upon ever more frequently – by both the spiritual and the material worlds.' She heaves a brave and tragic sigh. 'I met Danny during those years. He supports me in all that I do. He's my guiding light. And together, we moved from London to Netley Hall, to continue the work that the de Vere sisters began here back in 1923.' She smiles soppily at Danny for a long moment.

'Moving on, I shall talk,' about 'Channelling the Spirit'. I have to tell you that at this very moment in time, every answer we are looking for, all the truth we are seeking, lies within ourselves. The necessary skill, which we all possess and merely need to uncover, to bring to the surface, is that of listening to our inner selves and trusting our divine intuition. We have to be strong,' she continues, her voice rising in volume and conviction, 'in order to recognise that voice of intuition when it arrives. As I look at it, this is my higher self, telling me things I need to know. And you can all do the same, you can create that higher dimension within yourselves, tap into the magical opportunities around you, and allow something amazing to happen in your lives.'

Laura continues in this vein for some time, in fact for so long that I start to feel dizzy with the effort of trying to keep my mind rooted in the real world. She's said nothing of substance whatsoever and yet has somehow managed to impart a seemingly authentic air of other-worldliness to the room. I'm feeling increasingly disorientated, almost as though I've been hypnotised. As Laura's speech finally draws to a close, I look around the room to see that the group of students are rapt. Some, like me, are making notes as Laura speaks, but others are simply sitting still, eyes fixed on her, drinking every word in.

The more I see and hear at the Netley College for Psychic Skills, the more cynical and disillusioned I feel.

12

The open plan kitchen/dining area is also in the basement of the lovely Georgian mansion house, adjacent to our classroom. The food, which is brought to our table by the kitchen staff, looks fantastic. Laura and Danny lunch with the students, and the group is small enough to fit around one large farmhouse-style table, so that everyone has a chance to get to know each other. This is important, Laura says, because, 'This course, like the spiritual world itself, is all about connections. This is why we keep the groups small – so that we can connect.'

The food is indeed delicious, and Hilary compliments Laura on it. 'We employ an excellent chef,' says Laura. 'She lives in Micklehurst and, along with the rest of our small team, helps us to keep the college running smoothly. We like to take great care of our guests, and nutrition is of course the key to wellbeing. We grow our own vegetables and herbs in the kitchen garden.'

We tuck into our meal, and the conversation turns to ourselves and our lives in general, rather than our specific reasons for being at the college. It's a relief after the intense morning session. Hilary is the only one of the students who mentions children. All the others seem to be child-free, I note. I wonder whether it's usual for people interested in psychic studies to be childless. Perhaps parenthood helps people remain rooted in reality. Or maybe people with kids are simply too busy to think about anything other-worldly. What might Laura's take on this be? Maybe I'll ask if the opportunity arises although, of course, it might be a sensitive subject as she and Danny don't seem to have a family themselves.

After lunch – dessert isn't offered, disappointingly – Danny gets to his feet, raises a hand, and the room falls silent. It's the first time he's spoken to the students. I'd thought he and Laura would lead the classes together, but he seems to be the silent partner. Which is a pity, because he has a good speaking voice, well-modulated and educated in tone. A voice worth listening to. 'This afternoon,' he says, 'you're all free to follow your individual study paths. As you've seen from the timetables Laura handed out earlier, this will be the pattern for the week – you'll attend tutorials each morning, then be free each afternoon to think over what you've learned and continue with your studies or personal reflections. For this, you can either spend time in your rooms or one of the living spaces, or the library. If you'd like to follow me now, I will introduce you to the library.'

We all troop obediently up the stairs behind Danny. The library is on the ground floor. It's an extremely beautiful space, filled with wall to wall bookshelves and scattered with an array of very old but cosy-looking armchairs and sofas. 'Dinner will be served downstairs at seven,' Danny says, before he leaves the room.

Hilary is soon deep in whispered conversation with Charlotte in a corner of the library. Sophie retreats, probably to her bedroom. I listen as Chris asks Justin whether he'd like to go for a walk, a kind offer which, to my relief, is snapped up. Justin seems to have a need to talk constantly and I want to concentrate.

I stay in the library all afternoon, browsing. There's more to this stuff than I had realised. Volume upon volume, old and new, fill the library. The room is crammed with reams of information, and I don't know where to start. I pluck a few books from the shelves at random, take them over to a low, richly-upholstered armchair and begin to leaf through them. I start with a tome on the history of spiritualism, which turns out to be a surprisingly engaging book. I learn about the rise of the movement and the establishment of the spiritualist church. Arthur Conan Doyle himself, I discover, was a believer, and helped to establish a psychic college in the early twentieth century. Spiritualism was definitely a mainstream school of thought in the not-too-distant past.

I had a school friend, I remember, whose mother was a devotee of the spiritualist church. My friend – Denise, her name was – had been infected with its teachings. She once lost a bracelet in the park, and dragged me round with her for hours looking for it. It was like looking for a needle in a haystack, an utter waste of time. I thought. But then finally she'd kicked aside a pile of damp leaves as we went through an underpass and there it was, glistening silver against the tarmac. 'I knew I could do it! Spirit helped me!' she exclaimed as she bent to pick up her bracelet, and I thought, meanly, that she must have hidden it there herself just so she could try to impress me by pretending to find it.

Sometime during the afternoon Hilary leaves the library. Charlotte stays, getting her head down and studying hard. By contrast, I'm finding it difficult to concentrate, despite making detailed notes on the books I'm looking at. There's such a mass of information that I simply don't know what to believe, or how to separate the fact from the fiction. By the end of the afternoon my head is reeling with an impossible mixture of factual and spurious information on the nature of mystical phenomena. Perhaps Charlotte is getting some spiritual guidance to help her, because whenever I glance over at her she seems calm and contented, writing serenely. When the dinner bell goes at seven o'clock, she looks up from her notes as if emerging from a reverie and smiles at me warmly. We make our way to the dining room, where we sit next to one another and Charlotte talks for a while about how she misses her grandmother.

'I miss my grandparents too,' I say, truthfully. My mother had been orphaned long before I was born, but I'd loved my father's parents dearly.

'Do you speak to them, Robyn?' she asks earnestly.

'Um, no.'

'Have you tried?'

'I....' I'm not sure what to say. Of course I've never

considered speaking to my dead grandparents, but I don't feel that I can tell Charlotte that, since I'm supposed to be here to pursue my psychic studies. 'They don't answer.'

'Ah,' says Charlotte. 'That is a pity. I talk to my grandmother regularly.'

I consider this. Charlotte is so likeable and seems completely sane, yet believes she's in contact with her dead grandmother. I suppose if the idea gives her comfort it can't be a bad thing. Then again, when she introduced herself this morning, she said that she works with Tarot cards. Anybody who earns a living by drawing others into a fantasy world is definitely on shady moral ground, the way I see things.

I'm starting to think though, that the psychic career situation isn't completely cut and dried. You could say that if a medium genuinely believes in the existence of spirit world and in their own ability to converse with dead people, then they're not really actually fraudulently. In fact, if someone is seeking help from that quarter, it could be considered wrong for a 'psychic' not to try to provide assistance. Although of course, since it's fundamentally impossible to talk to the dead, it can't be right to pretend to…my head's spinning from the circular argument I've created in my own mind, and I decide to leave it for now. Maybe there are some things which just can't be worked out.

A few of my prejudices have been shattered already, though. I'd assumed that apart from being money-grabbing fraudsters in training, the students would be either strange or boring, or both, and that isn't turning out to be the case. It's almost a holiday-like atmosphere around the dinner table this evening, in fact. Everyone seems to be buzzing. Even Sophie has come out of her shell a little and is talking animatedly to Danny and smiling more than I have seen her do all day.

Justin is the only fly in the ointment. He's been for a long walk around the countryside this afternoon with Chris, who's now flopped into his seat at the dining table, declaring himself exhausted. Justin, on the other hand, is brimming with apparently boundless energy. He's talking non-stop to anybody who will listen, as if emptying a thousand fragmented and tangled ideas simultaneously from his brain. It's exhausting to try to follow even one of his many trains of thought. Fortunately, Laura and Danny's calm response to his behaviour has rubbed off on the rest of the group. By unspoken agreement, we take it in turn to listen politely to Justin's various strange ideas, whilst carrying on more normal topics of conversation around the rest of the table.

At the end of the meal Danny takes Justin off for what he says is 'private spiritual guidance.' I wonder what exactly this means, especially when Laura leaves the table soon after, saying she's going to join them. 'No dessert again then,' says Chris ruefully.

'Laura's opinion that sugar is an unnecessary addition to the human diet,' says Hilary. 'That's why there's no wine at mealtimes either.'

'Because it needs sugar to ferment?' I ask. 'Isn't that

taking things a bit far?'

Hilary looks at me sternly. 'Laura also believes that alcohol clouds the mind.'

'Well, durr!' says Chris. 'Isn't that the point?' and the rest of us laugh.

Despite the absence of alcohol at the table, we sit for hours chatting and it's late by the time I make my way upstairs. I move my laptop from its place on my bed, alongside the tangle of clothes and other possessions I'd left there in the morning. I haven't used it all day, having reverted to pen and paper for all my class notes. I'd intended to type these up before I went to sleep but instead I just write one word in my notebook, 'Tired.' I shower, then clamber dopily into bed and fall quickly into a deep and dreamless sleep.

13

I wake with a start. My ears are ringing and it takes a few seconds to work out what's happening, but as soon as I do – it's not my faulty hearing that's the issue here, it's the piercing shrill of a fire alarm – I leap out of bed in response.

I have no idea what the time is. The room is pitch black. I reach for my bedside light, but although the button clicks convincingly it doesn't illuminate the space. My brain's still sluggish, and precious seconds pass before I figure out there's no power. Above the ringing I hear loud cries of 'Fire! Wake up!' The voice is Justin's. It's strident and yet oddly dull and monotone, as though he's detached from what's going on.

I'm still dozy. Now I know it's only Justin sounding the alarm, I'm not sure whether to bother reacting or to just climb back into bed and put my head under the covers. There's no smell and no smoke, so there's almost certainly no fire. Justin is probably just delusional. He must have smashed the glass of one of the old, red fire alarm boxes I've noticed in the hallways. I sit down heavily on the bed but then stand again wearily. The memory of countless boarding school fire drills won't allow me to drift back to sleep in these circumstances. I can almost hear the insistent voice of my housemistress, Miss Tapper, 'Leave the area girls, take nothing. Never hesitate or your lives could be lost!' We used to stumble down to the playground in the middle of winter wearing only nightdresses, or even wrapped in towels straight from our baths. Anyone who took so much as a soft toy from her bed would be made to instantly regret it. Fire drills occurred like clockwork, once or twice each term, and Miss Tapper must have known that one day they would be good training for something.

The carpet is soft beneath my bare feet as I stumble out of the room into the disorientating darkness and make my way blearily down the stairs, still wearing the oversized T-shirt I've been sleeping in. I press a light switch on the wall in the hallway, but again nothing happens. The power is definitely off. I'm the first person to get downstairs, and I stand uncertainly by the front door. There's still no evidence of a fire, but Justin continues to shout and I can hear Danny too now, knocking on all the first-floor doors, rousing the other students. 'Assemble outside, everyone!' Danny shouts. 'In front of the building. You too, Justin.'

My eyes are getting used to the lack of light and I'm starting to see the blurry outlines of the hall furniture, and to make out the other students beginning to fumble hesitantly down the stairs. There's something out of place, I realise. It's the door to the room Laura had retreated to earlier this morning. Or was that yesterday morning, now?

The door she'd locked behind her when she'd caught me in the act of attempting to leave the drawing room and explore. Her office door. It's ajar.

I'm just pulling the handle of that door towards me when the hallway lights come on abruptly. I look up to see Laura striding along the corridor. 'It was the fuse box' she says. 'The main circuit was switched off.' She's fully dressed and wide awake. Interesting. So I wasn't the first person downstairs after all.

Lights are gradually flickering on all over the house, until the whole of Netley Hall appears to be blazing, although fortunately not with fire. I watch as the others come down the wide staircase, more confidently now that the lights are on. The students are in differing states of dress or undress and they move with varying degrees of urgency. Surprisingly Sophie, who I would have expected to be hysterical, seems completely unruffled, as though she's accustomed to middle-of-the-night disturbances. Hilary is the last down and she's not only fully dressed in one of her colourful outfits, but is carrying a large bag full of possessions. Miss Tapper would have made short work of her.

Justin has been ushered outside with the rest of the group and he's still yelling at the top of his voice, ranting not only about the non-existent fire now but about spirits and souls, ghosties and ghouls. From what I can see, he's taken a sudden and dramatic turn for the worse. The stream of consciousness spilling from his mouth is almost poetic, but it's disjointed and way more alarming than any kind of poetry could be. I can make out a few of the words and phrases, 'Across the river,' he shouts, 'along the way! Hey, Babylon, hence desire! The floods will engulf us all, so keep a straight path. Shekels and shackles, my friends, shekels and shackles.'

There's more in the same vein and none of it makes any sense at all. I can't help but feel scared at what seems to be Justin's total loss of control. He must be aware of reality on some level though, because he quietens as Danny takes hold of his arm and talks to him quietly. 'Listen to me,' I hear Danny say. 'There's nothing wrong with you. But people are going to think there is if you keep behaving like this.' To my amazement, within moments Justin is standing passively with the rest of the group, still muttering nonsense but at a much lower volume.

I'm shivering in my thin T-shirt. My arms and legs are completely uncovered and the night air is freezing. I wish I'd stopped to fish my dressing gown out of the wardrobe before I came outside. I smile momentarily as the image of Rick wearing the gown returns to me. But then I see my breath frosting in the cold night air and memories of the night we'd spent together assault my senses. It's just a few hours since I saw Rick and in any case our relationship is only in its fledging stage, yet I suddenly feel utterly bereft without him, and as alone as I have ever been in my life.

With a huge effort, I stop my thoughts in their tracks and concentrate instead on watching as Laura and Danny take a roll call. This night-time drama will make good copy I realise, bring my article to life. I note the reactions and behaviour of each student, looking for things I can use. Hilary, to my amusement, is insisting loudly that, 'I knew something was going to happen tonight.'

'Hindsight is a wonderful thing', I'll write when I report that comment. I watch Chris, in his pyjamas, talking quietly to Charlotte. Their heads are close together and it looks as though a romance might be budding. I can use that too. 'A psychic college might seem like an unlikely setting for love, but two of my fellow students only have eyes for each other.' Or words to that effect. I'll have to rely on my memory for all this of course, as for once I haven't got my notebook to hand.

Once everyone has been ticked off the list, we're told that we can return to our rooms. Danny has taken Justin aside and is speaking to him quietly while Laura beckons to the rest of the group to follow her. We assemble in the grand hallway huddled close, as if for warmth.

Charlotte is concerned for Justin. 'Shouldn't you call medical help for that poor boy?' she asks. 'He's clearly suffering.'

'The thing is,' says Hilary, 'He could be dangerous. What if he had set a real fire, instead of crying wolf? What if that's the next thing he does?'

'Unfortunately,' Laura says, 'there is no way to get emergency medical help for Justin without involving the police, which is often the worst thing to be done in these circumstances. He is only a young boy and I don't believe he's a danger to anyone. Let's hold on. Between us all, I am confident that we can help him. Tonight, I sense that Justin is at a turning point, a state of crisis, but if we act with care now, this could be a positive thing. This could be the beginning of his journey to wellness, although full recovery might be a lengthy process.' I can't see how she has reached this conclusion, but I say nothing.

Danny and Justin join us inside. 'I'm taking Justin down to the kitchen,' Danny says to Laura, as he leads the boy towards the stairs that led to the basement. Justin seems to be placid enough now. 'Come on,' Danny tells him kindly. 'We'll have a hot drink and a chat.'

'I'll join you in a moment,' Laura says. 'I could do with a hot drink myself.' She turns back to the group. 'Don't worry,' she says, as we all watch the backs of the retreating pair. 'Everything will be fine. Lock your doors though,' she adds, 'just in case.'

Laura goes downstairs after Justin and Danny, as everyone else heads sleepily back to their bedrooms. 'It's five am!' Charlotte says, and we all groan in response.

Five o'clock. Laura has either started work very early, or she's been up all night. I can't resist. I don't follow the other students, but instead, looking around quickly to make sure I'm not being observed, I duck into the room I'd seen open when I first came downstairs. I'd pulled the door almost closed just before the lights came on and, as I'd hoped, Laura must have thought she'd shut it behind her.

I close the door firmly behind me now, turn the light on

and look around. Good. This is, as I'd guessed, the college office. It's a large room, furnished with a couple of armchairs and two desks, with a computer at each. There are four large filing cabinets along one wall and I head straight for these. I don't know what I'm looking for but I do know I'll have to act fast if I hope to find anything.

I have anything between ten minutes and half an hour, I calculate, while Danny and Laura make hot drinks or whatever they're doing downstairs with Justin. I move quickly and carefully, checking my watch constantly. To my satisfaction, I find that the filing cabinets are unlocked. I open the first one and am peering into the top drawer, which contains what appear to be thick folders of notes, when I hear footfall on the stairs. Someone is coming back up already. I hurry to stand in the spot behind the door, where no one will see me if they glance into the room. Then I turn off the light and hold my breath. What on earth will I say if Laura or Danny find me here? My heart is hammering painfully.

Luckily for me, the door to the office remains closed and the footsteps continue up to the first floor. A narrow escape.

I leave the room, my heart still beating too fast. I pull the door fully shut behind me and hear the lock click into place. With any luck, Laura won't have realised she left the door open when she heard the fire alarm, and she will never know that I was there. I return to my room as quietly as I can, shaking with excitement as well as nerves. I'll have to get in again another time, I know, although I have no idea how. I can only hope that the room is left open again at some point.

It's now almost half past five in the morning, and I realise I'm still cold from being outside. I pull a jumper over my T-shirt before I get back into bed. It's only when I'm under the covers that I remember I haven't taken Laura's advice to lock my bedroom door. It doesn't matter, I'm not going to fall asleep anyway because it's almost morning and the pre-dawn light is beginning to colour the sky outside. Strange, I think sleepily, how safe I feel at Netley Hall, even though…and I'm out.

14

It's Wednesday, the second day of the course. There's a breakfast buffet laid out in the dining room and the other students are already eating and chatting. Nobody, including Justin, says a word about what happened in the night. I help myself to a generous portion of eggs, mushrooms and tomatoes and sit down next to Hilary.

'Have you seen anything of the famous college cats?' I ask lightly. 'I haven't spotted one yet, though I've been looking out.'

'Then you should keep your eyes open.' At that moment, a black cat wanders into the dining room and the other students gasp collectively.

'Right on cue,' I laugh, but Hilary just looks at me triumphantly, as though she, or the cat, has proved a point. I try to talk to her again, but she's clearly not interested. I've seen Hilary chatting away to the other students but whenever I try to make conversation with her, she just brushes me off. Oh well, her loss.

'The Art of Reading' begins on time. Laura leads the session again. Danny is present but from what I've seen so far, he doesn't seem to take any active part in the lessons. 'This tutorial is just a first step,' Laura says once we're all settled in our seats. The chairs are no longer arranged in a circle but in two short rows facing Laura and Danny, who are at the front of the room. 'You will begin to learn the art of reading, which you can do either with the help of the tarot, or by reading palms or auras. After a while it will become clear which art you each wish to specialise in. Do not expect spirit to come to you immediately. It will take a good deal of practice and experience before you can expect to become proficient in any of these skills. Learning to tune into the higher level is something which can take many years to accomplish, and each of our morning tutorials can only give you a glimpse of how it is done. We will consider the processes but there will be no formal tuition. The important thing, as always in these matters, is the feeling. The use of the senses. Do you all understand?' She finally pauses for breath, then looks around the room. Everyone nods intently, including me, although I don't really understand at all. No tuition? We're paying thousands of pounds for this course and she's just admitted that we're not going to benefit from any actual teaching. Well, I'm not actually paying, but that's beside the point.

'Now,' Laura says. 'We don't work with crystal balls here in the college, although some of you might choose to do so in your careers. As tools, they're no longer fashionable, and we have to consider what our clients expect from us. We're no longer concerned only with looking into the future or the past. A psychic medium can gain and share many different kinds of information from the spirit world. It might be that spirit instructs you to tell someone something important about their current life. Perhaps they are stuck in an unhappy relationship and you must advise them of the correct course of action. Or they want to meet a lifetime partner and they're hoping that you will be able to tell them whether and even how this could happen. Spirit may, if you are open, guide you in this path. It is a position of great responsibility.'

I'm unused to writing with pen and paper and am struggling to keep up with my notes. Laura certainly knows how to talk. 'Now, remember,' she continues, 'What you see, and what you say, could apply either to the person you are speaking to, or to someone they know. So, if you tell them they are unhappy and they deny it, you might recognise that the sadness you have sensed means that somebody close to them is unhappy. Perhaps, for example, they recently ended a relationship and the ex-partner is finding this hard to accept.' Statistically, I think, almost everybody must be close to someone who is unhappy, at any given time. You can't lose with this sort of a vague statement. As usual, I don't voice my opinion. Nobody here wants to listen to my cynical views.

Laura is still speaking. 'And how you construe the information that you receive from spirit might make all the difference. For example, if you see new love but your client tells you she is happily married, it could be that there will soon be a child in her life. And that child might not be her own, it could be that her sister is pregnant, or her best friend. Similarly, if the word Rose comes to you, that could apply to a person, or to the flower. Try to keep your language neutral, leave the various possibilities open. A reading, at is simplest, is a conversation. Often your client will tell you whether you are on the right track and as their faith in you grows they will offer more information.'

We're basically being taught techniques to con people, I think, scribbling my notes as fast as I can. Laura's lecture is constantly shifting and hard to pin down and everything she says is open to interpretation. But, although the notion of spirit guidance is mentioned occasionally, it's clear to me that Laura is feeding us information that will equip us to 'read' our clients without any help at all from the spirit world.

'One last thing,' says Laura, 'before you split into pairs to begin your practice. Remember, if you hit a blank, if you say something and your client doesn't respond, stay silent. Don't assume you have got it wrong. Move on and continue calmly in your reading, because the chances are that when the client gets home and has a chance to think things over, in the following weeks or months they'll realise there was some truth in what you said, although they might not have known it at the time. The spirit world is often ambiguous, capricious, in its delivery. Remain open and encourage your client to do the same. After all they have come to you for help.'

That, I reflect, is the trouble with the shady business of clairvoyance. Clients of psychics have either lost someone they love and are desperate to contact them, or they want guidance in their personal lives, assurance that they will find love or security of some sort. They must be desperate or gullible or both, to be asking for help from a person who they hope or believe is a representative of the spirit world. They're sitting ducks, vulnerable and ripe for exploitation. And because of this, the more of Laura's so-called instruction I listen to, the angrier I'm becoming, and I'm struggling now to stop myself voicing my feelings. It's a relief when she finally stops to announce that it's time to begin what she calls 'testing our abilities'.

'First,' she says, 'we'll simply form pairs, then sit together quietly and wait for spirit guidance. When something occurs to you, share it. Don't worry about whether you think what you're saying is right or wrong. At this stage, you're just learning to work with your intuition.'

Small, wooden folding tables leaning against the wall at one side of the room are pressed into action. I'm partnered with Sophie and we sit down opposite one another, the table between us. Both of us look awkward. 'Shall I go first?' I ask, and Sophie nods meekly. I take her hand. It feels slightly damp, and is limp and weak in my grasp, like a broken bird. I close my eyes for a moment, hoping that I look as though I'm becoming receptive to spirit guidance, then gaze deeply into Sophie's eyes. The urge to laugh overtakes me but I fight it back. 'I see an injury,' I say.

Sophie looks interested. 'I haven't hurt myself,' she says, 'But...'

I interrupt. 'There's a hospital. Surgery.'

Now Sophie is properly engaged. 'You're right,' she says. 'I had an operation last year. On my bunions. Both feet. Not very glamorous, I'm afraid.' She lets out a small laugh. 'But how did you know?' she asks intently.

I remain silent although I could easily say simply, 'Because I've been following the lesson'. It was hardly rocket science. I'd mentioned an injury and Sophie indicated that I was on the right track. From there it was a small leap to suggest surgery. As for how I'd started the 'reading', it's a reasonably safe bet that a number of people must either have injured themselves or been in hospital recently, or know someone this has happened to. As Laura told us, our 'insight' could apply either way. If Sophie had said she had not been injured, I could still have followed that path, suggesting that someone close to her had been hurt or had surgery. I didn't need to though, because I'd hit the jackpot at the start of the reading. The operation on her bunions clearly looms large in Sophie's mind, because she now treats me to a blow by blow account of the whole affair, including how long it took before she was able to drive again (ages) and how she coped mentally with the ordeal (badly).

Eventually I look up to see Laura standing by our table. How long has she been there? She's beaming at me. 'Well done, Robyn. Your client has opened up and is confiding in you. Fantastic. Keep going!' I'm oddly flattered. It's obviously nonsensical, and on one level I can hardly believe that I'm sitting in a room pretending to be psychic, but somehow it still gives me a warm glow to be considered successful at something and receive praise for it.

Laura triggers a strange mix of emotions and reactions in me. She behaved quite coldly and authoritatively yesterday morning when I arrived at the college, but she's kind towards Justin and she seems gentle and vulnerable in the company of Danny. I was pretty sure that she was just a con-woman when I was listening to her teach earlier this morning, and yet she's now very convincing in the role of wise teacher and role model.

'Continue your reading, please,' Laura says.

'Um...well...' I begin. Haven't I done enough for one session? Surely it should be Sophie's turn to read my fortune next. But I'm keen to try to impress Laura, so I duly take Sophie's hand and look into her eyes again. She's perked up and is waiting excitedly to hear what I have to say. She obviously enjoys being 'read'.

'I see lost love,' I say sadly, trying to sound detached, as if the message has come to me from nowhere. 'The end of a close bond.'

Sophie pales and her mouth becomes a wide 'O' of shock. 'My husband has left me!' she cries. 'My marriage is over. Everything is lost, everything! How did you know?' She's clearly distressed, and I feel unsettled by the strength of her emotion. I turn to Laura hoping for support. She says nothing though, and I catch an odd expression in her eyes. Suspicion?

If Laura wasn't standing by the table, I would have

assured Sophie that I'd just made a lucky guess, based on her dejected demeanour. I feel, though, that I should keep up a professional façade in front of Laura, so I don't answer Sophie's question directly. Instead, I say only, 'New love is closer than you think.' I'm speaking in a low voice, almost a whisper, and to my astonishment, Sophie seems to instantly spring back to life. Her face lights up and she looks suddenly younger and prettier. Her eyes are full of hope.

'How?' she asks, but I shake my head.

'Spirit is now silent on this subject, but spirit is sure,' I say mysteriously, and Sophie nods as though she understands this mumbo-jumbo perfectly. Incredible. A few well-chosen words and Sophie is practically eating out of my hand. I feel a heady sense of power. This is how it must feel to work as a psychic medium, getting instant respect when you make a lucky guess.

I've finished the reading and Laura is definitely impressed. 'Robyn has an unusual gift,' she says softly to both of us. She turns towards me, her voice pitched even lower. 'I thought as much, my dear, from the moment I first saw you.'

Did she? It certainly wasn't apparent at the time, when she glared at me forbiddingly then shoved me off to sit in the drawing room for ages. In any case, it's finally Sophie's turn. Laura wanders off to listen in to the other students, which is fortunate for Sophie because she has a memory like a sieve, appearing to have forgotten every single thing we've been taught this morning. She's literally hopeless at trying to read my palm, even though I give her several heavy hints.

Sophie soon stutters into silence. The other pairs of students also finish their conversations and Laura sums up by congratulating us on our efforts and encouraging us to continue our work this afternoon. 'This afternoon, I ask you to think on spirit and on your experiences practising the Art of Reading,' she says. 'You can either work alone or in pairs or groups. And please do use the resources in our wonderful library, because you will never find another one like it. There is an art in reading books as well as people. Trust the books and they will feed your minds and enhance your abilities.'

Trust the books? What is that supposed to mean? I take the notebook out from the small rucksack where I've been keeping it close to me at all times, and write down the phrase, which I intend to use to comic effect in my Globe article.

At that point, Danny pipes up. I'd almost forgotten he was in the room. 'Don't be afraid,' he says to the students, 'to open your minds to spirit.' I nod seriously along with the rest of the group while secretly mocking him.

It's lunchtime but I'm not hungry. I still feel upset, and a little guilty, at the strength of the emotions I've triggered in poor Sophie. Instead of heading to the dining room with the others, I decide to go out for a walk, get some space to think. I already have my purse in the rucksack, together with the notebook. I'm ready to leave.

Once outside, I realise how badly I'd needed a change

of scenery and some exercise. I quickly reach the end of the long driveway, then stride out through the country lanes, away from Netley Hall, almost joyfully. Eventually finding myself in Micklehurst village, I go into the only pub there, the Compass. I order a soft drink and a basket meal of scampi and chips. Then I return to my walk and a few minutes later, perhaps three miles away from the College, my phone pings and I take it out of my pocket to see that the signal icon has popped up. I'm connected again.

I call Katie, who sounds surprised to hear from me. 'I thought you'd be too busy to get in touch,' she says.

'I just need to hear a friendly voice,' I tell her. 'And a sane one.'

'Are they all raving mad?' Katie laughs.

'Not exactly. It's hard to explain. Being here feels like existing in some sort of parallel world where everybody lives by a totally different set of beliefs. It makes me feel a bit weird. Slightly out of kilter. The teacher even suggested that I had a special gift this morning and I didn't try to convince her otherwise.'

'Herd mentality can be infectious.' She laughs again. 'Still, don't worry about it. Chin up. Remember why you're there. Find out what's going on and report back to the paper. Stitch them up.'

'I'm starting to wonder why I'm still here, actually. I've seen enough already to write the article.'

'Stick with it,' my friend says. 'You don't want to be a quitter, Robyn. And don't forget, the paper paid a lot of money to send you on that course. They won't be happy if you walk out early. Just hold tight. It will soon be over. You'll have had a break from work and a new experience, and you'll feel all the better for it.'

I hang up, feeling much calmer. Katie's right. This could be my big opportunity to get my career on track. I need to stand firm, for as it takes to get some concrete evidence about what's going on at the college.

15

I return to Netley Hall in the early evening, just in time for dinner. Although nobody seems to have noticed that I've been out, leaving the college feels somehow trans- gressive. Laura had made it clear at the start of the course that we were free to come and go as we wanted but the subtext was that we would choose to stay on site and study. Apart from Chris and Justin on that first afternoon, I haven't seen anyone else leave the college grounds. I feel a lot calmer and more balanced for my time out though. Despite the fact that I slept so well last night, my head has grown muggy in this place from all the talk about spirit, the constant insistence that the unreal exists and is measurable. I'll get out for walks more often, I decide. Every afternoon, if possible.

Justin also seems to be feeling better. I observe him over the course of the meal. He's no longer talking non- stop on his own strange, improvised themes, but joining in with the conversation around the table, which as a consequence flows smoothly and is well punctuated with laughter. He's had a wash at some point and seems a lot more normal now that he's cleaner. The whole group of students seem very normal, I think, as I look around the table. In fact, apart from the slightly kooky appearance of a couple of them – Hilary's outlandish dress sense, Sophie's haunted look – you might think we were attending a course on residential writing, jewellery-making or crotchet techniques. I smile at the thought of the handsome Chris learning crochet. He's sitting next to Charlotte, whispering in her ear and she's giggling. I'll ask her what the state of play is there, when I get a chance.

I wonder about the tip-off that Jack had received about Netley Hall. Whoever it was, they were right about dodgy goings on. Laura and Danny are definitely crooked. What I'd like to know who blew the whistle on them and I have no idea how I'm going to find out, unless Jack decides to tell me himself. For now, though, the important thing is to get back into the office, find some evidence to back up what I know about the way Laura and Danny operate this college.

It's late again by the time I head up to bed but this time I manage to stay awake long enough to write up my impressions of the day. I don't use my laptop though. Instead I start a fresh A4 notebook, identical to the one I've been using in class. I'm surprised to find that I enjoy using pen and paper. It makes my thoughts feel more immediate and helps to make my writing flow more freely. I write about my experience of 'reading' Sophie, how impressed Laura was with my performance. I guessed about the divorce because Sophie seemed so sad and downtrodden, I write, and because she seemed about the right age to have suffered a failed marriage. I also note that Sophie's divorce must have hit her really hard, but perhaps she'd be better being single for a while, regaining her confidence before she enters another relationship. Looking over my work, I then add the words, 'Was it wrong to hint at new love?'

I continue to write in my notebook for an hour or so about the college and the other students, and it makes me feel much lighter. I think for a moment before I lay down my pen. What would I write, if I were channelling spirit? I let my mind float freely and then allow the pen to drift lazily on the page, forming words that I am only half aware of. When I have finished, I look down at the page. 'Life and Death' is written in heavy, looping swirls.

I check the clock before I get into bed. It's just before twelve. I fall asleep as quickly as I'd done the previous evening. I sleep dreamlessly and this time there's no disturbance in the night.

16

I wake at half past eight. It's Thursday already. The days are passing fast. I must have forgotten to set the alarm last night and now I don't have much time to get ready. I'm feeling well rested though. Rick was right, this assignment is a little like being on holiday. The accommodation and food are of a surprisingly high standard. I don't let myself dwell on thoughts of Rick, because I need to hurry. There's just enough time for breakfast before class starts at nine thirty. I check that my classroom notebook, the one I'm using for notes on my article, is in my rucksack. Leaving the identical one that I wrote in last night on the dressing table, I head downstairs.

This morning's tutorial is called 'Use of the Tarot'. Apparently, this means that we're going to continue learning the skills we'd begun to pick up yesterday, reading palms and auras. 'Charlotte, of course,' Laura says, 'is already skilled in the use of tarot cards. The rest of you worked very well yesterday using only your intuition, but sometimes other tools are necessary to channel spirit, or to inspire confidence in your clients. Trust is a vital ingredient of the therapeutic relationship.'

So we're therapists? Tarot counsellors? I snort inwardly

and when Laura takes out several packs of tarot cards and talks about how to use them for readings, I switch off mentally. This is one skill I am never going to need.

Laura eventually comes to the end of her Tarot lecture and then talks for a while about how to carry out a client consultation. 'Remember,' she says, 'It's the perfect opportunity to start a conversation. That is the essence of our profession. We begin conversations and then allow spirit to guide us. So, to start with, what you all need to do is tune into spirit and then free–associate. And do be open, and encourage your client to be open, to different angles. I spoke to you yesterday about how Rose could be the name of the person or the flower. Clients find names reassuring, it helps them to believe that you are receiving spirit guidance, encourages them to be more open. So, following on with this theme, bear in mind that people of a certain generation favour a type of name for their children and often these will cycle around from previous generations. Your grandparents might have had names like Molly or Jack, William or Daisy and so do many young children. If spirit gives you the name Tommy, that could be somebody's child, or their uncle who died in the Great War.' She's right. I read an article in the paper on just this subject not long ago, saying that many young middle-class girls now have the names that were once given to Victorian parlour maids.

Laura calls Hilary up to the front of the classroom for a demonstration. She takes Hilary's hand and looks at her kindly. 'I feel empathetic towards Hilary,' she tells us, 'and Hilary senses this fact.'

'I do,' confirms Hilary.

'Do you have a friend called Julia?' Laura asks.

'No, but I do have a friend called Julie.' Common names for people in their late forties or early fifties, I think. Louise, Julia, Jane. Emma.

'Has Julie been asking for your advice recently?' Laura says and Hilary nods, slowly.

'She's been talking to me about her problems. It didn't occur to me that she wanted advice, but now that you mention it, perhaps I should have offered some. Yes, I'll definitely do that next time. Thank you.'

Laura smiles, then turns to the rest of the class. 'It's all quite general,' she says, 'quite chatty. Keep it light. But if you get this sort of detail right early on in your consultation, the client begins to trust you and to open up. Another example. It's perfectly acceptable to ask people whether they have children. If a person says they have one, it's fine to ask if it is a boy or a girl. You can take things on from there as spirit inspires you, perhaps pointing out some of the characteristics of the client's child. Naming people, as I said, is a great way to establish rapport with the client, but spirit is not always as specific as we might wish, so sometimes we need to feel our way.'

We need to become experts in trickery, in other words. Next, Laura sends Hilary back to her seat and gives the class instructions on the use of intuition and the reading of body language. 'Use assertive body language,' she says, 'to give the impression of authority. This is purely in order to reassure your clients, because if they trust you they are more likely to let you help them.'

Laura then tells us about working practices. Confidentiality is apparently paramount, and we should never disclose the names of our famous clients unless we ask them if we can do so and they agree. We should also, she says, be upfront and fair in regard to what we charge for readings. 'Every psychic has their own way of working and each of you will develop your own personal code of ethics as your working lives progress.'

She then declares that the group should split into pairs again and continue to practice their skills. This time, I'm partnered with Chris. I've been watching him flirt with Charlotte again, over breakfast this morning. He was pretending to read her palm, saying that she was going to meet a dark handsome stranger and then flicking his own dark hair back dramatically. He makes her smile and it's nice to see.

I take his hand now. It's dry to the touch. 'I see water...' I tilt my head to one side, as if listening to spirit. 'You've just got back from holiday.'

Chris smiles broadly. 'A fortnight in Italy,' he says. 'How did you guess? Is it my incredible suntan?'

'No. I heard you talking about it at dinner last night.' We both laugh.

He pulls his hand away and then takes mine, making a show of scrutinising my palm. 'Watch out,' he says. 'A black cat will soon cross your path.'

I giggle. Yesterday morning at breakfast I'd told Hilary

I hadn't seen any black cats, but since then I've spotted plenty. In fact, the college is teeming with black cats, or as we are supposed to think of them, valued members of staff. 'But that's amazing. I tripped over a black cat on the way to the bathroom only this morning.' I free my hand from Chris's grip, then grab his again and peer at it closely.

'Don't step under ladders,' I say, 'and if you spill any salt at the dinner table, throw it over your left shoulder to knock the devil off.'

I look up to find Laura's eyes on me. She's been wandering around the room listening in to the various readings, as usual. She looks disapproving.

'This is not a laughing matter, Robyn. Perhaps we should move on, and let Chris read your palm. Or her aura, if you prefer,' she says to him.

He grins and takes my hand once more, looking into my eyes.

'There's someone new in your life.' I don't reply. 'You've met someone recently, Robyn, haven't you?' he insists.

'Okay, let's say I have. How did you reach that conclusion?'

'Because you're immune to my charms. I held your hand and looked into your eyes and your pupils didn't dilate, as they would have done if you'd felt any interest in that department. You're taken. And very much so – recently – because you're not even subconsciously considering a gorgeous prospect such as me.'

'That's ridiculous,' I say.

Laura is still standing by us. She's just told me off for being flippant, but perversely she's regarding Chris with approval. 'You're very observant,' she says. 'I'm guessing there's a reason why you have learned to watch so well.'

'There is,' he says, but he doesn't elaborate.

Laura does, however. 'I see a glittering career for you, Chris,' she says. 'You are wonderfully intuitive. And you have a special talent, Robyn,' she tells me. 'I saw the spark of it yesterday. Don't waste it. I think you should use the tarot in your readings. Clients respond well to that. The cards are starting points for conversations, remember? Let me run through the different sorts of packs again.'

17

I'm trying to look patient, but I'm not feeling it. It not that I couldn't understand the intricacies of the tarot cards if I concentrated. It's just that there's literally no point in me bothering to learn how to use these tools for fools. Laura doesn't wait for my response though, just tells Chris to partner up with Sophie, sits down at my desk and begins to speak at length about the origins of tarot and its supposed symbolism and significance. I give up resisting and try to focus on what she's saying. I suppose, if I learn how to read the tarot convincingly, it could turn out to be a useful dinner-party trick. I imagine asking my work colleagues whether they would like me to read their fortunes, and wonder what their reaction would be.

As Laura continues to lecture me on the properties of Tarot cards, I'm secretly smiling. This woman is supposed to be a professional fortune teller. I'm starting to wonder whether she might even genuinely believe in all the guff she spouts about spirit. Yet she has no idea that I am a journalist, although I've spent several days sitting in her lessons writing copious notes on all the other students and the events that are unfolding around me. She's going to get a huge shock when she reads next Saturday's paper.

Justin is sitting with Charlotte and I'm watching them surreptitiously as Laura drones on. I listen in as Justin recounts his recent experiences of life in his home town, Bristol, roaming around for days on end, seeing what he describes as visions of angels and hearing the voices of his family calling to him. 'You can't go around acting all crazy,' Charlotte says. I'm relieved. She's trying to bring Justin back to reality. Hurrah. But then she goes on, 'That's what I was like when I first started being psychic. Then I realised you've got to keep it to yourself.' I groan inwardly.

I have to admit though, that the boy's state of mind has vastly improved. He's now listening attentively to Charlotte, and in general he's communicating normally. He couldn't stop talking, or concentrate on anything that was happening outside his own mind, when he arrived at the college a few days ago. Since then he's spent a lot of time with Danny who has calmed him down immensely. In fact, the change in Justin is almost unbelievable. I remember Laura's words on Tuesday night, when he woke us all up because he was convinced there was a fire. Justin was having a crisis she said, and with care he should improve from this point. Was it a lucky guess or did she really have some kind of insight into his condi-tion?

Laura leaves my table and returns to the front of the room to address the class. 'Well done, all of you. That was a fantastic morning's work. We're about ready for lunch, but first I am going to talk briefly about stage skills. The term might sound a little cynical. This is not about acting, let's be clear about that, but there is, in our profession, some element of showmanship.'

'For example,' she says, addressing Sophie 'Would you rather have your palm read by a woman called Sophie or a clairvoyant named Cherie?' It's a leading question and Sophie, to nobody's surprise, admits that Cherie is a more attractive name for a clairvoyant. Laura inclines her head graciously. 'Also,' she adds, 'There may be times when you want some anonymity. You might be craving a normal conversation, you might need to confide in somebody else from time to time about your own problems. But if everybody, friends and clients alike, know that you have a spiritual gift, they will be looking for readings at every turn. Your night in a pub or restaurant with friends is just going to turn into a series of free readings. Using a pseudonym can be a wise precaution.'

'I'd like to be known as Madame Cherie,' Sophie says suddenly, and Laura congratulates her on the choice, saying that it strikes the right note. I feel a little uneasy. There's a faintly racist undertone in the suggested name change. Thoughts of Romany gypsies come to mind and I wonder why, in this day and age, it would be necessary to masquerade in such a way. After all, the celebrity mediums I'd researched a few days ago, back in London, have quite ordinary names like Derek or Susan.

I probably shouldn't speak out, but I do. 'Surely,' I say, 'going by a false name is misleading people? And the techniques you've been teaching us to read people, like guessing the names of their friends or relatives to win their trust. Isn't that cheating?' The other students are staring and I add hastily. 'I mean, surely spirit wouldn't approve?'

'Cheating,' Laura says sternly, 'would be making up things. What you will be doing, if you choose to follow your calling, is using your intuition, working to find clues, looking for guidance from the spiritual world for yourself and your clients.'

I make a note in my book to discuss this further with her before I leave. The list of questions I have for Laura is lengthening and I hope that before I leave the college I'll get answers to at least some of them. It will be useful to include her personal perspective in the piece.

'Can I add something?' Danny says. He's never really spoken out in class before and everyone listens attentively. 'I just want to say that it's important to protect yourself. You're all making brilliant progress and beginning to really connect with the higher level. Laura and I have been discussing how well all of you are doing. But I just want to make sure all of you are aware that you need to be in charge of when you contact spirit. You don't want spirit taking control, knocking at your door and coming right in whenever it chooses. You can be as open as you wish here, in the safe environment of the college, but when you leave you must make sure to set clear boundaries. You're a case in point, Justin,' he says. 'You are so open to the many paranormal influences around you. You are clearly gifted, but you will need more assimilation and training before you can carry out useful work in the realms of spirit. You need to work on your ego, your sense of self.'

I flinch. I'm expecting Justin to be either embarrassed or offended at being held up as an example to the class, but to my surprise he agrees with Danny readily. 'I do feel that I have a lot to learn,' he says and the rest of the group join in, chorusing that yes, so do they. I could teach them a few things myself, right now, I think bitterly. But that will just have to wait.

18

Yesterday I'd resolved to go out for regular walks, but instead I spend the afternoon and most of the evening in the college library. This is partly so I can gather material to inform my article, and partly because I've realised that I don't have much time left at Netley Hall. I need to get back into that office. Every hour or so I sneak out of the library to see if the door is ajar. It never is, and on the one occasion I spot Laura coming out of the room, she locks it carefully behind her. It seems that I'd just had a lucky break on the night of the fire alarm. I have no idea how I am going to gain access again. I'm now keeping my phone with me at all times though, in my rucksack along with my notebook and purse. If do get the chance to access the office, I'll be able to get instant photographic evidence of what's in those files.

I'm up bright and early the next morning and have time for a long, lazy shower before the work of the day begins. It's Friday and this morning's tutorial is called 'Feeling the Flow'. Laura says at the start of the session that it will consist of more 'practical skills' training and opportunities to practice on one another. It occurs to me that the last three days of 'Channelling the Spirit' have been almost identical in content. The only discernible difference is that the tutorials don't all have the same title. I wonder whether all the courses at Netley Hall are the same. One size fits all. And just two tutors for everything, only one of whom ever speaks in class. It's all rather half-baked. If I was a genuine student I would probably feel a bit cheated.

I'm partnered with Hilary, and I plunge straight in. 'I see children,' I say. 'Girls? Do you have daughters?'

'You already know I have children. However, I'll pretend for the purposes of this interview that you were not privy to this information.'

Ouch. 'They're almost adults now.' Even if I hadn't heard her talking about how her 'babies' are growing up too fast, I could have worked their ages out. Hilary is in her late forties, I'd guessed when I first met her, which would make her children teenagers, in all likelihood. My mother is around the same age as Hilary, but she was younger than the average parent when I was born.

Hilary nods. 'One of your daughters is very similar to you,' I say and she looks unwillingly impressed. I have been making the most of my time in the library to do extra reading on the techniques used in psychic practice. I've learned that if a person has two or more children, one will be more like their mother than the others. Also, one will be more creative, one more sensitive, one more academic and so on. Even if this isn't the case, the parents will often perceive them in that way.

'She's creative,' I say. 'Like you.' Hilary smiles. 'Does she dance?'

'They both used to do ballet and they study drama at school. One of them won't stop singing at the moment. She's happy because she's just got her own bedroom after years of sharing with her sister.'

'She's going to be a great success in the field of dramatic arts,' I say. Hilary looks interested. Of course, anybody would want to hear that their child is going to be successful. And with a drama teacher for a mother, there's a good chance that one or both children will have a stage-related career. I'm actually making this up as I go, but nobody can prove or disprove what I'm saying. And it's making Hilary feel good. Plus, she's warming to me at last.

Hilary then announces that she's going to read my aura. She makes her eyes unfocused, as if she has entered a trance-like state. 'I see silver.' She snaps her eyes open wide and stares at me searchingly. 'That means money. You're a wealthy woman.' I blush and she looks gratified. This causes me to bristle with annoyance. 'Red is for confidence,' she says then, 'and blue is for truth. You have these colours, but both are clouded, muddy. Which means that the red in your aura is the colour of anger, Robyn, and your blue is the colour of fear.'

It's all rubbish, of course. Hilary is waiting for me to say something, to give her some clues, but I remain quiet. Suddenly she hisses, 'Be careful! Someone very close to you cannot be trusted.' I feel a chill run down my back. It doesn't mean anything, I know. Anybody would be spooked by such a warning, even if they didn't believe a word of it. Again, I keep my expression neutral.

Hilary ploughs on. 'Change is coming,' she says, then repeats herself. 'Change is coming, very soon. You are stuck in the past my dear, frightened to move on. Is there a romance in your life?'

I smile tightly. I'm not giving anything away. I know these tricks. I've read up on them in the library. The suggestion that change is in the air can apply to almost everyone and everything and all of us are stuck in the past to some extent. As for romance, well anybody my age might have had a recent encounter. I didn't mind joking about it with Chris yesterday but I have no intention of discussing my personal life with Hilary.

'Romance? No, I don't think so.'

She's still gazing at me closely. Too closely. 'Oh, I do,' she crows. 'I think so. But you have closed your heart. You won't acknowledge the possibility of love. You are full of fear. I told you, I see it vividly, that muddy blue fear, right there in your aura.'

'Very good,' I say crisply. I've had enough of this now and I want her to stop but she presses on.

'What is it you're frightened of, Robyn? You've closed your heart to love. You've come here to learn and yet you've also closed your mind to the possibility of change.'

I don't answer. I know I should be more co-operative but I have no intention of talking about Rick to this woman. Insisting on budding romance in the face of my denial is ridiculous. I've told her she's way off track and surely if I was a real client it would make sense for her to accept that she's wrong or that I don't want to talk about it, and to move on to another aspect of the reading. As for closing my mind to learning, that's rubbish. There's nothing useful to learn at Netley Hall.

At last, she changes tack. 'I see great power here, she says, 'and also great responsibility.'

'Yes,' I agree, 'with great power comes great responsibility.'

'You're not helping me here.'

'You're right. My boss at work is very powerful and I feel a great responsibility to carry out my duty well. Law is an important business,' I say woodenly, recalling my cover story. There's an awkward silence. Luckily, just at that moment, Laura calls out, 'Time's up!' and all attention is focused at the front of the room.

Laura says simply that all is going well, and that we should find new partners to practice with. I'm paired with Charlotte. She says that I can take the first turn, and I decide to try an aura reading. Reading a client's aura makes it sound as though you're actually doing something, rather than just plucking insights out of mid-air. It certainly worked for Hilary. I begin with a general comment. 'There is happiness in your aura,' I say. 'I see orange, which means there is fulfilment in your life.' Charlotte nods and smiles encouragingly. 'You're fond of shopping. You particularly like to buy new clothes and you've splashed out a bit recently.'

'You're right,' she says. I'm watching her closely and can see that my leap of 'intuition' – which I know is anything but – has had an impressive effect. She has the same look in her eyes as Sophie wore on Wednesday, when she thought I'd magically divined that she'd had a bunion operation and split up from her husband. It's even more ridiculous that Charlotte has been taken in, since it's plain to see that she's been wearing brand-new, expensive clothes every day of the course.

I'm tempted to follow this up with something more dramatic. I take her hand and look closely at her palm. What was it we were told about ley lines? No, not ley lines, life lines. I pretend to be studying the lines on Charlotte's hand. I feel a faint stirring of unease, a slight twist in my stomach. Like Sophie, Charlotte's grip is weak and her palm is damp, but this time I suspect that the cause is something other than nerves. Laura pauses near our table and I suddenly can't resist the temptation to show off. 'There's something wrong,' I say. Charlotte stiffens in her chair. I feel a tug of remorse but carry on regardless. 'You have health problems. '

'What sort of problems?' she asks.

'I don't know exactly. An obstruction of some kind. Maybe a lump.' She's looking really panicky now and I try to backtrack. 'Look, maybe I'm reading the signs wrong. I'm sure everything is fine.'

Charlotte looks genuinely freaked out and I could kick

myself. What am I playing at? I wanted to impress Laura but I've really scared this poor girl.

Laura is standing very still. 'What does spirit say, Robyn?' she prompts eagerly.

I take a deep breath, close my eyes, then open them again, wide. 'Spirit says you will soon be well,' I tell Charlotte.

'I have breast cancer,' she replies. She gets up and, wobbling, makes her way to the door and disappears.

I feel nauseous. The air in the classroom has become heavy and oppressive and I rise from my chair, intending to follow Charlotte out of the classroom, but Laura touches me on the shoulder.

'Come on, Robyn' she says. 'You're doing brilliantly. Keep going. It's nearly lunch time.'

I'm doing brilliantly? It's lunch time? How can she be so callous? Food is the last thing on my mind. My attention is focused firmly inward, trying to work out why I said what I did. Hilary had upset and unsettled me with her reading and then I, in turn, shook Charlotte up cruelly. I feel terrible. Silently, I curse Jack for sending me into this situation. More than anything, I just want to go home.

19

Katie's words come back to me though. 'Don't be a quitter, Robyn,' she'd said on the phone a couple of days ago. It would be even sillier to leave now, when I'm so close to completing my assignment. So, when the class ends, I let Laura usher me straight into the dining room telling me as we walk 'not to dwell on sadness,' but instead to 'lift myself up to the power of spirit'.

Against all odds, the meal does make me feel better. Katie's cooking is excellent but the catering at Netley Hall is on another level entirely – although I have a feeling that she wouldn't appreciate me telling her so. The conversation flows smoothly as usual, despite Charlotte's absence from the table. Hilary is more relaxed now and talks freely about what she calls her 'spiritual awakening.' She was out walking her dog one evening when she heard someone calling her name. 'Nobody was to be seen. I looked around,' she says, 'and I suppose I should have been frightened, but I wasn't at all. I decided to follow the voice. It led me nowhere really, just around the streets, a different route home from my usual one. I heard the voice every few minutes, calling me, and so it took me and Pixie maybe twenty minutes longer than usual to get back from our walk.' Hilary pauses for a moment.

'When I reached the street where I lived, there was a vacuum. A gaping hole where my house used to be. The houses either side were damaged too. There'd been a gas explosion. It must have only just happened because I could hear the sirens in the distance, the fire engines and police zooming in. It turned out to have been a deliberate act of vandalism, although we never found out why. It was just a blessing that nobody was in any of those houses when it happened. Although we would have been at home, me and my little dog Pixie, if we hadn't taken a different way back. And that is when I knew I had to follow my calling. My life had been saved by spirit and I had to repay my debt by helping others.'

Around the table, the group are open-mouthed. I'm not surprised. That, I think, is quite a story.

After lunch, I wonder if I should hang around the college for the afternoon. Tomorrow is my last morning at Netley Hall and I should really be using every moment as an opportunity to try to get some evidence. I spent most of yesterday watching and waiting for a chance to get into the office though, and this morning has been stressful enough already. I decide it's more important to go for a walk again, to get some country air and some distance from the college. Gain some perspective.

Also, I want to speak to Rick. He's been on my mind since Chris and Hilary both talked about my love life and now I can't help wondering whether Hilary has, completely by chance, read the situation correctly. Perhaps I am holding back in some way. I'm at the brink of a new relationship, so why, when my phone finally kicked back into life on Wednesday, was it Katie I chose to call, not him? It's not as if he hasn't been on my mind. I walk until I am far enough from Netley Hall for the signal icon to pop up on my phone again, and then call Rick's mobile. I'm not sure exactly what I'll say and I'm aware of my heart beating fast when I hear his ring tone. I count to eight rings then put my mobile away. He's too busy to answer.

I try to relax. My head is clearing as I get further away from the college and I'm enjoying the fresh air as I stride out along the narrow lanes. It feels so good to be outdoors. I decide not to make any more calls. It's taken me most of the week to get used to not being connected but I don't really miss the phone and internet that much anymore. There's nobody I really need to speak to – I've already spoken to Katie once this week and I'm not going to try Rick again. I refuse to become an insecure, pining, female. I'll see him soon enough, and there'll be plenty of time for us to work out where things are heading.

Earlier in the day, Laura said that this evening's meal would be 'a celebration of all we have learned.' The food is, as usual, delicious, and the group seems even more animated than usual, although once again neither dessert or alcohol is served. I have to admit to myself that I feel better for their absence, although I don't think it would be an easy change to continue into my everyday life. I don't want to put a dampener on the few social events I still get invited to.

I'm glad to see that Charlotte has come downstairs to join us for dinner. She seems completely calm as she sits down next to me. 'I'm so sorry about earlier,' I say. 'I didn't mean to upset you.'

'It's not your fault. I was diagnosed about a month ago. They did a lumpectomy and now they're deciding whether to give me chemo or some other treatment.'

'You're so young. It's so much to deal with.'

Chris is sitting on the other side of Charlotte. 'My Mum died when I was fifteen,' he says. 'That's why I'm here at the college. Sometimes I feel that she's somewhere watching me and if it's possible I'd like to find out how I can speak to her. Not that I'm making much headway.' He chokes up with emotion and I remember Laura saying that something must have happened to make Chris sensitive. She'd been spot on again.

'Shit happens,' I say, hoping to lighten the mood.

'It does,' Charlotte agrees. 'Sorry I didn't tell you, Chris,' she adds. 'I just wanted to be normal for a change. I mean, I didn't want you feeling bad for me or anything. We've been having so much fun getting to know each other. Anyway,' she smiles brightly, 'Everything's going to be fine. I'm going to be fine. Robyn told me so.'

I had indeed, I remember, told Charlotte that 'spirit' said she would be well. I had no right to make this state-ment, but it does seem to have comforted her, and Chris too. I can only hope that positive thinking will have some sort of placebo effect and Charlotte will make a full recovery.

There's an short silence, but then Laura taps on a glass with her fork. 'This our last mealtime together and an opportunity to enjoy ourselves,' she says. 'But since it is our final evening, I want to talk briefly about the clairvoyant's code of conduct. There are just three things to remember. You will need to bear these rules in mind for the rest of your working lives. Firstly, remember that you will be giving only advice, not instruction, to your clients. Secondly, at all times when conducting yourself in public you should be kind, polite and responsible. And finally, when passing on a message, you must always say, "In the opinion of the spirit".'

'Is that a legal requirement?' I ask.

'Actually yes, it is.' I pretend to nod seriously, wondering whether any of the other students is thinking what I am. Laura has told us that legally, all psychic mediums must utter the disqualifier 'in the opinion of the spirit,' before offering any advice, or they risk being sued. If that's not a subtle admission of guilt and fraudulence, I don't know what is.

'One more matter,' she says. 'Think carefully about how to present yourselves. The jeans will have to go, Robyn. They don't give a professional impression to clients.' I can't disagree, although I don't really appreciate having my clothes criticised in front of the group. What about Hilary, I think, floating around in her clownish drapery. Why doesn't Laura pick on her? Then I remember how I'd assumed before setting off that all the other students would be wearing tie-dye and sequins. Another cliché busted. Apparently, we're expected to look professional.

As Laura continues her lecture, I nudge Sophie, who's sitting next to me. 'She's going to inspect our fingernails for grime next,' I say. I'm trying to make her laugh, but it doesn't work. Her eyes widen and she looks towards Laura fearfully. Poor Sophie seems terribly in awe of our course director.

After Laura and Danny finally say goodnight and leave the room, I crack a joke about how maybe we should devise a uniform and have make-up tutorials, and everyone laughs gratifyingly. I feel comfortable in this group, and it's a shame that I'm unlikely to see any of the other students again. After they read my piece in the Globe they're going to think they've been harbouring a viper. I've enjoyed their company though, and it's made me determined that when I get back to London I'll make an effort to meet some new people and get out more.

On the way back from dinner, I take a detour up the corridor to pass Laura's office. I'm almost certain I won't be lucky and I'm right, the door is closed and locked. Instead of heading back to my room though, I go to the library where I sit quietly in the dark. If I'm found, I'll say I was unable to sleep and that I've learned from experience that the best remedy for insomnia is to get out of bed and go and sit somewhere else until I feel tired.

An hour or so passes. My eyelids are beginning to droop. There's been no detectable movement, and I can't wait any longer. I'll just have to write the piece with what I've got. I'm climbing the stairs towards my bedroom when I glance across at the office door. To my amazement I see that it's slightly open, as if in invitation.

I practically jump back down the stairs and into the room. I realise that Laura has probably just popped out to the kitchen or bathroom. She could be back at any second and it feels as though I am taking a huge risk. But incredibly the exact file I am looking for – the one labelled 'Channelling the Spirit' – is on the desk right in front of me.

I could be caught at any moment but I can't resist this opportunity. I take out my phone, turn the pages of the file one by one and press the button on the camera silently and rapidly. Only minutes later, I have ample evidence to close this place down forever. I feel a warm glow of satisfaction and something else which I can't quite put my finger on. Could it be guilt? Regret, even?

No. Not possible.

But my heart is beating wildly all the time I am in the office and even when I get back safely to my room, having left the door ajar exactly as I'd found it, I'm still quivering with shock. I have every bit of proof I need. What an incredible, unbelievable stroke of good luck.

20

I rest so well and wake so refreshed that my first feeling on Saturday morning is slight disappointment that the course is drawing to a close. This is quickly replaced, though, by the thought that I will soon see Rick.

This morning we are just down for one brief lecture from Laura, the rather oddly titled, 'Until we Meet Again'. After that we'll be free to browse the library, meditate on what we've learned or simply chat.

It's interesting, I reflect, how often the things you dread most turn out to be perfectly fine in reality. Or even, as in the case of this course, really rather fun. And I have to admit I've learned a few useful things at Netley Hall. If things don't work out at the paper, I reckon I could make a decent living as a fortune teller.

I've read a lot in the library to add to what Laura has taught us over the last few days. She told us to use assertive body language to inspire confidence in the client and I've also learned about 'mirroring' – adopting the same physical position as the client, to make them feel at ease. I've also picked up how to make general statements that sound true, often because they're flattering. You feel a need to do the right thing in life…change is approaching fast...take every opportunity you are given...make the most of your skills and abilities...and so on. It doesn't really matter what you pretend to see or intuit as long as you have a receptive client. And, of course, the beauty of this career path is that dyed-in-the-wool cynics are unlikely to part with their cash for a consultation.

There are other tricks that a psychic medium can add to their skill-set. For example, when a client calls to make an appointment, you ask a barrage of questions about themselves and their lives. At the meeting, two or three weeks later, you can feed some of this information straight back to the client, who will probably have forgotten that she (ninety per cent of clients are female) told it to you herself on the phone a short while ago. In fact, during a reading an experienced clairvoyant often uses a skill known in the trade as 'parroting' – merely echoing information that the client is giving them. It's surprising how many people are so starved of attention, so grateful that someone is properly listening to them, that they don't realise they are being parroted. What's interesting is that in the manuals I've unearthed in the library, these tricks aren't billed as instructions on how to con people, but rather included as examples of how spurious mediums ply their trade. These people are so self-deluding it's crazy.

Laura begins her lecture by making sure that we all write down, 'The three vital rules from the Code of Conduct as I told them to all of you at dinner last night'. Once this is done, she talks about the importance of a positive mental attitude. 'If there's one thing that I want you to take home from Netley Hall,' she says, 'it is the importance of imparting positivity to your clients. A positive outlook can truly be life-changing. We are in the business of giving hope to our clients, hope for their own futures and for the future of our planet.'

I'm watching Laura closely as she talks about this and that, mostly repeating the things she's already said over the last five days. I don't bother to make notes. I have everything I need already. Finally, she clears her throat loudly. 'I am afraid to say that our time together is up,' she announces. 'We have arrived at the end of the class, and of the course. You have all been very perceptive, a really talented group of students. This is only a first level course though, with very basic teaching.' She then says that each of us should return to Netley Hall to practise our skills and develop our contact with spirit, if we choose to move onto the next stage of training. 'Danny and I do hope and believe that we will see all of you here again,' she says, 'some, perhaps, sooner than others. You are all gifted, to differing degrees...' at this point she eyeballs me, 'and with practice you will become more proficient. It is a matter of opening the third eye...' She's off again with her faux-spiritual nonsense and I sigh audibly. I don't want to listen to any more of this crap. I just want to get away from Netley Hall once and for all.

We've been invited to have lunch before we leave, and the others are all heading to the dining room. I'm tempted, but decide against it. I hurry to my room and pick up my

118

bag, which I packed before breakfast this morning. I glance around briefly. When I first arrived, I thought I'd be spending a lot of time in this room, but I've only really used the space to sleep and shower. As for my precious laptop, it has stayed in its sleeve throughout my visit. I've only written by hand and this may, I realise now, have played a part in the fact that I feel more grounded and relaxed than I have done for some time. All of us have benefitted from an enforced technology detox. Plus, of course, an alcohol and sugar detox.

I leave the room and close the door behind me, remembering to put the key back in the lock. I start to sneak down the stairs. I'm hoping to get away without speaking to anyone. There's no point in hanging around for goodbyes.

Laura, however, has other ideas. She's lying in wait for me in the hallway downstairs. 'I need to talk to you before you go, Robyn,' she says. She's gazing at me intently and I feel a surge of panic. What if she's realised that I've been sneaking around and she knows what I found? I can't stay and talk to her. I have to get out of here as soon as possible.

21

I can't physically push past Laura though, and I have an inbuilt horror of rudeness so I can't tell her where to go either. 'I'm in a hurry,' I lie instead. 'I have to get to Brighton station before one twenty.'

'Please.' The autocratic course director pleading with me. How can I resist? And anyway, there are a few things I should speak to her about, before I leave.

So I obediently follow Laura to her office. I hadn't had a chance to appreciate the décor on my previous illicit visits, but I notice now that the room is newly carpeted and better decorated than most of the other parts of the college I have seen. Laura seats herself in an armchair by a low table and I take the chair opposite. The effect is unnervingly intimate.

'You have the gift, Robyn,' she tells me abruptly.

Not that again. 'Thanks,' I say. 'But I honestly don't think so. I made a few lucky guesses, that's all.'

'It's more than that,' she insists. 'You're clearly not ready to acknowledge this, Robyn, but you do have a gift. You are a seer. The most important thing to remember, my dear, is that you must act responsibly. You must use your powers for the good of all.'

'It really was just guesswork,' I say.

'What you call guesswork, I consider to be intuition,' she counters. 'I heard you reading Sophie, and also Charlotte. And where did your knowledge come from, do you think? You are clearly guided by spirit.'

'No, really. I just said the first thing that came into my head. I was fishing for answers, using the techniques you taught us, and by some fluke I got close enough that the people I 'read' gave me the information I wanted. I'm not in the slightest bit clairvoyant. I don't believe in ghosts and I certainly wouldn't ever want to communicate with the dead even if I thought it was possible. You're wrong, Laura. You couldn't be more wrong. I do not have any gift.'

My voice is overly loud, I realise, echoing in the room. I hadn't meant to speak so forcefully but it seems to be the only way to get my message across. In any case, it's made no difference. My words don't seem to have had the slightest effect on the woman sitting opposite me, who merely smiles tolerantly as if speaking to an obstinate child. 'Nobody has to commune with spirits,' she says, 'unless they choose to do so. You needn't worry about that. But you do have a power. And I think you know it.'

I'm becoming increasingly irritated. Why does this woman persist in baiting me? 'Okay, let's leave the subject for now,' I say. I've tried, and if Laura doesn't want to listen it's up to her. She will find out the full truth when she reads my piece in the Globe next weekend. In fact, I'll send her a copy myself.

'Actually, I want to talk to you about something,' I say. 'I'm worried about Justin. I think he's mentally very unwell.'

'You are right,' Laura says calmly. 'Justin is psychotic. Which sounds alarming when used in common parlance, but if you look in the dictionary you'll see that the term psychosis means only a serious disturbance of the thoughts. He's improved greatly during the course of the week,' she continues, 'because he has been in the company of people who listen to him, without judging.'

'He could be a danger. To himself or others.'

Laura smiles again. 'The dangers presented by people in emotional distress are exaggerated. He won't hurt anyone. Justin is not a violent person. He's merely in a period of transition,' she says. 'If he is treated with kindness he will soon become lucid again, and Danny and I are committed to helping him in his journey. In fact, Justin is going to stay here at Netley Hall with us while his gift develops and settles. We will guard his welfare most carefully.'

Empty out his bank account most carefully, more likely. Ker-ching. 'Justin is going to be staying here? How much will that cost him?' I burst out.

'You don't need to worry about that.'

'And what about Sophie? She's a nervous wreck too.'

'She has also registered for the next stage.'

'Next stage,' I repeat dully. As if they're providing some sort of authenticated learning experience, a clear pathway to greater enlightenment, rather than day after day of brain-washing and play-acting. 'So, she's staying on at Netley Hall too. Can she afford it? Or is all her divorce settlement going to be sucked up in course fees? And why are you encouraging her in this Madame Cherie and crystal ball stuff? Isn't it a bit inappropriate, to say the least? Don't you think it's immoral to make money from people who are clearly in distress?'

'I'm surprised at your hostility, Robyn,' says Laura. I remember she still thinks I'm just an ordinary student. I don't reply and she continues to speak. 'Money is not the answer to everything, as you are well aware.' Laura is clearly probing for information but again I don't respond, and eventually she sighs. 'Alright then. Sophie, as you have rightly divined, requires confidence. Sometimes, the adoption of a new persona helps in these circumstances. Becoming Madame Cherie while undertaking the science of prediction – and she does, as you say, incline towards use of the crystal – may well lift her out her current depression and give her a purpose in life.'

The science of prediction? It takes me a moment to translate this phrase, then I realise Laura is talking about fortune-telling. 'Justin and Sophie are both mentally ill and you are encouraging them in their delusions,' I say. I'm angry because I have the whole picture now, and the files I photographed last night are all the evidence I need. Laura and Danny are not only deceiving and preying off their students but focusing in on the mentally ill, taking the richest and the most troubled onto their spurious courses, and milking them for all they are worth. It's unethical and highly dangerous. I can't challenge Laura with this – there's a strong possibility that she would try to take the proof I've garnered – so I just rise to my feet, ready to leave. I'm determined to get justice for these people.

Laura hasn't given up. 'When you are ready to talk about your powers, my dear, I will be here,' she says to my departing back as I exit the room. The crazy cheek of her. I am never going to see or speak to this woman again in my life.

22

Firmly up on my high horse, I stalk out of the college, slamming the heavy front door behind me. I'll walk to the village and call a taxi from the pub.

I don't really want to stop off at my parents' house. I'd rather go straight back to London, where I could relax and process my thoughts about Netley Hall, or maybe even push on and write up the piece for the newspaper this afternoon. Then I'd have a couple of days free, as Jack said I don't need to be back at the Globe until Tuesday. I could call Rick and see if he wants to come over this evening. I'm desperate to tell him what's been happening at the college.

But I know it would be unfair to my parents not to visit when I'm so close. I'll surprise them, I decide. They're always happy to see me – they'd welcome me with open arms if I turned up at midnight on any day of the week.

It takes longer than usual to walk to the village because I'm pulling my suitcase on its wheels. The pub is just opening and, since my mobile signal is still down, I go inside to make the call to the taxi firm. When the cab finally arrives, I'm surprised to see that it's driven by the same guy who took me from the train station to Micklehurst, on Tuesday morning. 'How did you get on, love?' he asks. I smile. The locals must be gagging to know what goes on at Netley Hall.

'It was interesting,' I say, and can't resist adding, 'If you get the Globe next Saturday, you might learn more.'

He doesn't ask why, just smiles back at me. 'I'll do that, love.'

The cabbie drops me in front of the Grand Hotel, which is on the promenade about a minute's walk from my parents' home. I love this house, which is where I grew up. Not many people have a sea view from their bedroom window. I particularly like the fact that it's at the centre of the hustle and bustle of Brighton and yet so large and peaceful inside. The back garden is a haven – a full acre of lushly tended greenery and one of my favourite places in the world.

I don't have a key with me, so I just knock loudly on the door. It's been newly painted grey, I notice. Although my mother will probably say that the shade is correctly termed 'mouse's ears' or 'elephant's breath.' Suddenly the door opens and she rushes at me, enveloping me in a hug. 'Robyn! I've missed you so much! We hardly ever hear from you. It's been weeks...months, since we've seen you.'

I interrupt. 'It's okay, Mum. I'm here now. You going to let me in?'

I follow her through the house and into the kitchen as she continues to chatter. 'I called the flat the other day, and that girl...'

'Katie,' I say.

'Yes, Katie...she said you were away for work and she didn't know when you would be back.' Strange. Katie knows exactly where I've been and she's well aware that the course was due to end this morning. Maybe she didn't want to pass on what she thought might be personal information, even to my mother.

'I've been so worried, Robyn,' my mum goes on.

'I haven't been far away,' I say. 'Just down the road, at Micklehurst. But there was no internet or phone connection there.' Which is bizarre, I realise, when the place is only ten miles from Brighton.

'Really?' my mother says vaguely.

'Anyway, you shouldn't worry about me. I'm an adult, remember? I've got lots to tell you about my week, by the way.'

She begins to bubble over with excitement at the prospect. 'Oh, that's great, Robyn. Brilliant. Your father's not here right now. He had to go to town for a meeting. He'll be back before dinner though and he'll be so pleased that you are staying over. It's just so lovely to see you!'

'It's good to be here,' I say, meaning it. I didn't say I was staying the night, but I suppose I should have realised I don't really have a choice after not showing my face for so long. I'll just have to go back to London first thing in the morning.

She busies herself getting me lunch. 'Just leftovers from last night,' she says. The plate is piled high with one of my favourite dishes, potatoes cut into wedges and dusted with paprika, to which she's added eggs and tomatoes. She sits down to watch while I eat it.

'How are you, darling?' she asks, looking at me searchingly. I smile back brightly.

'Completely fine!'

She looks as though she might be going to quiz me further but, takes a lighter tack instead. 'So, go on then, tell. What exactly have you been up to all week?' she asks. 'Why did you have to go away for work? That hasn't happened since you started at the Globe, has it? Have you been promoted? And where have you been? What did you do?'

'I'll tell you all about it over dinner,' I say. 'Save having to repeat everything to Dad. Where did you say he was?'

'Up in London. It's a work thing, some sort of takeover bid. The timing of the meeting means he would have come back late last night and had to leave again first thing this morning, so he just stayed over'.

'Really? A meeting in London on a Saturday morning? I thought he was tailing down his work commitments?' I wonder fleetingly whether my father might be having an affair and then dismiss the thought immediately. I can't see him as a Lothario, even if I try. He's no film star lookalike, unlike the debonair Danny. More your average, middle-aged, well-fed, balding businessman. 'Does he stay in town often?'

'Not really'. She shrugs, unconcerned, and I let the subject drop.

'How are you though, Robyn?' she asks. 'Are you eating properly? You look as though you've lost weight.'

'I really haven't. Katie cooks the most amazing meals for us both, practically every day. Sometimes I feel as though she's deliberately trying to fatten me up.'

'That's nice dear,' she says, sounding vague again. I get the impression she's only listening with half an ear. 'And what about your love life? Have you met anyone special? Anyone you want to tell me about?'

'Erm…not really. There's nobody new in my life.'

'I asked if there was anyone special, not anyone new,' she insists.

'Give us a break, Mum!' I laugh.

She pauses for a moment, then goes straight back in. 'You would tell me, wouldn't you dear, if there was anybody?'

'Of course, Mum,' I lie. It's not time to confide in my mother about Rick yet, I hardly know where we stand myself. In any case, I make it a matter of principle never to tell my mum when I am seeing someone. I would either get her hopes up or worry her, and there's literally no point.

23

Thankfully, my mother changes the subject again. 'Tell me more about your flatmate. Does she really cook for you both every day? Who pays for the food?'

'We share the cost. She's not bothered about money though. She's a barrister, Mum, she earns buckets. She cooks for fun.' I glance around my parents' house. It's immaculate, as usual. Once, my mother would have taken just as much time over her own appearance, but today she looks as though she can't really be bothered. The skin under her eyes is darker than usual, and the grey roots of her hair are longer than I ever remember seeing them. 'What about you? How are you, Mum?' She brushes off my query.

'Oh, you know. Fine.'

I head upstairs to sort myself out and by the time I come back down my father has arrived home. We hug. 'Great to see you,' he says. 'So where have you been all week? Your mother texted to tell me to hurry home. Apparently, you were waiting for me so you could tell us both about a big assignment you've been on.'

We're in the kitchen. Mum has laid the table and begins to serve up our dinner as I speak. 'Have you heard of

Netley College? In Micklehurst?'

Dad looks blank but Mum has suddenly perked up. 'The psychic college?'

'That's it'.

'Ooh!' she says. 'What were you doing there? I'd love to go on one of those courses!'

Dad is looking at her as though she's taken leave of her senses. 'Why?' he asks.

'Oh, it's so fascinating. The spiritual aspect of life. The idea of other dimensions. Mysticism. Kabbalah. I just want to find out more about it all.'

My dad cuts in. 'Don't be ridiculous, Beth. They're the biggest bunch of con artists going.' He turns away from her pointedly and directs his next words at me. 'So, why were you there, Robyn?' It's rude of him to snap at my mother like that, but I can understand his impatience. Who in their right minds would want to spend time at Netley Hall, if they weren't being paid to go there?

I tell them both about the course at Netley Hall and the various people I've met over the last week. As I recount my series of lucky guesses in the practice readings it all sounds increasingly outlandish. When I reach the climax of my story, telling my parents how Laura pulled me into her private office for a talk and told me to use my powers wisely, my father literally roars with laughter. 'Loonies!' he says, 'Crackpots!'

Mum is quiet. 'You shouldn't mock, Toby,' she says finally. 'We don't understand everything that goes on in this world.'

'You're right,' my dad tells her. 'But we know enough to be able to work out what's real and what's not.'

My mother has been drinking steadily throughout the meal. Dad and I had a small glass of wine each and she's finished most of the rest of the bottle. She never used to knock them back so quickly. She coughs now to get our full attention before she speaks, pronouncing each work over-carefully. 'I do think sometimes,' she says, 'that I am unusually intuitive.' That's true enough. Years of caring for me and my dad, combined with her sensitive nature, has tuned her into the needs of others to the point that she's perhaps even more aware of them than of her own. 'And,' she goes on, 'I wouldn't mind investigating further. Perhaps I really could take a course at the College. I don't think I'm exactly clairvoyant, but it wouldn't hurt to enrol on a short course and discover whether I have any potential... What do you two think?'

I am so surprised by the proposition that I can't come up with an answer, but I don't need to because my dad replies with an over-loud, 'No'.

He doesn't say anything else and my mother falls silent again. I don't like the way this makes me feel. On the one hand, she has a right to spend her time how she wants and my father shouldn't be giving her orders. And, it's not as if money has ever been an issue for the two of them. Why shouldn't she indulge her interests?

On the other hand, dabbling in courses on mediumship is not a harmless hobby. 'Mum, I really don't think it's a good idea,' I say, gently. 'These people are con-artists, and they prey on the vulnerable.'

My father looks interested. 'Do you have proof of that?' he asks.

'I suggest that you read my piece in the paper next weekend.' This is the second time I have powered my own publicity boat in the few hours since I left Netley Hall. I'll have to keep a check on that. I don't want to become a show-off. I make my excuses and head upstairs, trying as I go not to look at my mother who's sitting quietly, eyes downcast, the picture of a cowed and submissive wife.

Late that night, I lie in bed thinking through the events of the day and of past week. Strange that I'd had no trouble sleeping in the unfamiliar environment of the College but now, in my family home, the bliss of unconscious rest seems a mile away. My mind ticks over too fast, and thoughts tumble over one another in an unorganised fashion. I think about my mum and how my father's attitude towards her has hardened. And the drinking. That's not a healthy sign. She needs to get out more, to do something for herself.

It's nearly midnight and I'm finally drifting off to sleep when my mobile begins to ping repeatedly. All the messages that couldn't arrive at Netley Hall because of the blocked signal are coming in at the same time. I pick up the phone.

There's a message from Jack, enquiring about how I'm getting on at Netley Hall. He'll have to wait until I'm back at work to find out. Three from Rick. Then more texts arrive. Seven – and counting – all of them from Rick. The first couple are quite casual, in the tone of "Hey, Robbie, howzit going? ut there's increasing concern in the others. 'ARE YOU OKAY??? MISSED A CALL FROM YOU. WORRIED,' reads the last one so I text back.

'Don't worry, am fine. No signal at college. In Brighton, will call soon.' I turn off the phone and close my eyes.

I'll go to London first thing tomorrow, I decide sleepily. Decompress, write my piece. Call Rick. Maybe meet him for a drink in the evening and invite him to the flat after-wards. I have Monday off, so if he stays over he'll have to stagger into work alone... I'm just drifting off to sleep, smiling to myself, when I hear a knock at the door.

'Yes?' I say, trying to disguise my irritation.

'Robyn? It's me. Mum.'

'I know. I'm just going to sleep.'

'I just remembered – you know, the word for what I am. What I think I am. Not clairvoyant, but clairsentient. It means you sense what people are feeling.'

'Yeah, right. Clairsentient. Um, that's nice,' I say wearily. 'You know, I'm a bit tired, Mum. I'll speak to you tomorrow. Goodnight.' I shut my eyes tightly, flip onto my other side, and finally fall asleep.

24

Confused, I look across at the clock on my bedside table. It's almost ten and I've thoroughly overslept. I've been dreaming muddled, confusing dreams and now I feel dizzy and slightly sick. I try to orientate myself. I'm in… Brighton and it's…Sunday morning. I take a few deep breaths then get up and dressed quickly and make my way downstairs, still feeling flustered. I reach the kitchen and sit down heavily. My mother looks concerned. 'What's wrong, darling?'

'Nothing. I'm just trying to wake up, that's all.'

'You are staying for lunch?' I wasn't intending to, but I suppose I might as well. I'm feeling groggy and I'm not in the mood to rush off anywhere. I resist my mother's attempts to make me a cooked breakfast, knowing that lunch will taste better if I don't stuff myself with bacon and eggs now. Of course, this sets her off.

'I hope you're eating properly.'

'We had this conversation yesterday. You don't need to worry. Just look at me. I'm fine.'

We share a coffee and then start peeling the carrots and potatoes ready for lunch. My mother always cooks too much. 'So, what are you up to?' I say. 'What are your plans for next week?'

'I don't really have any.' She seems unconcerned.

'I did wonder. Don't you get bored?' I bite the bullet. 'Are you drinking a lot, Mum?'

'What do you mean?'

'I don't mean to be rude. And obviously it's your life, but well…it's just that…you overdid it a bit last night.'

Her laughter sounds brittle. 'I'm not turning into an alcoholic Robyn, if that's what you're getting at.'

'I wasn't trying to say that. It's just that…you seem to be at a bit of a loose end at the moment. Maybe a bit fed up? Or, like I said, bored?' I'm flailing around for words and wishing I hadn't started this conversation. It's fair enough, after all, if she doesn't want to confide in me. We finish peeling the veg in silence.

Dad shows up when the meal's ready. 'It's good to see you Robyn,' he says as we eat. 'It does your mother good to have some company. I've been telling her she should get out more.' Mum doesn't reply. There is an atmosphere in the room, and I wonder if it's always like that here these days – silent, awkward.

I stand up as soon as we've finished eating. 'I really must be getting back. I meant to leave early this morning.' I don't mention that I have tomorrow off work, or Mum will insist that I stay another night and I just want to get home now. I'm looking forward to seeing Rick.

My mum gives me a lift up to the train station. 'I can drive you to London,' she says as we pull up to the dropping-off point. 'I've got nothing else to do.'

'Thanks for the offer,' I say, 'But I've already bought the ticket and I'm planning to work on the train.' I feel a pang of guilt that my mother's life is so empty she'd rather spend her afternoon and evening driving to London and back than return home. It's not my fault, though. Anyway, I'm terrified of her driving. She has the most skewed sense of road positioning of anyone I ever met, driving so close to the kerb that I'm convinced we'll come a cropper at any moment. The five-minute trip to the station was nerve-wracking enough.

I'm just getting out of the Range Rover when she says, 'Thanks for your concern, Robyn,' and grabs what she can reach of me in an attempt at a hug. 'You're right, I am a bit fed up at the moment. Maybe it's just the menopause.' She attempts a laugh. 'Or a mid-life crisis. Perhaps I should take up a hobby. Like puppetry!'

Puppetry? How random is that? 'Are you sure you're okay, Mum?' I ask again but she only smiles in response. 'I'm always here,' I say. 'If you want to talk.'

'I know,' she says. And we leave it at that.

25

The journey passes quickly. Returning from Brighton to London feels as though I am transitioning from one life to another. From dependence on my parents back to control over my life and my choices. I've made a point, ever since I went to Uni, of being the only person to decide my life path. Of course, my grandparents' bequest made it possible, but I would have cut loose from my parents anyway. It was important to me.

I relish the journey and the walk home from the station. The trees are completely bare, as you'd expect in mid-winter, but there's a faint undercurrent of warmth in the air, which feels like a promise of spring to follow. 'Hi Joe!' I call to the hotel doorman, and when he waves back I cross over the road.

'Anything exciting happen while I was away?' I ask lightly.

'I don't think you'd want to know,' he says.

I smile. 'Has Katie been having wild parties?'

'No, just the one visitor. He stayed over. All week.'

He gives me a dark look and I wonder why. I'm happy for Katie if she's met someone. I'm also tired and I want to get into my flat and relax, so I just smile politely and briefly at Joe, and say I'll see him around. I'm not going to quiz him about my flatmate's actions. She can tell me herself who her overnight visitor was.

I'd texted Katie my arrival time and she's waiting for me. She envelops me in a hug. 'I've missed you,' she says. 'Silly, I know, but it's been so lonely here.'

'Has it?' I ask innocently. I lean away, to get a better look at Katie's face but I can't read anything there.

'I've cooked dinner,' she says. 'Macaroni cheese. Made just how you like it.'

'I'm still stuffed from lunch. My mum made a huge Sunday roast and I've done nothing since except sit on the train.'

Her face falls. 'Aw, come on. I took ages over this. Made a proper cheese sauce and snapped lot of little pieces of crispy bacon in. You can squeeze some in, surely.'

I'm irritated at Katie's insistence that I eat, and also by the fact that she's just blatantly lied to me about how quiet her life had been while I was away. 'What's wrong with you?' I snap. 'You're as bad as my mother. Always trying to feed me. I'm a grown-up you know. I can decide when I'm hungry.'

I'm not prepared for her response. 'That's pretty mean, comparing me to your mother when I was only trying to be kind. I don't know why I even bother. Bitch.'

The final word is said more quietly than the rest. For a moment, I wonder if I imagined it. By the time I gather myself Katie has flounced off into her room, slamming the door behind her. I stare after her in bewilderment. It's not the first time we've ever disagreed about anything – even a seemingly perfect flatmate has opinions of her own – but swearing at me is a first. I was looking forward to telling Katie all about my week at Netley Hall and to hearing, in turn, all about her new boyfriend. Now what am I going to do? How am I supposed to behave towards her, in the light of her declaration that I'm a bitch?

There's nothing I can do right now anyway, so I banish thoughts of Katie from my mind and call Rick. I can tell from his voice that he's happy to hear from me. 'Tell me everything!' he says.

'Let's talk over a drink.'

'At yours?'

'No, let's meet somewhere else.'

I'm actually pretty worn out. Emotions have been running high recently – all the stuff at Netley Hall, then my parents' weird behaviour and now Katie's sudden display of anger. But I'm keen to see Rick. I feel instinctively that being in his company will make things better. When I arrive at George's, the trendy pub on Kensington High Street where we've arranged to meet, he's already waiting at the bar, towering over everyone else in the room.

He sees me and waves me over, beaming. There's a brief moment while I wonder whether to hug or to kiss him. I can't decide which would be better, so I opt for neither and the moment passes.

'Come on, spill the beans. I can't wait to hear about

your week,' Rick says.

'Can't a girl have a drink before she gets a grilling?' I laugh.

'Yeah. Sorry.' We take a seat with our drinks, and I run though the main highlights of the week, ending with a brief recount of the visit to my parents and the revelation that my mother has announced herself to be clairsentient. It's intended to make Rick laugh and I'm pleased when he does, but I see a glint of curiosity in his eyes. 'Your mum's into psychic phenomena? What does your Dad make of it?'

'He's not impressed, obviously,' I say. 'Any sane person can see it's a load of bunkum.' Rick nods in agreement. 'But I still feel he should give her the benefit of the doubt. He seems to have changed recently…he's got a bit controlling.'

'That must be a worry for you.' Rick seems genuinely concerned. It doesn't feel quite right to be gossiping about my parents, but it's nice to be able to confide in someone.

'So, back to the college. What else happened? Tell me everything.'

'Well,' I say. 'Don't laugh. But the director of studies – Laura – thinks I definitely have the gift.'

Rick has forgotten that I told him not to laugh but I don't mind because I like the way his eyes crinkle as he creases up. 'Robyn, that's hysterical! Does Danny think you're gifted too?'

'I don't know what he thinks. He doesn't seem to say or do much at the college. He just goes along with Laura.

But honestly Rick, I think she might genuinely believe that I'm the next Doris Stokes. It's spooked me a bit.'

Rick's still grinning. 'I'm going to start calling you Doris,' he says. 'It suits you.' I don't smile back. 'Chill out, Robyn. They've obviously cottoned on to the fact that you're a journalist and they're winding you up. Trying to make you think you've got the 'gift' so you'll write a positive piece about the college.'

'I guess so. It doesn't really matter what they think anyway. I've got enough on the college to close it down for good. How have you been anyway? How was your week?'

'I missed you,' Rick says. I look up quickly, trying to catch the twinkle in his eye, but for once he seems entirely serious. 'You could say you missed me too.'

'I did.'

'So…' he says, 'Your place or mine? Bearing in mind that mine is overrun with parents and younger siblings and we wouldn't get any peace at all. And that yours is just a few minutes down the road.'

'Erm…mine? But bear in mind that I've had words with Katie and there's a bit of an awkward atmosphere at my place. She actually called me a bitch.' I tell Rick our run-in earlier, feeling the triviality of it as I relate the conversation, but he's listening keenly.

'It's okay,' he says finally. 'We'll keep out of her way.'

26

We're back at the flat in what seems like moments. 'Well Doris,' Rick says, sotto voce, as soon as we get through the front door, 'we'd better go and hide.' He takes my hand and leads me to my bedroom.

After we've got it out of our systems, Rick looks at me quizzically. 'Have you eaten? You said Katie offered you food but you didn't want it, and that's what you argued about?'

'I'm hungry now.'

'I have my uses,' Rick grins, and we creep out of the bedroom towards the kitchen. There's a huge bowl of macaroni cheese on the table with a note propped up on it that reads, 'Help yourself!' Rick and I take two forks and go halves, and I leave a note by the empty bowl to say thanks. It looks as though things are back to normal with Katie. Maybe she was just stressed yesterday.

I suggest that we watch something on TV, but Rick insists that we need to continue to, 'Keep out of Katie's way,' which is his explanation for the two of us staying alone in my bedroom for the rest of the evening. Not that I'm complaining.

The next morning, I wake and realise it's Monday. Rick

is already getting dressed and when he sees me open my eyes, he pulls a face. 'Some of us have to go to work,' he says pointedly. 'You can just stay there and relax.' He leaves me smiling in my bed like the cat who's got the cream.

A few minutes later, I'm making my way to the bathroom when Katie comes out of her bedroom dressed for work. She looks stunning, as usual. Sometimes I think it must be nice having to get dressed up. There's nothing stopping me from wearing decent clothes at the Globe of course, except the fear of looking out of place. Also, I'd need a lot of money to be able to dress in the sort of stuff Katie does. She might complain about not getting the best jobs, but judging by her lifestyle she's earning plenty. I envy her career. It's after ten and she's only now going off to work. She doesn't even work every day – as she's explained to me, all barristers are self-employed, so the hours they work are variable, depending on the jobs they're allocated.

'Where are you off to?' I ask.

'Court. I have to defend a client who's been accused of shoplifting. Of course, she's guilty as sin – they've got her on the security camera. But she's claiming to be innocent, so I have to pretend to believe her version of events. "Your Honour, the situation is this; a pack of two hundred Benson and Hedges appears to have transferred itself from the back of the supermarket tobacco booth into the bottom of my client's child's pram. My client declares herself powerless to understand it".'

Katie laughs and I imagine her swanning into the courtroom, drawing admiring stares as she speaks eloquently and amusingly in defence of her hapless client.

She's still smiling. 'Did Rick stay over, by any chance?' she asks.

I'm embarrassed and she rushes to reassure me. 'Don't worry, I didn't hear anything. I didn't even know anyone was here until I saw him leaving just now.'

I smile back. 'What about you?' I ask. 'Have you had any special visitors recently?'

Katie is wide-eyed. 'No. You asked me that yesterday and I already told you I haven't.' She's rattled, I can see that. I, in turn, feel slightly hurt. Clearly, she doesn't want me to know what she's been up to. But why not? If my flatmate has a new boyfriend, or even just someone who stayed over casually, why shouldn't I know about it?

I push on. 'You don't have to be all coy with me,' I say. 'I know we've never discussed this, but I really don't mind you bringing a man back to the flat.'

'That's very generous of you,' she says, looking at me oddly. 'I'll bear it in mind for the future. But I haven't had anyone staying here when you were away. Although if I had, why would I want to tell you about it?'

'Well, you know. Because we're friends.'

'Friends don't keep tabs on each other,' Katie retaliates, and while I'm still wondering how to respond she turns her back on me and stalks off.

I wish I hadn't tried to raise the subject. Just when she seemed to have decided to act normally again. Now there's going to be an awkward atmosphere and since I don't understand what I've done wrong, I have no idea of how to put things right. I stand alone for a moment in the corridor then sigh, head into the bathroom and shut the door behind me.

By the time I come out, Katie has left for work and I quickly forget about her because a text message pings in from Rick. He's asking what I'm up to and I text back saying I'm working on my piece and that I'll call him later.

I make coffee but, before drinking it, check my emails. They're mostly junk but there's one from Jack saying he's scheduled a meeting for tomorrow to discuss my piece. I'd better get started on that then. I dress quickly, then sit at my desk in the living room, near the window, and begin to sift through my notebooks from Netley Hall.

I write freely, not allowing myself to self-edit, just putting my thoughts straight onto the page. I'm in the zone and the piece is three quarters written when the phone pings. Rick again. 'You said you'd call me.'

'I said later,' I text back, with a smiley emoji.

Another ping. 'Want to meet for lunch?'

I hesitate. Is he a bit over-keen? Then I remember again what Hilary said at the college about me being frightened of commitment. Maybe she was right. Maybe it's time to trust my instincts and let go a bit.

'I need to finish this piece,' I text back finally. 'Can we just meet for a drink later? When you've finished work? Then you can come back to my place.'

His reply arrives immediately, 'Can't think of anything better. We should definitely keep out of Katie's way again…' I grin at the phone as I put it down. I feel slightly out of control, but it's not an unpleasant sensation.

I continue with my work. There's no point, I reason, when I'm writing for the paper, in anguishing over every word. It's not art, its journalism. And anyway, my writing reads best when I don't give it much thought. I let it flow, and finish by three o'clock, pleased with myself. I've produced a hatchet job on the College, including a description of the so-called lessons and giving full details of the evidence I found about the numerous deceptions practised by Laura and Danny. I enjoy writing about the cats but I stop short of mocking the other students. It's not their fault they're gullible and that their thinking is faulty.

27

It's a good feeling to have met my deadline with time to spare, and now the rest of Monday afternoon beckons promisingly. I'm basking in smug self-satisfaction when the doorbell rings. It must be Rick. I don't know how he managed to get off work early but he obviously can't wait until this evening to see me.

I buzz him up and stand at the open door to my flat, grinning stupidly. I'm high on anticipation as I hear the soft thud of his feet on the stairs…and then to my surprise I find myself facing a neatly dressed, petite woman. I blink and my smile slowly fades.

'Can I help you?'

'Robyn Walters? My name is Trudy Wright. I'm a private investigator.'

'And?' I prompt. 'How can I help?'

'Can I come in?'

I hesitate for a moment, then shrug and hold the door wide to let Trudy into my home. Like every visitor to the flat she's openly fascinated by her surroundings. 'Inherited wealth?'

'Sort of.' Coming from someone whose job consists of probing into other people's lives, it's not such an offensive question. I don't invite Trudy into the living room though or offer her a drink. We're standing in the hallway, under the chandelier, and I'm still waiting to find out what a private investigator wants from me.

'I was contacted by Laura Barker,' she says, once she eventually realises I have no intention of inviting her to sit down. 'Laura's an old friend of mine. She told me she has a hunch that you can help us with some enquiries.'

'Laura from Netley Hall?' Something doesn't ring true, but I can't put my finger on it. 'Look,' I say, 'Whatever it is she says I've done, don't believe it. The woman has some kind of a problem. She's convinced I have psychic powers.' I laugh to illustrate the absurdity of this, but Trudy doesn't react.

'Don't worry, you're not in any trouble. I just need your opinion on something. Laura told me she's never had a student as gifted as you before. That even her own skill is not as strong as yours.'

I'm open-mouthed. 'And you believed her?'

Trudy's silence tells me all I need to know.

'Look,' I say, 'Let me help you out here. Strictly speaking this is confidential, but the fact is, I'm a journalist. I work for The Globe. I was sent by my editor to write an exposé of the psychic college. Laura must have guessed I'd been sent from the paper, because she decided to try to convince me I have mystical powers in the hope that the College would get a positive write-up.'

Trudy smiles. 'Laura said you're a sceptic.' This is not the response I expected, and for a moment I consider asking her to pinch me, to make sure I'm really awake. 'The thing is,' she continues, 'I could do with someone like you to work with.' She must see the look in my eyes, because she takes a different tack. 'I mean, okay, if you say you're not psychic, you're not psychic. I know not everybody believes in clairvoyance.' She does though, is the sub-text. 'But I have a case that's bugging the life out of me. It's a missing child and she's only ten years old. Just let me tell you about it. Please.'

I'm a sucker for that please word. Also, if I listen to her, presumably she'll then go away. 'Go ahead,' I say, rolling my eyes. We're still standing uncomfortably in the hall. Hopefully she'll just say what she's got to and then she'll be gone.

Trudy starts to speak and she's soon in full flow, going on and on about the missing child. I don't pay full attention, but hear more than enough to know that, without magical powers, I can't help. I take in the odd detail – the girl's been gone for several days, she lives in Croydon, her mother's frantic – but mostly I tune out.

I begin to daydream, thinking back to the clairvoyant college and the various characters I've met there. Charlotte, Chris, poor, weak Sophie. Justin, and his amazing transformation. Hilary, who admittedly did make some clever guesses when she claimed to be reading my aura.

Trudy, I realise, has stopped talking and is staring at me. 'Sorry?' I say.

'Have you been listening at all?'

'Um…' I think quickly. I don't want to admit that I'd zoned out and so I cast around for a neutral comment. 'Why are you investigating this case?' I ask. 'Surely it's a matter for the police.'

'The police have brought me in as a consultant. I often work with them. Missing people are my specialty.'

I don't know whether to believe this or not, but Trudy's still showing no signs of budging from my hallway. 'Okay, well, I read about a missing child in the paper a week or so ago,' I say finally. 'She was about the same age as your girl – ten or so – and it was somewhere in London too. The police were all over it. Then she was found in her own house, under the bed, of all things. Maybe your missing kid will just turn up.'

'I haven't heard of that case,' Trudy says.

'It was in the paper. It wasn't a headline piece, just a paragraph in a side column.'

'Which paper?'

'Does it matter? The point I'm making is, hopefully this girl you've been telling me about will be found as well.'

She's still staring at me. 'Yeah, I guess. It's just that I usually know about stuff like that. I must have missed it somehow. What paper do you read, though?'

'I read them all,' I say. 'All the broadsheets, I mean. I'm a journalist and I like to keep up to speed.' I shrug. 'Look, I feel as though I'm being interrogated. Maybe you can look it up on the internet.'

Trudy's face remains impassive. 'Just keep talking,' she says. 'A young girl's life is in danger.'

'Yes, but this child I'm telling you about was found,' I say. I'm speaking slowly, hoping to sound more patient than I feel. I'm starting to wish I hadn't mentioned the newspaper article. I rack my brain for details. 'There was some man involved. Not in a sordid way, though. He was a relative, maybe, or a friend of the family. I can't remember. He obviously wasn't very bright, because she told him she was being bullied and he agreed to help her hide, so she wouldn't have to go to school for a day or two.' I pause. 'I think, when the alarm was raised, when the police got involved, this guy panicked and instead of letting on what had happened he kept on hiding the girl. It went on for a few days before she was found.'

'Okay,' said Trudy. 'Missing person cases are my thing, but I guess London is a big place. Anyhow, thanks for listening. I am sorry you don't want to work with me.' She's checking my face but obviously doesn't see any signs that I might have changed my mind about that, because when she speaks again she sounds resigned to the facts. 'Right. Okay. You don't want to get involved. Pity, but it's your choice. I'll see you around. I'll let myself out.'

I wait until the door has closed behind her before I speak. 'Bye,' I say. 'Good riddance.'

28

It's after six o'clock. Trudy has wasted too much of my time and now I'm hungry and a bit peevish. I make myself a sandwich and eat it quickly, wondering where Katie is. She always used to let me know if she was going to be out. It's lucky I've arranged to meet Rick for a drink, because I really need to speak to someone about all this. The more I think about the idea of a private investigator trying to recruit me to work with her as some sort of psychic consultant, the more unlikely it seems.

I glance at the clock again. Right, a quick shower and off I go.

Rick and I are meeting at George's again. It's unusually quiet when I arrive, almost empty except for a few well-dressed young couples scattered at the tables. The dimly lit room reminds me of the set stage in a genteel play.

I spot Rick standing at the bar and go straight over. I want to kiss or hug him but I don't know how he feels about public displays of affection, so settle for a smile instead. 'This is beginning to feel like a habit,' he says.

'Don't get too used to it.' I pause as the barman walks over to us. 'G and T please,' I say, then turn back to Rick.

'I have got to tell you about this.' I recount the tale of Trudy's visit and Rick listens, wide-eyed.

'That is completely bizarre,' he says finally. 'I didn't know the police in this country worked with private investigators.'

'I didn't know they ever did. Or that private investigators recruited psychics to help with their enquiries.'

'Yeah, weird. Although strangely enough, it has been reported that psychics have assisted the police in the past. Usually in the case of missing persons, in fact. And the police force do employ various outsiders as consultants, often with extortionate fees. I looked into that once... Anyway, what did you say to her?'

'What could I say? I mean, obviously I told her I have no 'gift' and I have no intention of working with her or the Met in any sort of capacity. She was a bit tough to convince, but she went off eventually. With any luck, that's the last I'll see of her.'

Rick is sipping his beer, his eyes fixed on mine. 'And what now?' he asks.

'Back to mine?' I suggest and he grins.

It's dark inside the flat. 'Katie's not home yet,' I comment as I flick the hall light on.

'Good,' says Rick, pulling me into his arms. 'Let's go straight to bed.' Which we do, and eventually we drift off to sleep in each other's arms.

I wake to a hammering on the flat door. My bedside clock says it's just after midnight. Katie must have forgotten her key. It's not like her to do that though, or to cause such a racket. And how did whoever it is get through the main entrance to the building, downstairs? Usually any visitors have to ring the intercom bell and be buzzed up.

I drag myself out of bed and head along the corridor. It's Trudy. 'Let me in,' she blurts out, pushing past me into the hall and slamming the door closed behind her.

'We found her!' she shouts.

'Who?' I'm befuddled by sleep but Trudy, by contrast, is wide awake and seems almost deranged with excitement.

'Pippa. The child I was talking to you about. I couldn't stop thinking about what you had said and then I looked on the internet for hours and couldn't find any case like that. You know, where the child had been hidden by a relative or friend. So I called Gino...'

'Gino?'

'Detective Inspector Gino Groves. From the Met. It was him who authorised me to use a psychic – I mean, said I could ask you whether you'd help us with police investig-ations. And he came with me – we drove to Croydon, to Pippa's house. Her Mum and Dad let us in. Pippa's uncle was there – he lives with the family. I asked to see the girl's room – said I'd had an idea about something...I could see from the uncle's face that...'.

As her voice tails off my head is already dizzy with confusion and dread. I know what's Trudy is going to say and I finish the sentence for her. 'The girl was there, in the house, hiding under the bed.'

Trudy is so overcome with emotion that I think she might be going to hug me. I take a step back, just in case. 'How did you know?' she asks earnestly.

'I didn't,' I say.

But Trudy is gazing at me as if I'm the Chosen One. 'You did,' she says. 'You knew.'

My stress levels are rising. 'Look, I don't have any psychic gift. I mean, I really don't.'

'So how do you explain it?'

'I told you, I read about a similar case in the paper. Similar, but different.'

'That's what I told Gino. But I can't find a trace of the story you told me about. Which means that Gino's not buying it. He wants to meet you. Soon.'

The hope in Trudy's eyes is heart-breaking. I can see, reflected in them, images of all the lost children she thinks I'm going to help her find. I have to put her out of her misery as soon as possible. 'Look,' I say, 'I don't mean to be rude, but do me a favour and get a grip. You found a little girl. Well done. I am genuinely happy for you. But leave me out of it. I don't want, need, or deserve any credit. And I don't want to be woken up in the middle of the night by somebody bashing at my door. All I did was tell you about an article I read about in the paper a week ago. It's just a coincidence that the cases are similar. A truly uncanny coincidence, but there you are. The world is full of them.'

'There was no similar case,' she insists. 'You have a power, Robyn, and if you use it to work with me, you can be a great force for good in the world.'

Something about this little speech reminds me of Laura's lecture before she left Netley Hall. I speak as loudly and clearly as I can, as if Trudy is deficient of understanding. 'Please listen. I am not, and I never will be, a psychic. I have no paranormal powers of any sort. I can't help you.'

'Work with me anyway,' she says. 'We need your help on a case, an important one. We can just call you an assistant investigator, if you want. Or better still, a consultant. You can be another pair of eyes and ears. Nobody is going to question whether you are just working with your intuition, or if you're particularly sensitive to nuances, or signals, or whatever. You could just have exceptional research skills. You don't have to have any special abilities. You can do, or not do, whatever you want. It's worth a try to us, Robyn. We – the Metropolitan Police Force, and me – are willing to invest in the chance, however small, that you might be able to help.'

I can't quite take this in. 'It doesn't make sense. I've made it as clear as I can that I don't have any powers and the only explanation for you still wanting me to work with you is that you still think I do. And if I agreed to work with you – which I won't, ever – you'd be watching me constantly, hoping all along that I'll come up with something. I can't operate like that. It would be a waste of everybody's time. It's madness. Please, just go now.'

'Just call me,' says Trudy, 'If you change your mind.'

I stare at her. 'It's not going to happen.'

She leaves reluctantly and I stand for a moment, trying to process the encounter. I shake my head slowly. There's no sense to be made of it. I remember that Rick is in my bed and pad softly back to the bedroom. I perch on the side of the bed. 'Did you hear any of that?'

He's wide awake. 'All of it,' he admits.

'What on earth is going on? All I did was tell her about something I read in the paper last weekend. And I only did that to get rid of her.'

'I have literally no idea. I think we'll just have to file it in the 'inexplicable' category for now. Let's talk it through tomorrow.' He wraps his arms around me and falls asleep almost instantly. I'm surprised by the strength of my feelings for Rick as I look down as him in my bed, already breathing deeply. He's right, of course, I should go to sleep too, and forget about this until the morning.

29

I close my eyes, but the peace of unconsciousness doesn't come as easily to me as it did to Rick. The problem is, I can still visualise that paragraph in the paper. I didn't dream it, I'm as sure of that as I can be. There's absolutely no doubt in my mind that I've read the report about a missing girl, exactly as I related it to Trudy.

Unbidden thoughts are going around in my head non-stop. If I'm ever going to get back to sleep I know what I have to do, although I don't like it one bit. I get out of bed as quietly as I can and pull on a pair of jeans and a jumper.

It's dark outside except for the moon, which is high and clear in the sky, almost a perfect sphere. It's cold, freezing cold, and I'm well aware of how crazy I must appear, after midnight in February, rooting around in a dustbin on the street. I sense that someone is watching me. Whoever it is clears their throat politely, waiting for me to look up, and I stiffen. Oh God, it's Joe from the Gainsborough Hotel. He's going to think I've lost the plot.

I look up reluctantly. It's not Joe, it's Katie, and she's regarding me with a mixture of amusement and alarm.

'What's up, bin lady?' she asks. I see a flash of

something that might be pity on her face and cringe inwardly.

'I just need to find something.'

'Okay, I'll help. Tell me what we're looking for.'

'It's in one of the broadsheets. One of those small paragraphs at the side of a page. A piece about a missing girl. It's from about a week ago, before I went to Netley Hall.'

'Why do you need it right now?'

'It's too cold to talk out here,' I say. 'Let's just carry on looking. I'll explain when I have it.' We haul out all the old papers from the bin where they nestle among plastic milk cartons and empty tins, and pile them up to bring inside. Between us, Katie and I bring the stack of newspapers into the kitchen, which we lay on the work surface and begin to scan through.

'It's lucky we separate our rubbish out now, into recycling and food waste and whatever. A few years ago, if you wanted a newspaper from a bin, you'd be rifling through it for hours and then if you were lucky you'd find a soggy mess, covered in eggshell and old teabags and rotten fish. Not that I did ever want to find newspaper out of a bin, as far as I can recall. Lucky it's not recycling week, too. Hurrah for fortnightly dustbin collections. Anyway,' Katie stops chattering for long enough to draw a breath, 'when are you going to tell me what this is all about?'

'Can we just finish looking through these first?'

'I'll tell you what.' My friend gathers up the papers we've already looked through and discarded. 'I'll take these back out to the bin. They do whiff a bit, now that I notice it. Then I'll make us a coffee while you finish looking and then you can explain what's rattled your cage.'

I spend another few minutes searching for the article before I reluctantly give up, wash my hands thoroughly and go through to the living room. Katie holds out the mug of coffee to me and I sip it as I gratefully sink into one of the sofas.

'Come on,' she says. 'Spill the beans.'

I recount the tale of Trudy's appearance and re-appearance at the flat. 'She went away eventually,' I conclude, 'but I'm pretty sure she'll be back soon. So I thought, if I can find the piece in the paper that I told her about, she'll understand that I really did read about a similar case, that it was just a coincidence. Then she'll stop insisting that I have some stupid gift.'

Katie nods slowly. She looks thoughtful. 'But don't forget, this woman – Trudy – came looking for you in the first place. Why don't you just go for it? Take advantage of the situation.'

'Are you suggesting I work alongside a private detective, assisting the Metropolitan Police Force? As a psychic?'

She laughs. 'Well, when you put it like that it does sound a bit daft. But it might be fun. You can do it along-side your job at the paper. Moonlight.'

'Look,' I say. 'Trudy wants me to help with missing persons cases. I can't help find anyone and I don't want to hold out false hope to anyone who thinks I can.'

'What's she like? The detective?'

'Nice. Really nice. Lovely. Apart from the fact that she's convinced I have supernatural powers. So obviously, she's completely nuts.'

'There's more to heaven and earth...' Katie begins and I roll my eyes in exasperation.

'Please. This is me, Robyn, you are talking to.'

'Yes, but think what this could be worth. If Trudy, and the police, think you're genuine...if you are actually genuine... Imagine what you could do with a psychic gift.'

'Oh, for God's sake, don't you start.'

'Think of your glittering future. You could learn the ropes with Trudy, then set yourself up as a one-person detective agency. You could do cheating husband cases, lost jewellery. Lost pets. You could make a fortune. You might get famous. You could become a psychic to the stars, like that woman who claimed to have counselled poor, troubled Princess Di every day for years.'

'I hate to point this out again, but it would be taking advantage. I haven't got any special skills. The whole thing is utter nonsense. And I'm not a con-woman.'

'Anyone else would just take the money and run,' Katie muses. 'But of course, you don't need it.'

I bridle at that. 'Look, I know I have the flat and yes, it's worth a ton, but I do need money to live on. I'm not as well off as you think. I can't just sell the flat, it belonged to my grandparents. It belongs to my parents too, in a way.'

Katie's obviously not listening. She grins. 'This must be a unique situation. I mean, I know psychics occasionally work with the police. But I've never heard of the force trying to recruit somebody as reluctant as you.'

'Well, I'm guessing that it's a case of Trudy offering my help rather than the Met actively seeking it out. I agree, though, it is bizarre.'

It somehow helps that Katie finds the situation funny, even though I don't, and I'm pleased to have had the chance to talk things through her. I was worried last night that our friendship might be disintegrating, but we seem to be back on track, which is a relief. I value her company...all my other friends seem to have moved on with their lives and I can't afford to lose Katie too. I thank her for her help with looking for the papers and go to the bathroom for a proper wash.

30

Clambering back into bed beside Rick, I feel much more relaxed. At least I tried to find the article. I can look properly on the microfiche files at the Globe tomorrow I think, drifting off to sleep.

I wake to see Rick leaning on one elbow, looking at me. 'Have you been watching me while I sleep?' I ask. 'That's a little creepy.'

He grins. 'I was using the power of my mind to wake you up. Morning, Doris.'

I laugh as he folds me into his arms. He feels strong and warm, and it's comforting to be held tight. 'I could get used to this,' I say, and then we're too busy to speak for quite a while.

Over breakfast I tell Rick that I've had coffee and a chat with Katie in the night.

'I thought you were tucked up next to me.'

'I couldn't sleep.' I don't tell him how Katie found me rifling through the bins in the dark. For one thing, I'm not sure what sort of image that would produce in Rick's mind, and for another I don't want him to know how much the whole business with Trudy has disturbed me.

'Does this mean that we don't need to keep out of Katie's way, now that the two of you are talking again?' he says. 'Pity.'

He's right, there's no reason why the three of us shouldn't socialise now. Except that I still haven't told Rick the flat belongs to me. I know I should come clean, but I want to be sure that he likes me for who I am, not because of what I have got. And I don't know how to begin to explain why I lied. Once you start lying there's no end to it. You can only sink deeper into the quagmire, trying in vain to remember what you said and why. I don't want to get caught in a crazy web of deceit, and so I'm just searching for the right words to try to tell Rick what happened, when I look up to see him gazing deeply into my eyes. He's twirling a strand of my hair around a finger. It's not surprising I've fallen for him, I realise. It would be impossible not to.

Rick speaks before I get the chance. 'I'm just thinking...maybe don't tell Katie too much about us.'

I laugh. 'Katie? Why not?'

'I just have a feeling she might not like it if she knows we're properly together.'

'Why? Because she wants you for herself?' I tease.

'Of course not. I just think she might feel...I don't know. Insecure. If she knows you're serious about someone.'

I think about this. 'Joe told me that someone stayed over with Katie, when I was away at Netley Hall. She denied it though.'

'And you believe her?'

I shake my head. 'I don't know. It doesn't really matter whether someone stayed over or not, anyway. It isn't really any of my business. It's just...confusing.' Rick hesitates as if he's about to say something else, but instead he just draws me in close. I want to lose myself in his embrace again, but a part of my mind remains separate, assessing the situation. Should I trust Katie, or Joe? And why am I sensing that Rick knows more than he is letting on?

'So, you're obviously not going to work with Trudy,' he says. I don't reply. 'Robyn, please tell me you're not considering giving up your career at The Globe to work with a private detective as a psychic advisor?'

'Katie thinks I should. Not give up my job, but work with Trudy some of the time. Moonlight.'

'Does she? Why? Is she into all that mystical claptrap too?'

'No. She just thinks it might be...interesting. Fun.'

'Which it might be, if this Trudy person was investigating other things. Like stolen cars or jewellery or whatever. But she's looking for missing persons. This is life or death stuff, if I get you right. Not something to get involved with lightly, or at all.'

'I know. That's what I told Katie.'

'So just forget about it, Robyn.'

Rick's right. Of course he's right. I need to put this whole stupid business out of my mind.

31

Breakfast over, Rick and I are travelling to work together and I'm in a good mood. It's a relief to be taking my usual tube journey. It makes me feel grounded to be back in the old routine. I've only been away for a week, but Netley Hall was such a different environment to the one I'm used to, and the people I met there were such a different crowd to those I usually mix with, that it feels like much longer.

I also like the feeling that I'm part of a proper couple, heading into work with my boyfriend. Rick holds my hand tightly all the way to work, his leg pressing firmly against mine, but when we reach the site of the Globe we enter the building separately, by unspoken agreement.

I've been looking forward to my meeting with Jack. I've written a good piece and I've got plenty of hard evidence to back it up. Netley College is soon going to be history, I think happily. I nod and smile at several colleagues as I make my way through our common workspace to Jack's inner sanctum. 'Robyn,' he says, as I take my seat opposite him. 'How did it go?'

I launch right in. 'Well, I've got a story for you. The College proprietors are definitely crooked. They are taking advantage of vulnerable people. It's all in the piece.' I've printed my article off at home and put it into a folder with the photos I've printed up. I offer the folder to Jack now, but he doesn't take it.

'Hmm,' he says. 'Do you have any proof?'

'Photographs of the files they keep on all their students. It's all in here.'

He still doesn't take the folder. 'Just run through it for me.'

I tell Jack about the file I'd found in Laura's office, stuffed with information on all the students on the course. 'Laura and Danny have a whole network of contacts that they use to exploit their students,' I say. 'The file I photographed includes information about medical issues, communications from other mediums that these people have consulted. Stuff about their relationships and financial situations.'

I pause momentarily for breath, and Jack butts in. 'The first rule of journalism is, don't speculate. What you found could just be explained as background material that the college keeps for all the students. We don't want to jump to conclusions, offend anyone, risk getting sued. Lots of people believe in this bunkum and it's harmless enough. Just write up a nice piece about what happened at the college, from a personal point of view. Make it real, write it so the reader imagines being there with you.'

I can't believe what I'm hearing. 'Jack, I have evidence of fraud at the college. Whoever tipped you off about the place was right. Laura keeps material on every student who has ever passed through Netley Hall.'

'Does she have a file on you?'

'Not on me, no. Probably because I booked in late, or because I went under a false name...'

'What exactly do these files say?'

Ah, I see the problem now. I haven't spelled things out clearly enough for Jack. 'Okay. Justin, for example. She knows he's mentally unwell, that he's been treated for psychosis. She knows who his parents are, where they live. The fact that they're wealthy.'

Jack shrugs. 'They're obviously well-off if they can afford to book him into Netley Hall. And they probably told her about their son's mental health issues. It's relevant information, if the college is expected to keep the boy safe. What about the others?'

'Charlotte is a chronic over-sharer on social media. Laura and Danny had printed out loads of stuff from her Facebook account, all sorts of personal information, including pages about her diagnosis of breast cancer.' Jack raises his eyebrows but doesn't comment.

'Then there's Sophie. She's consulted numerous other psychics over the last year or so, and they've fed everything they learned about her personal life back to Laura. That she's separated from her husband, that a divorce is the process of finalisation. Even that she's had an operation on her feet, and suffered emotional trauma in the process. These so-called clairvoyants must have some sort of a network system in place, sharing information about regular clients. Which they can then use to convince the clients of their supernatural powers. Jack, this is huge.'

'Anything else?' my boss asks. To my bafflement, his tone is neutral. He sounds almost disinterested.

'Loads more. Chris, one of the men on the course, was orphaned as a boy. I don't know how Laura and Danny found that out, but it's in his file. And there's information on Hilary too...'

I don't get as far as telling Jack about the notes on Hilary, which detailed her house being decimated while she was out walking her dog. He's already snapping at me angrily. 'I told you already, you can't mention finding those files. You broke into her private room. The paper would be sued. Even if you could prove that Laura and Danny intended to use the information for gain, it would be inadmissible as evidence.'

'I didn't break into anywhere,' I protest. 'I just walked through an open door.'

'You can't use it,' he repeats.

I'm still struggling to understand what he's saying. 'But...'

'You can't write that it's all a con without proof, and we can't use your illegally gained material as proof. And anyway, this is not the sort of article I wanted to see. Write about the food, the surroundings, what you were taught. Make it interesting, readable. Add some humour.'

Humour again. 'But you asked me to investigate! You said you'd had a tip-off about dodgy goings-on at Netley Hall.' Jack's face is devoid of expression. I have one last try. 'They keep the students cut off from the world, Jack, like hostages. There's no internet connection, no mobile signal. And then they carry out their brain-washing. Even I was starting to doubt my own sanity by the time the course finished.' I'm about to tell Jack about Laura insisting that I have 'the gift' and sending a private detective to my home to speak to me, but he doesn't give me the opportunity.

'Don't be silly,' he says. 'Just re-write the whole thing, Robyn. I want a nice, light-hearted article on my desk, first thing in the morning.'

I leave Jack's room feeling confused and angry. 'Don't be silly'? He's treating me as though I were a child having a tantrum. Write 'a nice, light-hearted article'? What on earth can he be thinking?

'Not a good meeting then?' says Rick, as I return to my desk. 'He's not sending you away again, is he?'

'I'll tell you about it later,' I say. 'I've got work to do.' Which is true... I have to somehow write an utterly sycophantic and completely non-judgemental piece about a college for clairvoyants and the people who run it, who are dodgy to the point of criminality and beyond.

32

My brain is foggy as I force myself to sit at my desk and open my laptop. I'm feeling disillusioned to the extreme. Jack's strange behaviour has brought the foundation of my career into question. What, after all, is the point of being a journalist if you can't expose the truth when you uncover it?

I'm so furious I can't concentrate on my writing. I'll take an early lunch, I decide. It will do me good to get out for a bit. As I close the computer I look around for Rick, hoping he'll be free to come with me. I really want to talk to him about what just happened in Jack's office. Rick, however, is nowhere to be seen, so I walk down to the river alone.

The Thames Embankment seems like the obvious place for a walk but when I get there it's so packed with people that instead I opt to sit on a bench, watching the tide of pedestrians milling around alongside the flow of the river, and the many boats drifting upon it. So many disparate lives, so many choices are on display here, from the City suits striding along with their briefcases to the group of hippies I spy floating down the river on a barge. And, what, I think, about me? What direction should I go in?

I mentally skim through my options. I could give up work. I could sell the flat or keep it and let it out, and use the money to set up a business of some kind. Or I could travel. I could do anything, really. Working at the Globe has been my dream for so long, though, that I'm reluctant to let it go. Jack might be a rubbish boss but he won't be there forever. Maybe I should wait and see how things develop.

I sit a while longer before the answer comes to me with a jolt of clarity. I know what I'll do. I'll work with Trudy after all. If you could call it work. I'll go along with her and it'll serve to take my mind off the business with Jack and the futility of my career as a journalist at the Globe, but I won't be burning any bridges in the process. I can still work at the paper, and moonlight with Trudy, as Katie suggested. Maybe I can even turn this to my advantage. I could write a piece about how the London police are wasting public funds by paying so-called psychics to help with their investigations. If Jack won't print it then I could use the article to try to get a job at another paper, or even go freelance.

At least I won't need to feel guilty about moonlighting. Any loyalty I ever felt towards the Globe seems to have been misplaced. Jack appears to have lost his senses, suggesting I ignore all the evidence and just write a stupid piece pretending everything at the college was fine. Maybe he has some ulterior motive. My thoughts spiral downwards again. My job and prospects are far worse than I realised. I am nothing but a puppet, with no hope of promotion or progression. But then it means I've got nothing to lose. Working with Trudy might be a complete sham, but it will definitely give me something new to think about.

I get my phone out and dial the number before I have time to change my mind. Trudy answers after just a couple of rings. I glance around quickly before I start speaking. This is not a conversation which I would like strangers to overhear, but fortunately there's no-one in the vicinity. 'Hi,' I say. 'It's Robyn Walters. I've been thinking about your offer and I'm willing to consider working with you. As an investigator, alongside my day job. You can call me a consultant if you want. But the condition is that you don't expect me to uncover anything using paranormal skills I don't have.'

She sounds unreasonably excited. 'That's brilliant news, Robyn,' she says. 'I'm so happy to have you on board. Can you meet me at the station in West Hendon? I'd like you to meet Gino.'

'Gino?'

'My contact in the Met. Remember?'

'Oh. Yeah. Okay.'

This moonlighting thing is taking off quicker than I'd imagined. I email Jack from my phone, telling him I'm not feeling well and I'm going home to re-write my piece on Netley Hall. If he doesn't like it, he can lump it. Then I make my way to the nearest tube station. It's not easy to reach West Hendon police station from central London. I have to change from the tube to the over ground train, to the bus. And all the time I'm navigating my way across the city, I'm trying to think about anything except what I'm doing, pretending to myself that this is a normal journey. I'm going…shopping, or something.

The police station is surprisingly modern and compact. I'd imagined such places were still rooted in the Dark Ages, but this one seems to have benefitted from a recent upgrade. I've texted Trudy from the bus with my ETA and when I enter the building she's already waiting for me in the foyer. She takes my hand and grips it firmly. 'I really am so pleased to have you on board Robyn,' she says. She's looking into my eyes and I can see she's genuinely delighted that I'm there. I don't think I have ever felt myself to be so much of a fraud.

Trudy takes me through a security door and leads me down a corridor to a room with a nameplate announcing its occupant as 'D.I. Groves'. We enter together and I size the policeman up as he moves out from behind his desk. He's about five foot ten, lean-faced, with bloodshot green eyes. 'Afternoon,' he says. He's looking at me with a distinct lack of enthusiasm and he doesn't offer me his hand to shake.

'Robyn Walters.' I say.

'Right. You can call me Gino. And now you and I are going out for coffee.'

'Why can't we talk in here?' I ask.

'Because I don't want any of my officers thinking I've lost my nut, letting some crazy private detective talk me into working with a supposed clairvoyant.'

I don't know how anyone in the building would have any idea what I'm here for, especially since we're currently behind a closed door. Gino's a senior police officer though, and I'm not about to pick a quarrel with him. I glance towards Trudy to see how she has taken being referred to as crazy, but her face is blank. 'I'll leave you two to it,' she says brightly. 'I'm going to grab myself a coffee.' I watch her back in disbelief as she disappears into the interior of the police station. She seems very much at home, but I suppose that fits with her story of helping the police with missing persons cases on a regular basis.

Gino and I walk in silence to a nearby café, where he insists on sitting at an outside table despite the fact that the temperature is not much above freezing. There's not even a heater out here to take the edge off. He claims that we're sitting outside to safeguard our privacy, which I think is odd given that he insisted on leaving his private space to conduct this meeting in a public place. The real reason becomes apparent when the coffee arrives and he takes a pack of cigarettes out of his pocket and lights one. The wind is blowing the smoke right over in my direction and I lean away. There's nothing I dislike more than passive smoking.

'Sorry,' he says, clearly not meaning it.

I forget to not wind up the detective inspector. 'Your problem,' I say. 'It's a death-wish.'

'What makes you think that?'

'What else can it be? Why do you think anyone with

176

any sense has stopped smoking? Or that most people don't even start now?'

'I just need something to put in my mouth…' he fixes his green eyes on mine until I blush, and then he laughs. 'I have a nicotine addiction. Not everything has a deep psychological explanation.'

I don't speak. 'Look,' he says, 'this isn't about my smoking. It's about you. Trudy talked me into getting you on board with this case. The only reason I went along with it is because there's no hope and the sooner the parents realise it, the better. Using a psychic is a last resort, and I've told them so. This is the end of a very long line of investigation.'

'What case?' I ask.

'Jordan Taylor.' He looks at me, waiting for a reaction.

I recognise the name but it takes a moment for the pieces to fall into place. 'The little boy who went missing on holiday? Ages ago. Wasn't it in Weymouth?'

'That's him. And it was ten bloody years ago.' Gino looks world-weary. 'The kid's gone for good. No doubt about it. He's not coming back. But his parents either won't believe it or they can't, and they've never let it go.'

The case of Jordan Taylor surfaces regularly in the papers and I'm well aware that his disappearance garners a lot more publicity than that of most missing persons, especially given the number of years since it happened.

'They badger the Home Office constantly,' Gino continues. 'They're very well connected and they've got public support behind them. Which means that the Home

Office pester us in turn, and then we have to make it seem like we're still looking for the kid, even though we've already exhausted every possible line of investigation. I'm in charge of the case, for my sins, and I really feel it's time all of us move on to something else. Which is why you've been called in. If it takes a so-called psychic to convince this couple that their child really has gone for ever, I'm going to do it. It's a last resort. After this, we move on. The Met has limited resources and there are other things we need to deal with.'

He pauses for breath, then looks at me curiously. 'So how on earth did you manage to convince everyone that you're psychic?'

'I'm not psychic,' I say.

'I'm not disagreeing with that. But Trudy believes you're the genuine article. And you did somehow find that Pippa kid. Explain that.'

'I didn't find her. All I did was read about a similar case in the paper and tell Trudy about it. You two found Pippa, not me. For some reason, you both seem determined not to believe my account of things.'

'You read about it in the paper, you say. Well, which paper? The Psychic News?' That's actually quite funny but I keep a straight face. 'Because Trudy's looked thoroughly and she can't find a trace of the thing you were talking about in any paper,' he persists.

I shrug but again I don't reply. After all, I know what I read. Eventually Gino breaks the silence. 'Okay, so you're a reluctant psychic.'

'I am not a psychic, as I already told you.'

'So why are you here?'

Good question. 'Because Trudy wouldn't take no for an answer. Plus, I've developed some problems at work. At the Globe. I thought this might make a change.'

'Right,' he says. 'And, of course, you're not influenced at all by the money, but I have to tell you that our usual consultancy fee is three thousand pounds a day. Is that going to be enough?'

33

Gino and I walk back to the police station without another word. The subtext to his silence seems to be that he's disgusted with my company, having formed the conclusion that I'm nothing but a money-grubbing hack without even any pretensions to a magical gift. The subtext to mine is probably shame, because I really can't blame this guy for resenting me. Three thousand pounds is a ridiculous amount of money to be paid daily. But then I didn't ask for it, he offered. No wonder the public services are all struggling to stay afloat, if this is the going rate for a consultant to the police force. Presumably Trudy is getting the same rate, which is doubly ridiculous.

When we arrive at the station, Trudy's waiting. Gino stalks away with just a curt nod in our direction. She smiles at me. 'All the details settled, then?' she says. 'We might as well get started right away, if you're free for the rest of this afternoon.'

'I guess I am,' I say. I follow Trudy to her car. It's a black BMW fitted with all the mod cons. Private investigation must be a lucrative business – at least if you get in thick with the police force. We've been driving for a few minutes before it occurs to me to ask Trudy where we're going. 'We're on our way to visit Jordan's parents,' she says. This statement makes me feel instantly nauseous. I don't want to face these people and their grief. I don't want to see the hope in their eyes when Trudy introduces me, knowing full well that I have nothing to offer them. It's too late to back out now though.

'Gino has said he's going to pay me three grand a day,' I say. I'm looking at Trudy's profile, interested to gauge her reaction, but she doesn't flicker an eyelid.

'That's the going rate,' she tells me.

'How come he's paying me?' I ask. 'And not you? Who am I working for?'

'You're acting as a consultant to the Met. That's the way he wanted it. They're paying me separately for my role in the investigation.'

I suppose it doesn't matter, and I let the subject drop. 'You're the only person I know who drives in London,' I tell Trudy.

'It comes with the job. I can't rely on public transport, I never know where I'll need to be next. Plus, I like driving.'

'Me too,' I say. 'There's just no point owning a car around here, for most people.'

'London's not the only place to live, you know,' Trudy says.

'It is, for me.'

'Why?'

'I don't really know,' I admit. 'I suppose it symbolises independence, freedom. And for a journalist, it's the only sensible place to be. Everything that matters happens in London.'

Trudy raises one elegant eyebrow. 'A lot of journalists freelance,' she says, then changes the subject. 'What did you make of Gino?'

'He is unlucky in love. He will soon go on a long journey...' I say in a faraway, trance-like voice. She doesn't laugh. What does she expect me to say about Gino? The man's an idiot. Anybody who spends more than a minute in his company can be in no doubt of that.

'I liked him,' I lie.

'Why?' Her tone is neutral.

'Because he doesn't have any expectations of my success.'

'That's fine then. At least you have a clear conscience, if you really don't believe in your gift.'

'I don't have a gift. And your acceptance of that fact is my condition of being here, remember? But if I can help you with your investigations, I will. Tell me about Jordan's parents.'

'Well. For one thing, they're shadows of their former selves,' Trudy says. 'Both used to be high-flying lawyers, both are now unemployed. They spend all their time trying to find their son and working on campaigns to get funding and public support for their search. They've pretty much lost touch with reality. It's a car crash.'

'Do they have other children?' She shakes her head. 'I suppose that's a good thing. I mean, the others, if they had any, would be affected by the loss of Jordan too. The whole family would be destroyed.'

'Or,' says Trudy, 'The parents might have held themselves together for the sake of the kids they still had. Who knows?'

We're in Richmond, pulling up in front of a palatial building. 'It's good that they managed to hold on to their home,' I observe.

'They were both invalided off work on generous packages. Also, they have friends in high places. Money's not a problem. But the house is a wreck.'

Now that the car is stationary, I can see for myself how neglected the place is. Paint is peeling from the door and the window ledges, and the front garden is a tangle of undergrowth. It looks more like a squat than the home of a well-to-do, still-young couple. The front door is ajar and Trudy pushes it open and walks in.

'I suppose you told them we were coming,' I say.

'Yes, they're expecting us. But the door's almost always open anyway. I keep telling them to shut and lock it. They've been burgled several times and they're lucky they've never been seriously injured. They won't listen though.'

Trudy sighs. She doesn't need to explain, I know exactly who they keep the door unlocked for. The two-year-old child they lost, the twelve-year-old son who might one day just walk in. Who probably already does, every night in their dreams.

As my eyes adjust to the lack of light, it's increasingly obvious that the condition of the house is truly shambolic.

This must be the most squalid home I have ever entered. I scan the hallway to see that the dust is thick on every surface, and the floor is lined with litter that must have blown in from the street. The carpets are so badly stained that the only decent thing to do would be to throw them out and start again. I see a faint, quick-moving shadow dart into a doorway. It could be either a cat or a rat. The smell is so overwhelmingly foul that I have to fight the urge to gag.

Trudy calls out and when the couple emerge from the darkness at the back of the house, she says simply, 'this is Robyn.'

Lucy and Lionel Taylor are well-spoken and polite but, as Trudy had implied, they appear distant and dead-eyed, as though they've been hollowed-out. We follow them through to the kitchen where we all sit. Trudy and I politely decline Lucy's offer of a hot drink and the couple don't seem surprised. I guess it's been a long time since any guest accepted refreshments in this wretched house.

Once they begin to speak about their child, they seem to come alive. They're clearly obsessed with the search for Jordan. They've enrolled their friends, their wealthy families, and all the connections they've made in law and government from both of their illustrious careers, to help them over the last ten years, but the sad fact is that Lucy and Lionel are probably the only two people in the world who still believe there's any hope of finding their son.

We sit in that dingy kitchen for what seems like hours and all I can do, as I listen to the devastated couple, is wish I could help them. Finally, they finish their long recount of the search to date. 'Are you the psychic?' Lucy asks suddenly. 'They promised to get us a psychic.'

I glance at Trudy, but she doesn't speak. 'I would like to help find your son,' I say.

I want to say something else but I am casting around helplessly for inspiration, and Trudy taps my arm gently. 'Come on, Robyn. Time to go.'

I stand up to leave with her, but then on impulse change direction quickly, to face Jordan's parents again. 'Could I have a look at Jordan's room, please?' I ask. Tears are pricking at the back of my eyes, and I have to summon all my resolve to stop them breaking through.

'Of course,' says Lucy, 'you can go anywhere you want.' Lionel nods eagerly.

'Maybe just have a look around on your own,' Trudy suggests. 'We'll wait in here.'

I move from room to room quickly and quietly. There's nothing much to see downstairs apart from the squalor I've already noted, so I make my way and quickly find the room that must have been Jordan's. I glance around. From what I've seen so far, it must the only area of the house that's clean and tidy. It's also crammed with what must have been the boy's belongings, a vast array of toys and books.

I know the police must have been here on more than one occasion, looking for clues, and anyway Jordan has been gone for so long that there couldn't possibly be anything useful to find. So I don't look for anything in particular, but just stand in the centre of the room and try to stay open, to see if anything comes to me, any idea or connection. There's a book on the small table by the boy's bed. War Horse. I pick it up, turn it gently in my hands. I feel only a deeper sense of the sadness which already pervades this house.

Then my legs go shaky and I sit, suddenly, on the toddler-sized bed. What am I doing? Trying to connect with something other-wordly? I don't even believe in this stuff. But even though I've only just met them, I'd do anything to help the couple downstairs, to get rid of the haunted look in their eyes. And who am I to shut my mind to any possibility of spiritual phenomena? I realise, suddenly, that Hilary was right. I am scared. Scared that this 'spirit' notion might actually exist. Because if it did, where would we all be? Not knowing what is real and what isn't, whether or not we can trust the evidence of our senses. Disregarding the laws of science and physics, constantly trying to tune in to another level or channel. How confusing, how disorientating that must be. That's why it's always been something I've shied away from. I want to live in the here and now. I want to stay sane. And yet here I am, after just a brief visit to this bereft and empty household, attempting to make 'spirit' communicate with me.

My legs still feel weak as I go back down the stairs. I can't hear any voices in the kitchen but when I enter the room they are still all sitting at the table. Three faces are looking at me eagerly, hopefully.

I smile faintly. 'Anything?' asks Lucy.

'No. Or only...I was wondering about the book on Jordan's table,' I say. 'War Horse? Quite a read for a two-year-old boy. Was he very...advanced?'

It's Lionel, not Lucy, who replies. 'I'm reading it,' he says. 'I've always done it. Ever since Jordan was...since he left. I choose books I think Jordan would like, and I read them for him. I know it doesn't really make sense. But it makes me feel as though he's...'

'As though he's here,' I interrupt and Lionel looks up at me, tears in his eyes.

'Exactly that,' he says.

34

Trudy and I finally leave the Taylors' house and we've been driving for a few minutes before Trudy speaks. 'What were you doing up there? In Jordan's room?'

'If you really want to know,' I say, 'I was wandering around, picking things up, hoping for some intervention from spirit. That's how crazy those poor desperate people made me feel.'

'I'm sorry, Robyn. I should have prepared you better for meeting Jordan's parents, not just sprung it on you.'

'It's worse for them,' I reply, and for the rest of the journey we remain in silence. It's just after seven o'clock when Trudy drops me off at the flat. I sit quietly in the living room. My mind is empty and I feel numb. I'm unaware of how much time has passed when my phone rings, making me jump. It's Rick.

'Where did you disappear to?' he asks.

'I'm surprised you noticed. It's not as if you're in the office much yourself.'

'Well I was today, and you were supposed to be having lunch with me.'

Whoops. 'It was a really bad meeting with Jack. I had to get out for a walk, think things over for a bit. I looked for you but you weren't around, so I went out alone for an early lunch. And then things happened…' I trail off. If I'd remembered that I'd arranged to eat with Rick and waited for him, I realise, I probably wouldn't have ended up calling Trudy and meeting either Gino or Jordan's parents. It really had been one hell of an afternoon.

'You sound tired,' Rick says. 'Shall we meet up tonight? You can tell me all about it.'

'I'd love to. I really want to see you. But I'm really sorry, I can't. We'll have to have a night off. I need to re-write my Netley Hall piece.'

'Why?' he asks. I remember that he doesn't even know the outcome of my meeting that morning and quickly explain that Jack is refusing to believe that anything's awry at Netley Hall, despite all the evidence, and has told me to write a 'nice, light, humorous' piece instead. Rick is sympathetic. 'We're just the minions, Robyn,' he sighs.

I put the minimum of effort into writing the new version of my Netley Hall article, and am finished by nine. I could have seen Rick after all, and I'm on the verge of calling him to suggest that he comes over to spend the night when I hear Katie's key in the door.

'Hi!' she's smiling cheerfully. 'Have you eaten?' It's a welcome question. 'I'll do a stir-fry,' she says. 'Come and talk to me what happening at your work, while I cook.'

I sit at the kitchen table watching as Katie chops peppers and slices carrots, quickly and skilfully assembling a rainbow dish for the two of us. As she prepares the food, I tell her how Jack surprised and upset me with his rejection of my article this morning. 'I've decided to work with Trudy after all,' I announce.

'Ooh!' Katie says. 'Exciting!' She's agog as I relate the details of the meeting with Gino and the case I've been asked to help with.

'Jordan Taylor. I know that name.' Of course she does. Everyone does. And knowing Katie, she's probably read all the opinion pieces on it as well as the factual reporting. 'That is one high-profile case,' she continues. 'Personally, I always wondered if the parents were involved'.

I'm shocked. 'They've done everything they can to find their son, for ten years,' I point out.

'I don't know. Sometimes when I see them on TV, on news conferences, I get the impression that they're enjoying the publicity.'

'You couldn't be more wrong,' I say. 'There's no way that Lucy and Lionel have anything to do with Jordan's disappearance.'

'I thought you said you're not psychic.' I ignore this dig and we shelve the subject and sit down to watch the TV. I'm not happy with Katie's attitude though, and I feel relieved when, after just a few minutes, she gets up and goes back to her room. Now I wish I'd called Rick after all, but it's half past nine now. Too early to go to sleep, but just a little too late to call and ask him to come over.

It's Wednesday morning and I'm back at the Globe. Rick's at his desk and I wave to him but don't dare go closer because I'm aching to touch him and don't know if

I would be able to resist. I don't want everyone gossiping about us.

I think for a moment about the mechanics of moonlighting. How can a person work two day jobs? The Globe keeps me pretty busy – how will I get time off to meet with Trudy? Fortunately, Jack inadvertently comes to my rescue. There's an email in my inbox from him, asking me to write a feature on women who work as opposed to women who stay at home with their children. Another glossy space filler, in other words.

'Do your research around town,' the message ends. 'No hurry. Don't feel you're tied to the office.' It's almost as if he knows I have other demands on my time.

Rick has left the building once again, so I work through lunch. I write the piece quickly. My research consists of reading a couple of internet articles on the subject of whether it's better for children for their mothers to look after them full-time or go out to work, then re-hashing the arguments and coming to the conclusion that it should be a matter of individual choice. 'Clarice,' my invented working mother source, says that not having her at their constant beck and call has made her three kids more resilient. 'Jolie,' my pretend stay-at-home mum, is quoted as saying, 'Jack and Yasmin are so much happier than their peers because they have my undivided attention.' I then find a quote from a child psychologist who says that there are pros and cons on both sides – and the job is done.

I don't send the piece to Jack yet though. I'll keep it in

hand, email it to him on Friday. It'll be good for a day off tomorrow, which I can spend with Trudy, passing 'Go' and collecting three thousand pounds, while pretending to be doing my research.

I email Jack to say I've made a start on the article and will be meeting and interviewing mothers at a local playgroup tomorrow to round it out. I also tell him what I'd gleaned from my conversation with the Brighton cabbie. 'If it's true that London councils are giving the homeless one-way tickets to seaside towns, it's a scandal. Is it okay with you if I research and write a piece on this?' I write.

He mails back almost immediately. 'Good work re the mother thing,' he writes. 'Enjoy toddler group tomorrow. But no article on the homeless will be required. The Globe doesn't really do campaigning on social issues. Leave that sort of thing to the Guardian.'

I'm irritated, but not surprised. I don't expect much from Jack any more. I suppose I could write a piece on the subject of the homeless anyway, though. It might come in useful one day, if I do decide to go freelance. I make a note on my phone so I don't forget.

Rick hasn't come back to work, so I text him. 'Fancy a drink tonight?'

'Of course. Where?'

'My place.'

'My favourite venue,' he texts back, with a kiss-blowing emoji.

I find the emoji with the heart-shaped eyes, think for a

second but then decide against it and send the smiley-face one instead. One step at a time.

35

Katie isn't around, which means I have to cook for myself. My culinary skills might not be great but I can rustle up an omelette, and I fry up some mushrooms and onions to go in it. Rick turns up at around eight. I open a bottle of wine and we sit in the kitchen. 'Sorry I haven't seen much of you,' I say. 'There's been so much going on in the last couple of days.'

'I started to wonder whether you were going off me.'

I laugh, because I know that there isn't a chance of that happening and I'm pretty sure he knows it too. 'Listen, I've got news. I've decided to work with Trudy after all.'

'You're joking.' He looks at my face. 'Okay, you're not joking. But why on earth would you want to do that?'

'There's no future for me at the Globe. And the Met are going to pay me, you won't believe how much. Also, it could be interesting.' I tell Rick about my proposed exposé of how the Met are wasting public money.

'You said you weren't going to get involved with that.'

'Look, it's different for you,' I say. 'You've worked at the Globe for exactly as long as I have and you have a glittering career. Mine, by contrast, hasn't even started to take off. Then just when I think I've done some real investigative journalism and finally written something that's worth reading, Jack refuses to publish it. It's quite a knock, Rick, and I don't know where to go from here.'

'Whoa,' he says. 'Hold your horses. I'm just worried about you. You seem to be getting involved in something you're not completely happy about and I just wanted to point out that you don't have to do it.'

I soften. 'I know you're looking out for me,' I say. But there's no need. I know what I'm doing.'

Do I, though? Do I really?

Rick stays the night again and the next morning, Thursday, I wave him off to work. 'Remember,' I say as he leaves, 'if anyone at the Globe asks, I'm researching an article.'

'As you say, Doris.'

Then I go to work with Trudy and, by extension, for the Greater Metropolitan Police.

We meet at ten o'clock, in a café near my flat. It's called Benny's and, unusually for the area, specialises in the all-day English breakfast. I watch as three men on a nearby table, who must have come from work at the building site opposite, tuck into huge plates piled high with sausages, eggs and beans. Rick would like it here.

Trudy orders us both a coffee and we sit down at a corner table. 'Can I ask you a personal question?' I say. I continue without waiting for an answer. 'What's your connection with Laura? And why do you believe so strongly in her powers?'

'That's two questions.' I smile politely. 'Okay,' says Trudy, 'I've known Laura for about fifteen years. When I first came to London I was very young, still a teenager, and completely alone. There was a time when I lost my way and Laura gave me hope.'

'Specifically?' I ask.

'I was seventeen. I'd been having a hard time with a boyfriend. I moved to London to be with him but it soon became clear that things weren't going to work out. I was stuck in a dead-end job and I didn't know whether to stay or go home. I'd never seen a psychic before but I was desperate for any guidance I could get. Laura was working out of a department store then, with a bunch of other women. Mystic Angels or something, they called themselves.' Trudy pauses.

'She mentioned that she started off working as part of a team,' I say.

'Right. So, it was a Saturday, and I walked straight in and Laura read my palm, and she was amazing. She saved my life.'

'Specifically?'

'She knew without being told that I was having boyfriend trouble. I'll always remember her words. She said, "You'll be alright. But not with him." Then she advised me to stay in London and join the police force.'

'Really? She told you to join the police? In so many words?'

'I don't blame you for being sceptical. But Laura knew so much about me, she reassured me, told me everything was going to be okay. And she was right.'

'Anyone could have reassured you.'

'I could trust her. It was instinctive. She had authority.'

I think back to Netley Hall and how quickly Laura had all the students practically eating out of her hand. She did have an air of authority. And vulnerable people need something to cling to, understandably. But Trudy's not a teenager anymore. She's an adult with a responsible career. She should know better by now.

'But you didn't join the police,' I say.

'I did. I worked on the force for twelve years before I set up my agency. That's how come I regularly get brought in to help as a consultant. It's my bread and butter work.' So Trudy used to be a police officer. All the more reason why she shouldn't be so gullible. 'That's not all,' she continues. 'I went back to see Laura again about four years ago, and she told me about my sister's illness. Sylvie had been having symptoms for a while, but wouldn't go to the doctor. Laura said it was her stomach and that she must get medical help and if she did it would be alright, but if she didn't go, that would be the end of her. I took her to the GP myself, she got sent for tests and it turned out to be cancer. She had surgery and has been in remission ever since.'

'Was it cancer of the stomach?' I ask.

'Bowel,' Trudy says. She's looking at me askance. 'Look, Robyn, spiritualism is not an exact science. I know you're cynical. But you can't deny that there's something in it. There is so much in this world that is unexplained.

So many supposed coincidences.'

'But,' I say, 'they probably are just coincidences. Or if not, there might be other explanations. I mean, maybe you joined the police force because Laura suggested it to you. In other words, she didn't predict your career, you just followed her guidance. And can't you see that she operates by a system of guesswork? She asks about your family, you hesitate, she detects a problem, guesses it's your sister... Honestly, in the classes at Netley Hall, Laura expressly teaches students how to read people, what to say. I was quite a good student, as it happens. It doesn't make me psychic.'

Trudy won't be convinced. 'I have the utmost faith in Laura's abilities,' she says. 'I trust her absolutely.'

'So why didn't you ask her to help you find Jordan Taylor?'

'When Jordan's parents asked us to find a clairvoyant to help with the case and Gino authorised it, I did turn to Laura, but she told me she was unable to help. And then she recommended you instead.'

I'm getting impatient. 'Listen,' I say. 'She's got it all wrong. I duped her into thinking I have supernatural powers. It seemed quite funny at the time. Although when I upset one of the other students, by talking about her illness, I felt rotten...'

And blow by blow, sitting opposite Trudy in the café, I tell her every detail of what happened at Netley Hall. Finally, I sit back. 'You see now? It's a pity really. I could have done with earning three grand a day but I wouldn't feel comfortable with myself letting you continue to think I'm psychic.'

I'm waiting for her to get up and walk out. I suppose that means I'll have to try again to make it work out at the Globe, or figure out another course of action, but at least I'll know I did the decent thing. But to my surprise, Trudy remains seated. She's lost in thought for a minute and then she looks up at me and smiles. 'Look Robyn,' she says, 'You've been completely upfront with me, and I'm grateful. But I'd still like you to help me with this investigation, if only because two minds are better than one. I'll never mention the possibility of you having any sort of supernatural abilities again. Gino's happy to have you on board and he never believed that you had any sort of a gift anyway. You said yourself that you could do with the money. So why don't you just make the most of this opportunity?'

I wasn't expecting this. Three thousand pounds a day. And I won't be doing anything wrong, won't be deceiving anybody. 'Alright,' I say. 'I'll give it a go.'

36

Talking Trudy through everything that happened at Netley Hall has taken almost two hours. It's midday now and both of us are ready for another coffee. Trudy goes to the counter and brings the drinks back to the table.

'I just want to run my flatmate's theory on this case past you.' I report what Katie said about Jordan's parents being somehow implicated in his disappearance.

'She's not the only person to say that sort of thing. Sometimes the parents do turn out to be the perpetrators, and obviously we've had to investigate Lucy and Lionel's involvement as a possibility. But there really isn't any sign of that.'

'I just don't think any child's parents would behave in that way,' I say. 'It would take bottomless reserves of deceit. And Lionel and Lucy are so clearly heart-broken.'

Trudy sighs. 'You're right,' she says, 'Those two are innocent. Although it's hard to know, sometimes, what people are capable of. You'd be surprised how often I get taken in, even after all these years.'

I wouldn't be that surprised, actually. Bearing in mind that Trudy believes in psychic phenomena, she's obviously never going to win any prizes for the UK's most cynical private investigator. 'Tell me, how's this going to work?' I ask. 'How do you usually go about finding missing people, when you work with the police?'

'I was going to ask where you want to start, actually,' Trudy says. 'In the normal, course of things, well... usually we have something to go on, in the beginning. People to talk to, witnesses. People who just happened to be around when the kids – it's mostly kids I investigate – go missing.'

'And then what?'

'We follow up leads. There's usually a limited time before things escalate, if they're going to. A window of around 48 hours. Either the person turns up, or the body does, or someone comes up with some relevant information for us to follow up...' The way Trudy says, 'the body' so casually makes me feel queasy. I don't want to think about dead bodies, especially where children are concerned.

'Then we just keep going with the investigation for as long as it takes. I get a lot of informers. Not just from the public but also from the criminal fraternity. Even the most hard-bitten criminals don't like paedophiles, so they often tip off the police, or me. I still have a number of contacts from my time in the Met. In fact, missing child cases are usually easier to solve than when adults disappear. In Jordan's case, of course,' she goes on, 'everything has been looked into already, time and again. We've interviewed every person, followed up every possible avenue, so many times over the last ten years. So, what do you think?'

I have literally no idea what I think, but Trudy seems to be expecting me to make some insightful comment and I don't want to disappoint her. 'Um…can you go through it all with me now? And let me have all the paperwork and access to the computer files, later on? If I'm going to work on this case, I want to do it properly.' So, for the next three hours, Trudy talks, while I give her my full attention and make notes on what she's saying.

It's lucky that Benny's offer an all-day breakfast, because it's three o'clock before we stop for lunch. We don't go for the full English, but instead both choose poached eggs on toast. Neither of us have much of an appetite after the things we've been discussing. After eating, we leave the café and spend the afternoon walking around the area. Trudy remarks on the elegance of Kensington, its many pretty houses and gardens, but the beauty of my neighbourhood is lost on me. I listen as she continues to talk about the events surrounding Jordan Taylor's disappearance, attempting to fix the details in my mind as we go.

It's complex. The police have followed hundreds of lines of enquiry and interviewed seemingly thousands of people in connection with this crime and it's hard to concentrate on everything Trudy is telling me. Eventually she stops talking. She promises to send me over all the paperwork and arrange access to all the computerised police files as soon as she can. I promise in return to do my best to work through it at my earliest opportunity.

Then we say goodbye, and go our separate ways.

37

The next day is Friday and I'm back at work at the Globe. Rick makes silly faces at me across the room all morning and I try to ignore him. Eventually he rolls his chair over to my desk and whispers, 'Let's spend the whole weekend together. Starting tonight.'

'My place, I suppose?' I whisper back, and he grins.

'Naturally.'

We leave the building separately, since Rick says he needs to go home to get some things. An hour after I get home he arrives at my door. He has a rucksack flung over one shoulder and is holding a huge bunch of flowers. We go straight out, to a Chinese restaurant he knows in Covent Garden. He's booked and ordered ahead, and within minutes of our arrival two waiters begin to place a huge array of dishes on our table. 'That,' I say when they eventually finish, 'is an enormous amount of food.'

'It's not going to be a problem,' Rick assures me.

We roll back to my building just before midnight. I have to hush him on the stairs and we're giggling by the time we get through the flat door. The lights are all out and I'm pretty sure Katie isn't at home, which is exactly what we'd been hoping for.

I wake up smiling and turn to where Rick should be next to me in the bed, only to find that he has disappeared. I get up slowly and head to the shower. I let the hot water rush over my body, enjoying the sensation and trying not to think about where he might be. He's back by the time I come out of the bathroom. 'Coo-ee,' he calls. 'Breakfast.'

I make my way to the kitchen, my hair wrapped in a towel turban. Rick has laid the table with coffee and pastries. I recognise the napkins. He must have been down the road to Benny's. 'I borrowed your keys,' he says. 'Hope you don't mind.'

It would be churlish to complain, faced with this morning feast. 'It's fine.'

'So what do you want to do today?'

'I haven't thought about it.'

'Camden? The market? I like shopping.'

'I can't even tell if you're joking.'

'I'm not.'

The tube is quiet and we soon reach our stop and begin to weave our way through the busy streets. Camden Market used to be one of my favourite places to visit when I first arrived in London. I love the vibrant, multi-cultural atmosphere. I stop at one of the stalls to buy Rick a shirt. It's royal blue, soft linen. He then insists on buying me a heavy silver box chain in return. 'A neck chain used to be a symbol of slavery,' he says, as he stoops to fasten it around my neck. 'You're mine now.' I feel a shiver travel the length of my spine.

We walk along the waterway. It's still February, so the weather is cold but the sky is bright and the air feels fresh and clear, and these things more than make up for the temperature. The canal path is another lovely part of London, passing Regents Park and London Zoo, but I'm not looking around, so the surroundings are just as wasted on me today as they were on my walk with Trudy yesterday. I'm too busy basking in Rick's company. We talk about books we've read, holidays we've taken. I get a glimpse into his home life. He's fond of his younger siblings, refers to them often. I thought I'd already grown to know him well during the three years we've worked together, but now our conversation is becoming more personal and I'm beginning to see a new, softer side to him. Also, he likes shopping. He's starting to seem almost too good to be true.

My mind drifts and I think for a moment of Jordan Taylor. His parents must have been this happy together, once, before the loss of their child had de-railed them. Life is so unpredictable. We never know what's around the corner. In which case, we should enjoy each moment as it happens, I reflect, deciding to put all thoughts of Jordan out of my mind for now and make the most of my weekend with Rick.

It's a busy couple of days. We're out all day on Saturday and on Sunday we get up early and head to Euston to the Wellcome Collection to see the new Teeth exhibition, then travel back to Kensington and go to the Science

Museum. We eat out again and it's early evening before we get back to the flat. The place is dark and feels subtly different. It takes me a minute to work out why. Usually Katie would be there, and probably cooking. But there's no smell of food in the place and there hasn't been all weekend. I raise the subject as Rick and I drink coffee in front of the TV.

'I don't know where she could have gone.'

'Don't fuss over her, Robyn,' Rick replies. 'Katie's an adult, she can do what she wants. She doesn't have to check in. You do you.'

'I thought you were doing me.'

He laughs. 'It's an expression my little brother uses. It means focus on yourself and stop worrying about other people.'

'You do you. I like that.'

'Anyway, surely she's just gone to see her family,' Rick says.

'I've never heard her talk about them. Not in all the time I've known her.'

'That's odd.'

'I guess. I never really thought about it before.' I shrug. After all, I don't visit my parents often either.

In any case, I don't take Rick's advice to leave Katie to it. Instead I text her to check that she's okay and within a minute I get a terse reply, saying she's absolutely fine and I should stop fussing. Interestingly, she's echoed Rick's exact words.

38

On Monday morning Rick and I travel into the office together again. Within an hour of our arrival, Jack emails, asking me to produce an article on women with hidden alcohol issues. That's an easy one. I can write it off the top of my head, using my own experience as a source. 'Beth's daughter Robyn says she had no idea that her mother was using alcohol as a crutch until she went home one weekend to find her completely sozzled.' Maybe I should anonymize the piece though.

The day at work passes quickly. Getting ready to leave, I reflect that it's only been two weeks since Jack sent me to Netley Hall, and so much has changed in my work life since then. Jack has started me commissioning me to write regular, if meaningless, features. Plus, of course, I now have a part-time job moonlighting as a consultant to the Metropolitan Police.

Rick and I steal a secret goodbye kiss in a corridor before I head off home. I take my usual Tube journey and Katie is back at the flat when I get in. She greets me briefly but she doesn't say where she's been and I don't ask. She doesn't offer to make dinner and I don't ask about that either. It's clear that things have changed at home as well as at work, and I'll just have to get used to the new normal.

February segues into March. The weather changes almost imperceptibly as winter gives way seamlessly to spring. After a few weeks of working with Trudy, I have settled into a routine. I spend Tuesdays and Thursdays with her, and on Mondays, Wednesdays and Fridays I base myself at the Globe. Having two jobs means I have to manage my time carefully, although working with Trudy is hardly demanding. Mostly we just walk around London near Jordan's old playschool and his home, or sit in cafés or restaurants discussing the case. I know as much as she does now about his disappearance, and although I haven't met all the people that the police, and Trudy, have interviewed, I spend a lot of time trawling through all the files that have been written on each of them.

I draw up a list of suspects, based on the reams of material the police have collated over the ten years they've been conducting this case. There are files on every individual the Taylors came into contact with on their holiday in Weymouth – other people who were holidaying in the same hotel, for example, as well as those who worked there. There are also police files on each member of the Taylors' extended family, as well as all of their friends and acquaintances. Also, of course, any known offenders within a thirty-mile radius of where Jordan went missing have been investigated to within an inch of their lives.

Each person who might have been connected with the case has been interviewed, not just once but several times over the years. Everything that has been said is recorded in the files, whether it is fact or speculation. And what strikes me as I read through this material, is that everyone who was asked about Lionel and Lucy has said that both parents had worshipped the ground their child walked on. The only faintly negative comment about Lionel and Lucy in the files comes from a young nursery nurse who worked at Jordan's pre-school. In her words, the couple were 'rather entitled.'

The Lionel and Lucy I'd met had no shine of entitlement about them, but I suppose it might have been fair comment at the time. People like them, who'd enjoyed all the benefits of money and education, probably did take their good fortune for granted in their daily dealings with others. I ask Trudy about Lionel and Lucy again, 'You said the police have looked into the possibility that Jordan's parents might have been behind his disappearance?'

'Like your flatmate, other members of the public suggested that they could be involved. Perhaps that they lost their temper with Jordan and there was an accident which they tried to cover up. But as you'll see in the files, there's not a shred of evidence. Nothing on their clothes, their cars. No dodgy phone calls or acquaintances. They're squeaky clean, the pair of them. They don't deserve this – nobody does.'

Jordan's parents are the first people I cross off my list of possible abductors of their son. But then for the others, I set up a new system on my computer. It's something I can build up over time, and which will work alongside my constant perusal of all the evidence. Under the name Jenny Hunter, I establish social media accounts on every single platform I can think of. Facebook, Twitter, Instagram, Reddit – you name it, Jenny Hunter is on it.

I find a profile photo for Jenny on the internet. She looks young and friendly, but trendy. I build up a backstory for her. She works for a marketing agency. My plan is that, acting as Jenny Hunter, I will 'befriend' or 'follow' each of the suspects on my list, if they have accounts on any of these social media platforms. If they don't appear on social media, or if any of their accounts are closed to people they don't know, I will befriend their friends, their acquaintances, their employers or employees. I'll make connections with other members of the public too, to disguise any pattern in my actions which might alert a guilty party.

I'm laying a trap. It's going to stretch across the internet. I'm building a web of connections which is intended to reach everyone who has ever been at risk of even the slightest hint of suspicion in the Jordan Taylor case. It may take me weeks, months, even years to reach everybody on my list, but if anything ever happens in any of these people's lives and it's recorded by any person who knows them even slightly, I'll see it and I'll act. At the very least, it gives me the illusion that I'm doing something useful.

As winter gives way to spring, I see progressively less of Katie. She rarely cooks now, even for herself. She's like an elusive shadow in the flat, and when our paths do cross she seems withdrawn and distracted. She doesn't ask about my work or my life and if I try to ask about what she's up to, she only answers my conversational gambits in monosyllables. However hard I try, she doesn't appear to be interested in anything I have to say.

I can't figure out why our friendship has failed. One day I suggest that we talk things through but Katie rebuffs my approach, saying only that everything is fine and I'm only imagining problems. On a practical level I know I should forget about it and move on. But I find it hard to accept the change in her attitude without understanding it. My mind keeps finding its way back to the problem, worrying at it, trying to ferret out a solution.

I try to talk to Rick about it but he isn't interested. 'Sometimes friendships just end,' he says. 'Stop trying to analyse everything. And I did suggest, remember, that we didn't let Katie know how close we are. You've got a boyfriend, she hasn't, and she's jealous. She's a little strange, Robyn. Maybe you're the only person who never saw it before. Don't worry about her. You do you, remember.'

39

If Jack has noticed that I'm absent from the office on regular days each week, he doesn't say a word. In fact, I get the impression that I could turn up to work just once a week or once a fortnight without any repercussions, as long as I continue to hand in any articles he commissions. It's an odd arrangement but it seems to work for us both.

I feel lucky that I have Rick to fill the gap in my life left by the decay of my friendship with Katie. He's spending almost every night at the flat now, although I resist his efforts to get me to meet his family. For some reason I can't define, I feel a bit awkward about that.

It's early April, and the winter seems a distant memory. One day, late in the afternoon, I'm at home. I've read through Jordan's case files for what must be the twentieth time and now I'm busy socialising as Jenny Hunter on various social media accounts. My network is growing. Some of the suspects are willing to connect and to my surprise, some of them even discuss Jordan's case on their accounts openly. I suppose so much time has passed since his disappearance that any warning from the police not to talk about it wouldn't seem to matter anymore. Other suspects are much more private – some of them aren't on social media at all, but then I have managed to find links to most of them, through relatives or friends. It's amazing how much digging can be done on the internet.

After my initial dismissal of Jordan's parents, I've been slow to cross suspects off my list. I'm gradually whittling it down though, based on what I've discovered about their lives and their behaviour. As a general rule, the individuals who are most protective of their personal information, who are either not on the various platforms, or who have their security settings at the highest levels, are the ones I continue to investigate. People who share every tiny detail of their lives on social media, I reason, are unlikely to be capable of practising sufficient subterfuge to keep the secret of Jordan's disappearance for ten years.

I raise my head and sniff. Something smells good. Katie must be cooking. She hasn't spoken to me for weeks, apart from in monosyllables. She's hardly ever at the flat and although I'm not complaining because it gives Rick and myself space, I'm curious about where she spends her time. She doesn't usually bring friends back here. Perhaps she's preparing a special meal for someone this evening. Maybe I should leave her to it. I could call Rick and arrange to meet him somewhere.

I'm in the act of picking up the phone when there's a knock on my bedroom door. Katie sounds hesitant. 'I've cooked,' she says. 'Your favourite – chicken and chorizo stew.'

She's smiling, friendly, when I enter the kitchen. It's

like old times – at least, I hope it is, although the sudden change in her attitude makes me feel uneasy. She pours me a glass of wine and I sip it, feeling body and mind relax as the alcohol spreads its warm glow through my body. Katie sits with me at the table and we watch the stew bubble away in its glass pot.

She's the first to break the silence. 'I haven't seen much of you for a while.'

'I know. I've been busy.'

Her expression is neutral. 'With Rick? Or with your private investigator friend?'

'Both. Things are going well with Rick, and Trudy is keeping me pretty busy. We're together for two days a week, talking about the case, looking for clues and leads. It's like I'm living in some sort of detective story. Although in fact we're busy doing nothing really. We're not getting anywhere.'

'So does Trudy still think you have a gift?' She says it mockingly.

'I think she's finally accepted, on a rational level, that I'm not gifted in that way, but part of her still hopes that spirit will suddenly descend on me and I'll magically solve the case. It's weird because she seems so sane most of the time, but she's completely off the wall when it comes to this supernatural stuff.'

'So how exactly do you and Trudy spend your time together?'

'We literally just sit in cafes and chat, or walk around, or drive about in her car. We've already trailed through all the old reports, re-examined the files on everyone who's connected with the case.' I don't know why I'm confiding in Katie when she's been ignoring me for so long but I suppose the alcohol has helped to loosen my tongue. She must be thinking the same thing, because she pushes the wine bottle towards me and I refill my glass. She doesn't take another drink for herself.

'So, you're moonlighting from work. Which mostly involves wandering around or having coffee with Trudy.'

'That just about sums it up.'

'And how does that work with your day job?'

'On the days when I'm with Trudy, I tell Jack I'm out on a story. I always find pieces to file, somehow, mostly fabricated, but who cares? Who's to know, these days, what news is real and what's faked? Or Trudy sometimes feeds me stories from her work. Small things usually, column fillers...'

'And what happens when the penny finally drops and the police realise you're not going to be able to find the kid? You just part ways and carry on at the Globe?'

'That's the thing,' I say. 'Whether we find Jordan or not, Trudy wants me to continue working with her, on similar cases. I could carry on like this indefinitely, apparently, as long as Gino goes along with it. And she reckons she can persuade him.'

Katie regards me with interest. 'Really? Gino being her contact in the Met, I assume? Well, this is amazing. Will you get a bonus for each person you find? That is, if you do find someone?'

'It's not a joking matter,' I say, but she's still smirking as she serves up the two bowls of chicken and chorizo stew.

The fact is, in some ways working with Trudy is not as easy as it must look from the outside. As the time passes, Jordan's case is increasingly playing on my mind. I think about him in the present tense now, willing him to be alive. Sometimes I lie awake at night, thinking of the small boy I've seen in photos taken when he was just two years old, and wondering how he would look now, at twelve. The police have commissioned an artist's impression every year, showing how he might have changed, but I find it difficult to believe in these images. To me they are composed largely of guesswork. Sometimes I dream about the child too. When I wake I don't recall the detail of my dreams but I do know that he is alive in them, well and happy. It's wishful thinking, I know, and in the mornings after those dreams I struggle to get out of bed and on with my day.

40

It's a Wednesday evening. It's May now, still early in the month but the weather has turned hot overnight. The TV news reports keep announcing that we're breaking records, as though the scorching weather is something to celebrate rather than a worrying symptom of global warming. Rick and I are together in the flat. He's watching some obscure sport on television and I'm sitting by him, embarking on a piece that I've provisionally titled 'Fox hunting still happens'.

He glances over at the screen of my laptop. First, I enter the words 'does fox hunting still happen' into my search engine and this turfs up various internet treasure. I begin by looking at Wikipedia. I learn that although hunting foxes with dogs was banned in 2004, people still follow scent trails instead of foxes. And if they do find a fox, they are allowed to flush it out with dogs so that it can be killed by a bird of prey. In other words, they've found a way to get around the law. I close the Wikipedia page then start to write fast, trying to report the facts simply and dispassionately.

'What made you think of writing about hunting?' Rick asks.

'Oh, one of the girls at work was talking about going hunting at the weekend,' I say. 'I thought it had been banned so I decided to look into it. I'm going to round the piece out with something about big game hunting. You know, those chaps who have been pictured killing lions on safari in Africa and looking ridiculously proud of themselves. I'll get one of the research assistants at work to dig up some photos for me. Then I'll sum up by saying at least we've tried to legislate about cruelty to animals in this country but that perhaps the law needs updating. That's it.'

'Google and Wikipedia. Is that the extent of your research?'

'That's actually quite extensive for me.' I tell Rick about Clarice and Jolie, my made-up sources for the feature article I wrote when I first started moonlighting, about whether mothers should go out to work. It's supposed to be amusing but he doesn't laugh.

'You don't approve.'

'I didn't say that. It's your decision how you write your pieces and if Jack wants to print them, that's up to him.'

'But?'

'Well, looking at the wider picture, maybe you should think a bit about your career. You're a brilliant writer and you work so quickly. I'm honestly in awe of you. But maybe journalism isn't your thing.'

'That's a bit harsh.'

'I'm sorry,' Rick says quickly, 'I don't want to hurt your feelings. I'm just thinking out loud really. Actually, there's something else I wanted to talk to you about.'

He seems suddenly hesitant. 'What?' I ask.

'I was wondering...since we've been together a few months now and it's going so well...I mean, I really like you. And you're not getting on with Katie. She's so up and down in her behaviour, and I know it upsets you. It's going to get uncomfortable for you staying here, if it's not already. So, what do you think about us moving in together? Getting a flat of our own?'

The last sentence comes out in a rush and Rick's voice is pitched about an octave higher than usual. He must have felt nervous about making this proposition. My heart leaps at the thought of waking next to him every morning. And yet, I realise, I can't agree to move in with Rick. He still thinks this place belongs to Katie. I can't move out of my own flat. It feels like the completely the wrong time to reveal my dishonesty, just when he's asking me to move in with him. So, heart sinking, I lie again instead. 'I don't know if I'm ready for that yet,' I say. 'I mean, I really like you but I've never lived with a man before...'

'No worries,' he says. But I am worried. How am I ever going to resolve this mess?

One night a week or so later, I'm lying on my back in bed, gazing up into the darkness. I've been awake for several hours already while Rick has been sleeping soundly beside me, but now he stirs. 'What's the problem?' he asks.

'What problem?'

'You just sighed rather loudly. Loud enough to wake me up.'

'I was just thinking about Jordan Taylor.'

'No progress, I suppose?'

'None.'

'It's the middle of the night, Robyn. This thing is really getting to you. You're losing sleep over it. How long are you going to let it go on for? How long have you been looking for this child already?'

I sigh again. 'Months, I suppose. I'll talk to Trudy about it. See if she wants to call it a day.'

The next morning, a Tuesday, Trudy and I are sitting in the Southbank Centre. Alongside Benny's café, it's one of my favourite places for our meetings – it's always cool inside, and the open space and civility of the place appeals to me. Trudy and I only ever really talk about Jordan so although we start with polite chat about the weather, when she suddenly says, 'Do you think he's alive?' it's no effort at all to switch subjects.

'I hope he is. I want him to be. But I have literally no idea. I have no way of knowing. You do understand, don't you, that I have no mystical abilities? I mean, I told you at the start what happened at Netley Hall. I don't want you to hope that I'm going to have some sort of magical insight one day.'

'I do get it,' she says. 'We're on equal terms, Robyn, as investigators on this case. And I appreciate all the thought you put into it.' She's more right than she knows. I rarely switch off from the case now, day or night. 'Just stay with it,' she continues. 'That's all I want from you.'

So I decide to let things keep rolling on. Trudy, inexplicable as it might be, is happy with the arrangement. And working with her is not an uncomfortable arrangement for me, apart from the way poor Jordan's plight plays on my mind. Trudy is my only point of contact with the police force. I haven't had to go to the station or meet Gino again, which is a massive relief. Trudy has told me that he is willing to go along with my employment unless and until she tells him it's no longer working.

41

Although I have a renewed clear conscience, I can't deny that trying to help Trudy investigate Jordan's case is feeling increasingly pointless. I'm spending far too long reading through old files, or wandering around familiar areas of London and talking about the same things. I'm getting bored. Trudy has already told me there's no point in interviewing everyone again but one day I think of something we could do.

'Why did the Taylors go to Weymouth?' I ask. 'They were high-flying lawyers, working in government. A run-down seaside resort seems a strange choice of holiday destination.'

'They said it seemed too much like hard work to take a toddler abroad. When Lucy was young her family used to go to Dorset, so it was a nostalgia thing. It was the second year running that they'd taken Jordan to the same place. The first time he was only a baby.'

'Let's go to Weymouth,' I say. 'Next week. Tuesday.' And she agrees.

May has ended now, and the Tuesday I've arranged to meet Trudy is the fourth day of June. The weather, mercifully, has changed from boiling hot to comfortably warm. It's a perfect day to get out of the city and down to the seaside. I feel slightly high, almost disassociated from reality. Because, although I haven't told Trudy, somewhere at the edge of my mind I'm hoping that, if I venture to the place where Jordan was lost, I'll get some sort of hunch. It's a crazy little hope, because the rational part of my mind knows nothing like that is going to happen in a million years and that the lack of sleep must be getting to me.

Trudy arrives to collect me from the flat just after nine. Joe the doorman is watching from over the road and I wave at him before I get into her car. 'You do know,' I say as we set off, 'that this isn't going to lead anywhere?'

She shrugs. 'I keep telling you, whatever you want to do, it's fine with me.' Fine with her, fine with Gino, fine with Jack. I don't seem to be making any impression on the world, nobody cares if I'm around or not. Except Rick, of course.

Once we're out of London and on the motorway, I relax. It's a long time since I went anywhere out of town. I can't remember when I last had a holiday, in fact, unless you count the week I spent at Netley Hall at the beginning of the year. Perhaps Rick and I should go away somewhere together. France, or Spain perhaps. I remember what he said, about re-thinking my career. I could forget journalism and just write whatever I wanted all the time. Fiction. I wouldn't need to be tied to any place then.

Right this minute though, I don't feel in a hurry to

change anything in my life. Trudy is happy with my efforts and I'm being generously paid. Jack doesn't seem to mind what I get up to, so my job at the Globe is secure. My friendship with Katie might have gone belly-up, but she's hardly ever around to bother me and the last time I saw her she behaved quite civilly. Also, for the first time in my life I have a steady boyfriend. All is good. It's time to stop worrying and start living.

Trudy is a good driver, confident, and she clearly knows her route well. 'This journey used to take a lot longer,' she says, 'when Jordan first disappeared, back in 2008. But the roads to the coast got sorted out for the London Olympics a few years later.'

'How often do you head down this way?' I ask.

'At least once a year. Much more frequently in the beginning.'

We don't stop on the way so we make good time, arriving at our destination by late morning. Trudy parks near the seafront and we walk down to the beach. 'That's the spot where Jordan disappeared,' she says, pointing.

'Tell me exactly what happened,' I ask. I've heard the story before, but I want to listen to it again in the location where it took place.

'Lucy and Lionel were right by their son,' she says. 'Both of them. We're not just taking their word for that, there were other holiday-makers on the beach, people they knew from the hotel. It's clear that they were really attentive, playing with their boy, taking turns to walk with him to the water or to build sandcastles. They were marking Jordan, both of them.'

'And then what?'

'Neither of them know. Nobody knows. One second he was there, the next he wasn't. The beach was busy. They raised the alarm in minutes. But there was no sight of him. Nobody remembers seeing a boy crying, or being pulled away by anyone else…it's a complete mystery. As though he simply vanished into thin air.' She sighs.

'And what happened in the aftermath of his disappearance?'

'The entire Metropolitan Police child investigation team was mobilised from day one,' she says. 'I worked with them full-time at the start. We camped out here for the first week or so. We were called down from London immediately because the Taylors both had high profile jobs and there was a suggestion that there might have been gang involvement in Jordan's disappearance. We worked with the local bobbies, day after day, searching for any trace of the boy. We interviewed anybody who'd been near the beach, the hotel where they stayed. After a few weeks, the Met left the investigation here to the local police. We went back to London and interviewed every one of Lucy and Lionel's friends, relatives, work colleagues. We kept on the case and we kept liaising with the Dorset force. Literally for years. My involvement tailed off, of course, so that after a while I just worked with the police for one day a week, then one day a fortnight. And now, ten years on, I'm just paid to invest-igate for one day a month. Gino wants to close the case, but every time he tries he comes under pressure from the Taylors to open another line of enquiry or go back over the old ones. Eventually, Gino gave me responsibility to keep the case going. I can call in the police to help whenever I feel the need and Gino is still in charge officially, but he says there's no hope at all. Once or twice a year I come down here to follow leads…which always turn out to be nothing. I…' Her voice trails off and I wait for her to continue.

When she does, she nods slowly to herself as she speaks. 'I just feel so sad about this case, it's kind of eaten away at me over the years. I just keep hoping I'll find a clue about what happened, get some sort of closure for the Taylors. I don't want Gino to close the police file on this completely, even though I know it's the practical thing to do. And it's inevitable, imminent. We've had ten years to get to the bottom of this, and our time's about to run out.'

I wish I could say something to comfort her, but there's nothing. The feeling that I might get some kind of inspiration has dissipated and I can see it clearly now for the delusional hope that it was. We linger at the seafront for a while. Fifty feet away, a Punch and Judy show starts up and is soon in full flow. The shrieks of the puppets in the striped tent are unpleasantly shrill, jarring on my nerves as they carry down the beach. 'Oh yes, you did! Oh no, I didn't!'

Punch is battering Judy. Sausages are involved. Trudy sees the expression on my face. 'It's passed as entertainment on this beach for more than a hundred years, you know,' she says, trying to pacify me.

'Well, it's one tradition that should be done away with,' I insist. 'It's horrible.'

We walk from the beach to the nearby shops. Along the way Trudy points out various places the Taylors visited on their holiday – a bowling complex, a soft play café. As we walk I'm scanning the area, looking for somewhere Jordan could have been taken, somewhere nearby he could have been hidden until the fuss died down. But then I know Trudy must have done the same thing countless times as she's walked this route over the years. If there were ever any clues, there are none left now.

Eventually we stop for something to eat in a run-down burger joint. We order absently. I'm still thinking about Jordan and his family and suddenly I realise there's one place Trudy hasn't showed me. 'You said the family stayed at a hotel,' I say. 'Where was it?'

'It's gone now,' says Trudy. 'It was a small family hotel, right by the beach. I wanted to stay there too, when I was investigating the case. But I ended up being billeted with a local officer's family instead. The hotelier shut the place right after Jordan disappeared. She was too upset by the whole business to carry on working. She said she needed a break and as far as I know, she never re-opened the hotel. It's not even there now, the site was sold and re-developed years ago.'

'What's her name?'

'Helen Watkins.'

I remember now. I've followed her on social media,

along with the many others on my list of suspects. 'Do you know where she is now?'

'She moved to a small town in Devon. Walkford. We've visited regularly, to re-interview her. She's still traumatised. Never had children of her own, always wanted them, and can't bear to think about the pain that Jordan's parents must be suffering. Once or twice I've had to dissuade her from getting in touch with them personally. People mean well, but Lucy and Lionel have had enough to deal with over the last ten years. They don't need to constantly experience the grief and sympathy of strangers.'

More people were affected by the loss of a child than you might think, I realise. The hotelier, the friends of Jordan's parents who still funded their search and tried to support them emotionally. And any parents of young children, although strangers to that family, might feel a kinship with Lionel and Lucy, might have the details of this case seared into their brains. They would keep eagle eyes on their own children for weeks, months after it happened. Perhaps even for ever.

We continue to eat, although I don't think either of us are relishing the food. 'What about the other guests at the hotel?' I ask. 'Did you check them out? Look into their backgrounds, and so on?'

'Of course,' Trudy says. 'They were all above board. All devastated by Lucy and Lionel's loss. Most of them were families with young kids of their own. Again, we've followed up all of these people at least once a year, and never found anything new or relevant to Jordan's disappearance.'

'That's weird,' I say suddenly.

'What?'

'Don't look now, but that guy over there in the corner, with the woman and the two children.'

'Right. Not looking.'

'He works at the Globe. On the reception desk.'

'So he's on holiday with his wife and kids. Not that weird.'

'It just seems strange seeing him, you know, out of context. And I hadn't imagined him having a family. He's young to be married.' Trudy's right though, it's not that weird. I remember having the same feeling when I was a child. I was out with my mother on a Saturday and I'd seen my English teacher shopping on Brighton high street. She was wearing a leather jacket, had her long hair loose. She was the epitome of a cool biker chick. She had a whole different life outside the classroom and I'd felt the same jolt of disconnection then that I do now. I wave to the reception guy on our way out of the café and he waves back, although to my gratification he looks just as surprised to see me as I'd felt a minute before. The world is full of coincidences, just as I'd often told Trudy. But they are just coincidences, and when we start to interpret them as having some sort of meaning we get onto shaky ground.

Trudy and I arrived in Weymouth before eleven, and we don't get back on the road until eight in the evening. It's been a long day, I think, watching Trudy's silhouette as she drives. It's still light, and the motorway is uncannily quiet on our side, heading into London, but the lanes on the other side are jammed with with traffic, a lot of it almost stock still. There appear to be thousands of people heading to the coast, even though it's mid-week.

I text Rick to tell him I've been held up and won't be able to see him this evening, and he immediately texts back with a barrage of sad-faced emojis, followed by a single poo emoji.

'Boyfriend?' Trudy asks, glancing over to where I sit in the passenger seat.

'Yes.'

'Is it serious?'

'It is,' I say, smiling contentedly.

42

That night I get home late and fall straight into bed. I'm exhausted. But the trip to Weymouth has brought Jordan's disappearance to the forefront of my mind, and now I can't let go, can't stop thinking of it. I dream, and when I awake there are tears streaming down my face. I can't remember the details of the dream, except that at one point I was inside the red and white striped Punch and Judy tent. There was gritty sand under my feet, darkness and the smell of damp canvas surrounded me, and above I could hear the ugly puppets shrieking, 'Oh no, she didn't!'

On a rational level, I know that none of this means anything, that my unconscious mind is simply processing the events of the previous day, searching for answers to things that have worried me. But as I shake the memory of the dream off, I am left feeling oddly flat and emotion-less. Completely unlike my usual self.

I remain unsettled. It's a Wednesday and I know I should head to the Globe but I can't face it. I'd like to see Rick though, and I don't want to wait until this evening. I try and fail to reach him on the phone but around lunch time I finally track him down to the Horse and Cart. He's standing at the bar, chatting to someone, and he looks genuinely pleased to catch sight of me. 'Doris!' he exclaims and the guy he's standing with does a double take.

'Private joke,' I say, holding out my hand to Rick's friend. 'Robyn Walters.' He smiles back but soon makes his excuses and drifts off.

'Sorry,' I say to Rick. 'Didn't mean to interrupt.'

'What's up?' he asks. 'You don't look quite right.'

'Nothing that you can't sort out,' I smile. 'Skive off work with me?'

'You're a bad influence,' he grins.

We take our time walking back to the flat across London. The sky is blue above our heads and the warmth of the sun feels comforting. I talk to Rick about the night-mare I had last night and how I'm becoming increasingly obsessed with finding Jordan. He looks concerned.

'I'm not going to say I told you so,' he says, 'but you will remember I was concerned about you getting involved with Trudy. I told you to put an end to it.'

'I can look after myself...' I haven't finished speaking, but he interrupts.

'I know you can. But I want to look after you too.'

We reach my building but just as we're about to go in I glance over the road to the Gainsborough. Joe waves and we cross to speak to him. 'How are you?' I ask.

'Good. And you?'

'Great. This is Rick,' I say. It's about time I introduced

them.

But to my surprise, Joe nods. 'We've met,' he says.

Rick shrugs and smiles, then tugs my hand to pull me into my building.

'I didn't know you knew Joe?' I ask when we're inside the flat.

'I've just spoken to him once or twice on my way in here. I think he was trying to suss me out. He seems to think it's his job to protect you, rather than the hotel.'

'He's sweet,' I say. 'And I think he does look out for me. He never liked Katie very much, and he's turned out to have been right on that one.'

'He doesn't like her? Why?'

'He's always made snide comments about her. He was on about her having an overnight visitor when I was away at Netley Hall, don't you remember? I asked her about that and she denied it. That's why we originally fell out. She accused me of spying on her.'

'Interesting,' Rick says. 'Do you think she's seeing someone?'

'I think she'd tell me herself.'

'Unless she doesn't want you to know about it,' he comments.

'I don't want to provoke her...' I start to say, then stop and change tack. 'Okay, I'll talk to Katie when I next see her. Happy?'

'Ecstatic,' he says. 'But not a patch on how I am going to be feeling about ten minutes from now.'

It's a few days before I even see Katie. One morning, Rick's still asleep and I'm in the kitchen cooking breakfast when she comes into the room.

'Cooking?' she asks. 'For Rick, I guess. You never cooked for me.'

'You never wanted me to. The cooking was always been your thing.'

She changes the subject deftly. 'You two are practically joined at the hip.' She doesn't say this as though it's a good thing.

'Maybe you should introduce us to your boyfriend. We could all go out somewhere together,' I suggest.

She looks startled. 'What do you know about…' she begins to snap, then picks herself up. 'Oh, very clever. Yes, okay, I did have a boyfriend, but it's all over now. I would have loved a double date otherwise.' Her tone of voice is unpleasant.

'I'm sorry to hear that,' I say.

'No great loss,' she replies. 'I've moved on.'

I don't know what else to say so I make myself busy with the bacon and eggs. Then I carry the tray of food carefully back into my bedroom, and Rick pulls himself up to sitting as I place it on the bed.

'I just spoke to Katie,' I tell him. 'Took her by surprise, asking how her boyfriend is. She admitted that she did have a relationship but it's over.'

'And?' he asks. 'Did she say who it was?'

'No.'

'Did you ask her if somebody stayed over when you

were away?'

'No. I suppose they must have done. It doesn't really matter now, does it?'

'No.' He looks uncomfortable.

'Rick, is there something on your mind? Something I should know? Because if so, I would appreciate you sharing it with me.'

He shakes his head slowly. 'It's nothing. Just me, over-analysing things. All this investigative journalism thing is getting into my personal life. My bad.'

'You're bad?' I ask, confused.

Rick laughs. 'It's an expression. You really need to meet my family, get up to date with the lingo. How about it? This weekend?'

'Another time,' I say. It's not the first time he's asked, or the first time I've refused and I'm grateful he doesn't question me about my response. It just feels as though Rick introducing me to his family as his girlfriend would make our relationship seem sealed somehow, final. I don't know why this bothers me, but it does and I don't want to have to try to explain it to him.

43

The year is opening out. June ends, July begins and as the days become increasingly hot and sultry, I am lulled into a sense of calm.

I have established a regular routine. I still go to the Globe building three days each week. I quite enjoy writing features now that I've given up on any hope of moving across to news reporting. I'm making a bit of a name for myself in fact, getting two or three pieces into print most weeks. It doesn't seem to matter how silly my ideas are or how sloppily researched, Jack goes along with them. It's only when I suggest doing something serious, like the homeless article, that he vetoes it. Which is strange, but as I'm no longer emotionally invested in my work at the Globe, I just let it all slide by.

At home, however, the situation with Katie is worse than ever. I'm with Trudy one Thursday morning. We've bought takeaway coffees and are sitting in the by the Round Pond in Kensington Gardens watching the ducks and coots, as they skit along on the surface of the water.

'How's life?' she asks. 'All going well with that boyfriend of yours?'

'It is,' I say, 'but not with my flatmate.'

'What do you mean?'

'Generally, she's just unfriendly and sarcastic. It's been going on for months. I don't get what her problem is, and she refuses to talk about it. She just says nothing's wrong and then goes out, or off to her room. There's an atmosphere, all the time, and it's really not pleasant. But now she's done something which is completely off the wall.'

'What's that?'

'She sacked the cleaning lady and told me she'd left of her own accord. I only found out because I bumped into Lisa on the high street.'

Poor Lisa. She'd been really upset, didn't know what she'd done wrong. Especially as Katie hadn't given her the chance to talk to me about it, just said we didn't need her, gave her a week's severance pay and sent her on her way.

'Why would she do that?' Trudy asks.

'That's what I asked. She said it was supposed to be my job to do the cleaning, but I'd just farmed it out. Then I said we'd only agreed that I should clean because she was going to do the shopping and cooking but that she seemed to have given up on both. It turned into an all-out slanging match.'

Trudy looks thoughtful. 'She sounds a little unbalanced.'

'I think she might be. Rick reckons she's upset because I've got a steady boyfriend and she hasn't.'

'Could be awkward for her, living with a couple who

are all loved up…'

'That's the other thing,' I sigh. 'I want to ask her to move out. Partly because Rick wants us to live together.'

'Why's that a problem?'

'It shouldn't be. But I told Rick that Katie owned the flat, because…'

'You didn't want him to think you were rich.' She's caught on quickly. 'Why don't you just tell him the truth?'

'I suppose I'll have to. It's just been so long…I've let so many opportunities to do that slip by. I don't want him to hate me.'

'He won't. Just sit him down and explain things. Then you can get rid of that ghastly woman and move your boyfriend in instead.'

'And get Lisa back.'

'The cleaning lady? Can't you do that anyway?'

'I tried already. I told her it was just a misunderstanding, but Katie really upset her. There's no way she'll agree to come back to work as long as Katie's still living here.'

'Get rid of Katie.' Trudy says again.

I tell her I will, and I mean it. I definitely will. I just need to build up my courage to speak to Rick first.

44

Weeks slip by. One Friday late in July, I decide to spend the afternoon at home. I tell my colleagues at the Globe I'm going out to interview somebody who was planning to set up a dog café in Islington. My interviewee is, in fact, non-existent but it's a fair excuse for a few hours off work. Nobody will notice or care if I don't actually turn in the article.

I'm still dividing my week between the paper and Trudy. She and I talk the Jordan case through interminably. But whenever I can get some extra time to myself, I work on my own list of suspects. I spend hours on Facebook and all the other social media platforms. Gradually I eliminate more names from the list. My access to the people I'm still tracking has widened as I slowly find and link with more people who know them. I'm aware that all this may come to nothing but, in the persona of Jenny Hunter, I keep a regular check on all my suspects to see if anything unusual pops up online.

After a few hours on social media, I switch track and start work on my next article for the Globe. It's a feature about women who are single by choice, another re-hash of a subject that is covered regularly at every level of the media. I give my piece a new spin by including statistics from a recent study which has found that women are happier after divorce, and draw the conclusion that from a female point of view it is definitely preferable not to get married.

This time, I write the piece off the top of my head, not bothering to do any research at all. Who cares, honestly about these sorts of features? One day the media takes one stance, the next it changes, according to the zeitgeist at the time. It's usually either about filling spaces on the page, or promoting somebody's new book. I'm starting to feel that journalism, like every sort of work and leisure activity, is ultimately pointless. They are all just different ways that humans have invented to keep ourselves occupied, to stop ourselves dwelling on the bigger questions such as why we are even here.

I shake myself. I'm not usually given to such morbid trains of thought. Of course, work is necessary for most people. We're dependent on it for our survival. And perhaps, I reason, that explains why I'm feeling jaded. Money is no object for me these days – I have more than enough to live on and have, in fact, saved a substantial sum this year. I'm like a bird in a gilded cage. I don't even need to think for a living any more.

The month of July is almost over. I've just got back from another day of fruitlessly wandering around with Trudy. She's dropped me outside the flat. I see Joe outside the Gainsborough and cross over. I'm not in a hurry, have no plans for the evening, and feel a bit guilty that I haven't stopped to speak to him much recently.

We chat for a few minutes about how hot it is and how we shouldn't complain. What would the English find to talk about, I wonder, if not for the endless vagaries of our weather system.

'How's your police lady friend?' Joe asks.

'Fine.' He's digging for information. He's seen Trudy coming to meet me regularly for a while now and of course he's curious – Joe's always curious. But I can't even begin to tell him that Trudy's actually a detective and that I'm working with her, as a consultant to the Met. I haven't even told my parents…it would just be too weird. Although my mum might actually be proud of me if she knew that I'd been recruited on the basis of my supposed psychic abilities. I smile to myself briefly, thinking of her claim to clairsentience. Then I look at the doorman again.

'Joe,' I say, 'Tell me about what you said a few weeks ago, about Katie having someone stay when I was away.'

'I told you already.'

'I asked her about it,' I say. 'She said she had a boyfriend but it's over now.'

He doesn't respond. I sigh. 'Okay. Who was it?'

He hesitates. 'The thing is, it's someone you're very close to. I don't quite know how to tell you.'

'Right,' I say. 'Thanks, Joe. I'll ask her myself.' I'm filled with righteous anger and I storm over the road, upstairs and into the flat. I find Katie sitting in the kitchen.

'Hi Robyn,' she says. 'Who's rattled your cage? What's up?'

'I'll tell you what's up.' I'm so furious that I am struggling to speak. 'I can't deal with this. You've doing my head in for months, Katie, acting nice one minute, nasty the next. I'm fed up with giving you the benefit of the doubt. Who exactly is this mystery man you're sleeping with? I'm giving you one chance to tell me, and if you don't, then Joe will.'

'What mystery man? Who's Joe? Oh, the creepy little doorman from the Gainsborough. You've got him spying on me now, have you? What did he say?'

'That you've been sleeping with someone close to me.'

She looks down for a moment, then brings her head up and glares straight at me. The expression on her face is chilling. 'Right. You asked for it. Remember, it was him who didn't want you to find out. I would have told you. Also, it ended ages ago, before it began really. It was only a fling, while you were away. And it's your fault, for telling him I owned the flat. He lost interest as soon as I told him it wasn't true. And went back to you.'

I blink. A fling, while I was away? 'Telling him you owned the flat... Are you trying to tell me you've been sleeping with Rick?'

'Look,' Katie says, 'It's better that you know. He's only after one thing from you, and it's not the thing most men are after. He only wanted me because he thought I was loaded and he ended it when I told him I'm not, that this place belonged to you and not me. I wanted to tell you, and I almost did. But…you seemed so happy. I didn't want to spoil it for you. It's been really difficult for me, Robyn.'

I stare at her. 'Then maybe you shouldn't have fucked my boyfriend.' I don't often swear but there are times when no other words will do. It's a mistake though. The language seems to flick a switch in Katie. Her eyes blaze with hatred.

'How dare you speak to me like that?' She's practically spitting with anger now.

I stand very still and stay quiet. My stomach has contracted with fear, although there's no actual physical threat. She just seems so…menacing, suddenly. I wait to see what she's going to do next. I'm wondering if I should say anything to try to calm her down, but at the same time I'm trying to plan my escape from the kitchen and from the flat.

Suddenly she changes again and becomes meek and contrite. 'I'm so sorry Robyn. I didn't mean to scare you. And I didn't mean anything to happen with Rick. We'd been for a drink and…' She smiles at me timidly but I cut her off mid-sentence.

'I don't want to hear it. I want you to leave my flat.'

'I've got nowhere to go.'

'Why should I care?' I say and I realise it's true. It will be a relief when Katie has left my home and my life.

'I've got something for you, Robyn,' she says then. She fishes into her handbag, pulls something out and hands it over. It's a piece of newspaper, folded and yellowed. I open it out and scan it. I can hardly believe my eyes. I'm looking at the article I was searching for when I first met Trudy all those months ago. The piece about the missing child who was found unharmed in her own home. The totally coincidental case that echoed the one Trudy was investigating, the thing that convinced Trudy I was definitely clairvoyant, that led her to insist that I work with her, turned my life upside down.

I'm staring at Katie in disbelief. 'How did you...why?'

She holds out both her hands, palms up. 'I don't know. When we were looking for the newspaper outside, you seemed so upset. But you hadn't told me what it was about, and I wanted to know. I found the piece, then put that paper aside, thought I might show it to you later, we'd have a laugh about it. Then you told me why you'd been looking for it and − I don't know why − I still hung onto it. Once you'd decided to get involved with Trudy it was too late to own up to what I'd done, and it didn't seem to matter anyhow.'

'You messed with my life, Katie. That child's parents actually thought I might be able to help him. I've been going crazy...started to almost think myself that I might have some kind of psychic gift.' I just can't fathom that I'd once thought this person was my closest friend. 'What have I ever done to you?' I'm shouting now.

'You haven't got a clue,' she shouts back. 'You're so spoilt you don't even realise how lucky you are! Swanning around like you haven't got a penny to your name, with your battered old brown handbag that just happens to be vintage Gucci. You've never even had to clean your own toilet!'

'Well, nor have you for the last year! Anyway, I have since you sacked my cleaning lady!'

She suddenly laughs. 'Robyn, what's happened to us? I can't believe we're arguing about the cleaning. Look, I'll make some coffee. Cook us something to eat.'

Coffee? Food? I say nothing and when she speaks again, she sounds subdued. 'I'll move out.'

'You'd better. Right now.' I turn my back on Katie and retreat to the safety of my bedroom. I can hear her packing her stuff, opening wardrobes and drawers. She must have flung everything she needed into a case in record time, because a few minutes later I hear the door to the flat slamming behind her. Good. I leave my room, take a chair from the kitchen and place it under the handle of the front door, just in case she comes back.

I'm still trying to take in what just happened. I really did feel scared, facing Katie in the kitchen. I don't believe she would have hurt me but there's no way she can redeem herself after this. She can't ever share my home again. I'm going to be completely alone, I realise, without a flatmate or a boyfriend. Without any career prospects either, because I can't work as a psychic advisor to the police indefinitely, not without making any break-throughs.

Then I stop myself. What am I thinking? How can any of this be true? Who do I trust, Katie or Rick? Rick is one hundred per cent solid. There's no way he's been sneaking around with my flatmate behind my back. It's just Katie trying to wind me up. I don't even bother to phone him. Instead, I decide to get an early night. It's all fine. I'll talk to Rick tomorrow and we'll put all this straight. I'll explain about owning the flat too.

Must remember to get the locks changed, is my last thought before I fall asleep, smiling to myself at the thought of asking Rick whether he wants to move in, now that Katie has gone.

45

I'm exhausted after the showdown with Katie. I sleep for longer than I should and get to work late as a result. Not that anybody seems to notice. I'm surprised my colleagues aren't jealous of all the time I spend out of the office these days, but I suppose they're too busy trying to further their own careers.

Rick's at his desk and I go straight over to greet him. 'What sort of time do you call this?' he grins. 'You lead a charmed life, Robyn.'

'Early lunch?' I ask and he laughs.

We leave work and head to 'our' café in Borough Market. We're holding hands, but it no longer matters whether anybody from the Globe might see us. After all, we'll soon be living together.

Rick orders his usual massive baguette and I ask for a salad. I wonder how to open the conversation, and decide to keep it neutral. 'I need to talk to you about Katie,' I say.

He looks sheepish. 'I'm sorry I didn't tell you about that,' he begins.

'About what? What do you mean?'

'She called me. She said you knew.'

'Katie called you? She told you I knew what?' My head's spinning. How did Katie even get Rick's phone number? 'You mean, it's true?' I snap.

'Just let me explain…'

'Let you explain? You must be joking.'

'Just listen,' he says. 'There's a reason I didn't say anything before now…'

'I don't want to hear anything you've got to say.'

'But…'

'And I don't want to see you ever again. We're over.' I'm fighting back tears as I leave the café. I was in love with this man. I allowed myself to trust him and the whole time our relationship was based on a lie, a cheat…

I don't know how I'm ever going to get through this.

For more than a week I don't go to work at the Globe and nor do I see Trudy. I plead illness to both my employers, but really I'm grieving for the loss of Rick – and perhaps also for the hopelessness of the situation with Jordan. The nightmares about the child intensify. I feel that if I don't act soon something awful, something final, will happen.

One day I go to Katie's room. She's left a lot of her stuff here and I need to think about clearing it out. I open the door and then stand in shock at the threshold. I've hardly been out of the flat recently, so I don't know how Katie's managed it without me seeing or hearing her, but every item of her belongings has vanished from her bedroom. I try to call her mobile to ask her to return her key but the line is dead and I have no other way of contacting her. I must remember to change those locks, I think wearily.

Rick keeps trying to call me and leaves a number of text messages but I press delete without reading them. I know I can't avoid him for ever. After all, we work for the same newspaper. But I just need to get my emotions on a more stable footing before we come face to face again.

46

Trudy arrives at my door one Saturday morning. She has chocolates, which she holds out to me. 'I know you said you were poorly but I thought I'd drop in. What's up?'

I invite Trudy in reluctantly but once I've made us both a coffee and we've started on the box of chocolates, I realise it's a relief to have someone to talk to. I tell her what's happened with Katie and Rick and she sympathises. 'He sounded as though he was a decent guy,' she says. 'But then I suppose you can never really know what someone's capable of.'

She's right. I think of the scene with Katie, in the kitchen, when I'd been scared that she might attack me.

'You never talk about your personal life,' I say to Trudy. 'What did happen with that teenage boyfriend of yours?'

'All that was a lifetime ago. I dumped him. I'm married now, with two kids. Laura was right. I'm fine, just not with him. You'll be okay too,' she says. 'Broken hearts mend.'

I smile as though I believe her. 'On the bright side,' I say, 'Katie has moved out.'

'That is good news. Now, I need to talk to you about

something. Do you know, it's exactly six months since you started working for the Met.'

'I suppose it must be.'

'It was the tenth of February,' she says. 'And today is August the tenth. You haven't been out of this flat for a while by the look of you, but it's hotter than ever out there. Do you remember how cold it was the first night I came here?'

I do remember. After Trudy had left, I'd rooted around in the outside dustbin until my fingers were numb, looking for the newspaper article about the missing child to prove that what I'd told her was true. I think of the tattered piece of paper that Katie gave me the last time I saw her, get up to fetch it, and hand it to Trudy wordlessly. She reads slowly then looks up at me.

'Well,' she says, 'I have news for you. You'll be pleased to know that Gino has decided it's time to call it a day. He's ended the investigation into the Jordan's case.'

I should be feeling pure relief but oddly my emotions are more complicated. 'What made you decide to do that?'

'Well, obviously we've been trying to find him for long enough. And this,' – she glances at the newspaper clipping she's still holding, 'illustrates that you were only telling us the truth all along. That you never had any sort of psychic abilities.'

I'm staring at her. 'But you said you didn't believe any more that I had a gift? We've had so many conversations about that. I explained to you what happened at Netley

Hall to make Laura think I was psychic.'

She sighs. 'I still couldn't help hoping there might be some…spark of inspiration. Something. I suppose it was hope born of desperation. To be honest, I never even looked for this article.' She flutters the piece of newspaper at me. 'Laura was so convinced that you were genuine and I didn't want to find anything that might dissuade Gino from letting me take you on.'

I want to be angry with Trudy but I can't. 'At least you've seen sense now.' I say.

I expect Trudy to make her excuses and leave. After all, this is a working day for her. But to my horror, instead she produces a bulging folder and starts to take papers and photographs out. 'Can you take a look at these?' she says. 'Then we can decide where to start. The folder contains, I realise, the police paperwork on another missing person case.

'No!' I exclaim. 'I haven't got anywhere with Jordan, what makes you think I am going to succeed with this? I don't want to be part of the misery of any more families, Trudy.'

'The thing is,' she says, 'I think Jordan is probably dead. And you don't want to communicate with spirits – and I don't blame you – so you won't be able to find him. But maybe some of these other kids might still be alive.'

'Hang on. I thought we were now operating on the assumption that I definitely don't have a psychic gift? As evidenced by what I told you about Netley Hall, and by the newspaper article I just handed you? You said that yourself, less than a minute ago.' I take a deep breath. 'I can't handle this, Trudy. We're literally going round in circles. I wish I could help. But I can't figure it out…what you want from me just doesn't tally with the abilities I have. I keep telling you that and you've seen it for yourself, over months. Now you're holding the concrete proof and you still won't take it on board.' It's all mumbo-jumbo, I want to say, but I hold my tongue. Let Trudy take comfort from all that mystical stuff, if that's what she wants to believe. But she can't involve me on that basis.

'If I can't find Jordan,' I say, 'I'm not going to be able to find anyone else. It's over.' It's the second time I've dumped someone in a week and it doesn't feel great.

Now that I'm no longer working with Trudy, I should feel lighter, but I don't. In fact, I feel worse. I'm frightened to sleep because when I do the bad dreams descend upon me and overwhelm me. I miss Rick, although I don't want to admit it even to myself. And I don't like being alone. Sometimes I hear a noise in the flat and think Katie must be home but I get up and look and there's nobody there. I'm starting to fear for my sanity.

I have a job to do though. I turn Katie's old room into an office and set it up as the centre of my investigation. Gino and Trudy might have given up on it but I have no intention of doing so. I feel like I am falling apart – I have no friends and no relationship. But I am going to do the best I can to find this boy.

I assemble everything in this room. All the police files, which Trudy didn't take with her when we parted ways. My own dwindling list of suspects. And in pride of place my laptop, from which I operate all of the fictional Jenny Hunter's social media accounts. I've recently installed face recognition software on the computer and programmed it with all the pictures of Jordan as a child as well as each of the annual police impression portraits of him. I've also set up social media alerts so I'll know when any of the remaining suspects post anything on any platform. Trudy might think I've given up but I'm playing a waiting game, and I won't stop investigating the disappearance of Jordan Taylor until I have exhausted every single possibility.

47

First of all, though, I'm going to visit Netley Hall. I want to talk to Laura Barker. I dial the landline number, picturing the big old telephone in the hallway ringing. When I say who I am, Danny sounds unsurprised. 'Laura has been waiting for your call,' he says.

'Oh yeah, I expect she knew I was going to phone.' He doesn't appear to get the joke.

He passes the phone to Laura, who agrees that I can come to the college. There are no courses running today, since it's a Monday. I don't even bother to email an excuse to Jack about where I am. If he thinks about me at all, he'll probably just assume that I'm still unwell.

I don't think Laura or are Danny are actually dangerous but since I am going to face them down, I decide to take the precaution of letting someone know where I'll be. I call my Mum. 'I'm coming to Brighton this morning,' I say. 'Can I borrow your car? Just for a few hours?'

'Of course. Are you going to Netley Hall?'

'How did you guess?'

'I'm clairsentient,' she says. 'Plus, there's not really anywhere else around here that you'd need my car to visit.'

Uncharacteristically, when I get to the house my mother just hands me the car keys, without attempting to make me stop for a chat or for lunch. I promise I'll be back in a few hours and she nods, seemingly unconcerned. Driving after all this time takes a little adjustment but I enjoy the sense of freedom and independence and find myself wishing the journey was longer.

As I enter the long driveway leading up to Netley Hall, I feel a strange nostalgia for the grand old building. It's an odd feeling and I can't quite place it, but I feel as though I've come home in some way. There must be a reason for this and I wonder briefly what it is. Is it possible that I became a little institutionalised during my short stay? Or am I simply hankering for the comforts I recall of my days here?

Danny greets me at the door with apparent enthusiasm. 'You're just in time for lunch,' he says. We head down to the basement where not only is Laura already seated in the open-plan kitchen and dining area but so, to my amazement, are Justin and Sophie. I try to hide my surprise, and greet everyone politely.

Steaming plates crammed with gammon and fresh vegetables are brought to the table and conversation is delayed while we eat. Yes, I think approvingly, it was definitely the food I missed about this place. Sophie and Justin make their excuses after they finish eating, and head off up the stairs. I turn to Laura.

'Why are they still here?' I ask. 'You must be milking them for all they are worth.'

She smiles gently. 'You shouldn't jump to conclusions, Robyn. Justin and Sophie are both staying with us free of charge.'

'Why? Are you running some sort of cult?'

Laura smiles again. 'So charging them would be bad, but letting them without paying is equally suspicious. In any case, you must have seen that Justin is very much better.'

He had indeed behaved like any ordinary young man while we ate lunch. There was no trace left of his psychosis, no strange ramblings or pronouncements. I don't say this to Laura though. Instead, I say, 'I suppose he still believes he has supernatural powers?'

Laura nods regally, as though there is nothing wrong with this. 'Justin's parents are very pleased with the trans-formation in him. We have given him the confidence to believe in himself. In another society, he would be hailed as a shaman.'

'But he's deluded.'

'That's your interpretation. And not a very kind one, in my opinion.'

I don't like the comment but refuse to take the bait. 'What about Sophie? She doesn't seem much better.' Poor Sophie, she had been as nervous as ever throughout the meal.

Danny speaks then. 'Sophie's problems are not easy ones to solve. She has been with us for more than a year already.'

'Really? You're saying that she was just posing as a

student, on Channelling the Spirit?' I remember Sophie coming down the stairs that first morning, how I had asked why she'd been allowed to her room when I wasn't, and she was unable to answer. 'But why?'

'We don't divulge the personal circumstances of the students to each other, so everybody who comes to Netley Hall assumes, as you did, that Sophie and Justin are also new. That way, they don't have to explain themselves to the other students, they are just treated on an equal footing.'

It doesn't make sense. My face must show my puzzlement. 'It's part of the reason why we are struggling financially,' says Laura. 'Those who can't afford our services, receive them gratis. But thank you,' she continues, 'for your article about Netley Hall. It has gone some way to improving our situation.'

I feel a rush of irritation. 'I didn't want to write it that way,' I say. 'I wanted to expose the college, but my editor…'

'Jack told me all about it,' Laura interrupts.

I stare at her. 'Jack?' I repeat dully. 'Do you two know each other?'

'He's an old friend. We needed some positive publicity, so I contacted him at the paper.'

'You mean he sent me to write about the college at your request?' I suddenly get a flashback to the evening Trudy first arrived at my door, asking for Robyn Walters. Laura knew me as Robyn Bennett, or so I'd thought. I hadn't realised at the time, but she must have been aware of my real name all along, to have passed it on to Trudy.

'He said you're a good writer. He said he couldn't guarantee you'd write something positive about psychic abilities, said you were too hard-headed for that, but he said he'd make sure the piece was entertaining and that it would raise the profile of the college. He's a good man.'

That's what I used to think. 'He was wrong to use the Globe to promote your interests.'

'Jack and I go back a long way.'

'Tell me about it.' I don't mean it literally but she tells me anyway.

'His wife used to come and see me as a client, a long time ago. She became a friend, and we stayed in touch after she married. Then recently she contacted me asking for help with their teenage son.'

'Is he psychic by any chance?' The sarcasm is wasted on Laura.

'He was deeply troubled. Spirits were visiting him at night, he couldn't sleep, he was becoming unwell. I told them to remove the mirrored wardrobe doors in his bedroom, that were acting as a portal to the other side. He recovered.'

I struggle to keep the smirk from my face. Spirits stopped coming though the mirror portal, I think. Yeah, right. Or maybe Jack's teenage son just got better because he gave up smoking dope. It's not worth trying to dissuade Laura though, and the sincerity with which she relates this little story has answered one question. It's clear that she really believes in her supernatural abilities.

'So why are you telling me about your connection with Jack?' I ask.

The couple both regard me serenely but as usual it's Laura who replies.

'You are in need of all the facts now, Robyn,' she says. It's her usual oblique, mystical sort of pronouncement. She's trying to make me believe that she has some sort of special insight. I ignore it and continue to question her.

'You said the college has been struggling. Why?'

'Some people were critical about our methods. They posted negative reviews on the college website, claiming that we'd been taking advantage of the mentally ill, encouraging the psychotic to believe they have paranormal abilities.'

'And you refute that?' I say. 'Isn't that just what you did with Justin?'

'No.' She says it firmly, authoritatively. 'I told you, we helped him.'

'So why isn't there anything on the internet about the College?' I ask. 'I didn't find any negative reviews, or any information at all except what's on your website.'

'Jack dealt with that for us.'

'But why did he take down all the reviews? They can't have been all bad.'

Laura shrugs. 'An over-zealous employee, apparently. Ask Jack.'

'The thing is,' I say, 'What you're saying doesn't add up. Your course fees are sky high. Even if only one or two students paid for each course, you'd still be raking it in.

Other psychic colleges have numerous tutors. This is a one woman show. Although of course, there is Danny.' I turn to him. 'What do you even do?'

'I'm a trained psychologist.'

A psychologist. That might explain how he'd managed to build a rapport with Justin, to calm him down so quickly and effectively.

'We've got a huge mortgage,' Laura says. 'And we don't run this place on a budget. Everything is done properly. You can look at all our records, Robyn, if you don't believe us. I stay up half the night sometimes working on the finances, trying to make sure we can pay all the bills.'

'Ah,' I say. 'Finally, I understand. Netley Hall is basic- ally providing a public service. It's a charity for waifs and strays. With a qualified psychologist to counsel those students who other people might think have mental health problems, and help them to realise that they are, in fact, psychic. I'm so sorry. I can see now that I totally I misun- derstood your motives.'

48

This time the sarcasm isn't lost on Laura, but she remains calm in the face of my provocation. 'If you've already got everything worked out, why did you come here today, Robyn? What do you want from us?'

I sigh involuntarily. 'Here's the thing. Thanks to you and your friend Trudy, I'm working with the police, trying to find a missing child. And it's getting to me. I have this crazy feeling he's alive somewhere, even though I know that's not possible. I'm losing the plot. I'm racked by nightmares. And I need an out. I need you to under-stand that I'm not psychic,' I'm speaking slowly now, 'because somehow the idea has got inside my head and it won't leave me alone.'

'You have to trust yourself, my dear,' she says.

'I am not psychic!' The words explode from my mouth but Laura merely smiles.

'The things you knew about Charlotte's cancer and Sophie's divorce. You couldn't have known them other-wise.'

'I got that information from your files. I thought Trudy must have told you that. I know you two are in touch.'

'She didn't need to tell me, I knew already. I left the

office door open for you. But that was after you had made those readings. I wanted you to see the proof of what you had said, to understand how gifted you are.'

I think back. 'You left the door open for me? On the Friday night?' Laura nods. 'But that was the second time I went into the office. The first time was on the first night of the course. Tuesday. The night of the fire. The door was ajar. I went in, I read the files and then I went back to bed. Then for the rest of the week I waited for another opportunity to get back in. That time, I took my camera, for proof.'

Laura's staring at me, clearly trying to process my words. 'You're telling me you already knew about Charlotte's cancer,' she says slowly.

'Of course. Just like you did.'

'And you had prior knowledge of Sophie's operation and her divorce. Before the readings.'

'Yes. Because all of it was in your files.'

'But,' she says, 'I read your notebook. You left it in your room. You wrote about your lucky guesses, your intuitive leaps. You wrote about spirit. There was automatic writing, across the pages. I remember the words. 'Life and death.'

'Laura,' I tell her, 'when I stayed here, I kept two identical notebooks. I had one of them with me, all the time, in my rucksack. That's the one I used to write my class notes, and observations and ideas for my article. The other one was a decoy. In case you came snooping in my bedroom, spying on me. Which I know now that you did.'

There is silence as Laura and Danny absorb the implications of what I've said. I can't read his expression but she looks wounded and betrayed, which I find slightly ridiculous seeing as subterfuge is her specialist subject.

'So, you really don't have any powers,' she says finally.

'As I've said all along.'

'You don't believe in spirit at all.'

'Nope.'

'So,' says Danny, 'you think that Laura and I are charlatans. In which case, again, why have you come here today?'

'I don't have a psychic gift,' I say. 'But that doesn't mean the possibility doesn't exist – I mean, that nobody else has any powers. I don't believe in it personally but I'm starting to accept that I don't know everything. And I'm scared. I need help. The nightmares. They don't make sense and I just want them to stop. I thought maybe you could do something…I mean, maybe if you have the gift, you could find Jordan…' My voice fades away. I know how pathetic I must sound.

'Maybe,' says Laura, 'the child has gone for ever. And perhaps your nightmares illustrate this. You have tuned into the universal consciousness, whether or not you wanted this to happen.'

I don't think so. I think I am just generally troubled and my subconscious is trying to deal with the disturbance in my mind by throwing up frightening dreams, as a sort of puzzle for me to solve. But for once I don't argue. I've asked Laura for help, so I have to listen to her theories without objecting. I look down at the table, and when I look up she's still regarding me steadily.

'When I first became psychic,' she says, 'I was inundated with messages from spirit, clamouring for my attention. My parents took me to a doctor who said I was mentally ill and he prescribed medication. For a while, I floundered. Then I met Danny. And under his guidance, with his support, I chose to believe in my powers, to follow my own path in life, and to help others who are lost, as I was once. I've never looked back.'

She's opening up to me and on one level I feel touched. I also can't help thinking, sceptically, how much easier it must to be believe you have a special gift than to accept that you are mentally ill. I glance at Danny. If he's really a psychologist, surely he should have some sort of scientific understanding. But he's only nodding in agreement. 'If you believe you have magical powers, why do you feel the need to keep files on your students?' I ask.

At least Laura has the grace to blush. 'It's just the way we work. I feel that the more we know about people, the greater chance we have of helping them.'

'All of you are cheats. You have this whole networking thing going on.'

'I do have some contacts in the world of spiritualism.'

'From your days with the Mystic Angels?' I ask, but if I'm expecting a reaction from her, I don't get one.

'From the many years I have worked in this business,' she replies with dignity.

Can't she see how shifty she sounds? If mediums across the country are banding together, sharing information about their clients, it can't be anything other than fraudulent, even if they somehow convince themselves that they are doing it with the best of intentions.

'What about the internet and mobile signals? How did you block those? And why?'

'We haven't blocked anything. We just don't have access around here.'

'Netley Hall isn't that remote. Other people in the area must be able to use their mobile phones.'

'It's the countryside and there's some kind of a blind spot in the system. I'm sure the neighbours have found ways to get connected, but here at Netley Hall we've chosen not to. We really believe it's good for mind and body to have a break from all that.'

'And your website? How do you keep in touch with the rest of the world?'

'We dial up the internet when we really need to, through the telephone line. I told you before Robyn, we're not incommunicado.'

'I felt as though I'd been taken hostage when I was here. As if I'd been brainwashed.'

Laura and Danny both laugh. 'I think you're being a little over-dramatic,' she says. 'Our students don't feel trapped or stifled. They see this place as a refuge, a haven. We have people who return year after year for our courses and to catch up with us.'

'What about the Church?' Laura looks puzzled. 'The

Spiritualist Church?'

'What about it?'

'Other psychic colleges in the UK seem to have links with that church.'

'Netley Hall is secular,' Danny says.

'We see ourselves as providing a kind of security that is separate from religion,' adds Laura.

'Most people nowadays,' says Danny, 'tend not to go to church. But they still need links with the spiritual world.'

They've clearly thought this thing through. I'm starting to lose my focus again. 'You mean,' I say slowly, 'that because people don't get comfort from the church, including the spiritualist church, you fill the gap.'

'We try to help. We provide a therapeutic environment.'

That's their story anyway, and they seem to be sticking to it. I decide to leave the subject for now. So,' I say, 'about this boy.'

'Jordan?'

'Yes. Can you tell me how on earth should I set about finding out what happened to him?' I feel stupid asking, but I'm desperate.

I needn't have wasted my breath. Laura looks into the distance for a while, then eventually she speaks. 'The answers, Robyn,' she says, 'are all within yourself.'

'Great. Thanks. Thanks a bunch.'

49

Before I set off back to Brighton, I sit outside Netley Hall in my mum's car, composing an email on my phone to Jack, asking for a meeting with him first thing tomorrow. I need to get a few things straight with that man. But when I try to fire the message off, there's no internet signal. Is it really true that there's no coverage in this area? Such a simple solution. I should have looked into that, but I suppose I hadn't bothered because Jack said he wasn't going to print the piece anyway.

I drop the car off back to my mother and stay for a quick cup of tea in the garden. She must have been watering it night and day, because even in this heat it's lush and green. I am slightly taken aback that she doesn't ask about what I was doing at Netley Hall, or even about my life is in general, and she doesn't even protest when I say I need to get back to London. She seems to be, in fact, more relaxed and self-possessed than I have seen her for a long time.

I send the email to Jack when I get home and the next morning I'm at work, facing him. 'Robyn,' he says. 'I haven't been impressed with your recent performance.

You're hardly ever here, for one thing…'

'I know,' I say abruptly, 'about your connection with Netley Hall. Why you sent me there. To get positive publicity for your friend.

He looks startled, but rallies fast. 'Look,' he says, 'It's life. These things happen.'

'But they shouldn't, and you know it. It's not ethical to use the paper for personal gain. How much did Laura pay you to talk up the college?'

'She didn't pay me. She was an old friend in need. I did her a favour. It's not something I make a habit of and I'm not proud of it. But it's done now.' As if it doesn't matter anymore.

'It's not acceptable.'

'You said that already.'

'And you tampered with internet records of the college. Got rid of every trace of Netley Hall, not just the negative reviews.'

'Well, I didn't do that personally. It was all taken care of by a handy little intern, a computer whizz. Who didn't question my authority.' He's looking me over his glasses and he doesn't need to say the next words, because we can both see them hanging in the air between us. 'And neither should you.'

I push on. 'While we're on the subject, I never wanted to go to Netley Hall in the first place. Why do I get all the rubbish jobs?'

He doesn't try to deny it. But what he does say shakes me more than if he had. 'Just because your father bought you the chance to work at this paper that doesn't mean I have to treat you with kid gloves.'

I stare. 'That's not true.'

'I assumed you knew,' he says. He looks at me askance. 'I'm sorry if you didn't. But it's true. Your dad pulled some strings on the old boys' network, and gave the editor-in-chief a back-hander to sweeten the deal.'

I feel a surge of anger towards my father. What made him think he could just buy everyone and everything?

Jack's expression had softened, but now it hardens again. 'Anyway,' he says, 'You're not exactly the blue-eyed girl. I know you've been playing hookey for most of this year. Arsing around pretending to be a psychic, supposedly helping the police with their enquiries, and getting well paid for it.'

'How do you know about that?'

'Laura told me. Your detective friend is quite pally with her. How much does the Met pay the pair of you?'

I don't have to tell Jack but I want to see the look on his face when I do. 'They're giving me three thousand pounds a day.'

He whistles. 'You've got it made, Robyn,' he says. 'Look, maybe you should stick with it. We're doing fine here. I don't mind you not turning up at the paper every day and I'm happy to keep printing your pieces. Let's just forget this conversation and both move on. You're onto a cushy number, so don't rock the boat.'

I don't reply, but simply get up from my chair and leave the room. The reality is, it doesn't matter what I do, or don't do. The boat is rocking all by itself and it won't stop until the case of Jordan Taylor reaches its resolution.

50

Back at the flat, I knuckle back down to my investigation. I spend more time on social media, many hours every day now. There were answers to the Netley Hall situation, I think, and there will be answers to Jordan's disappearance too. Nothing is unexplained in the end. You just have to know where to look.

I can't believe I was stupid enough to ask Laura for help. I'll keep my own counsel from now on. I closet myself in the flat. I'm finished working with Trudy and I'm confident that Jack will keep my job open, so I just leaving things hanging at the Globe. Jack's not going to take action to end my career, because he knows I could ruin his too if I blow the whistle on his connection with Laura. For now, finding Jordan is my only work.

I've been living off toast, when I remember to eat at all, but I still have to leave home occasionally for supplies. One day I return from shopping, pack everything away in the kitchen and then enter my living room to find Katie sitting on the sofa, bathed in the early evening sunlight which pours in from the long window behind her. I feel an instinctive lurch of fear.

'I wanted to return your key,' she says innocently. She's behaving as though it's completely normal to let yourself into someone else's home and sit there waiting for them to arrive.

'Leave it on the table,' I say warily. I'm creeped out by her unexpected presence. If I'd got around to having the locks changed, this wouldn't have happened.

'So, you'll be off now,' I suggest hopefully.

She doesn't move. 'Look,' she says, 'I'm sorry, Robyn. I really didn't mean to scare you that day. I didn't mean to say all those things. I was upset. And the other thing, it's not how I told you. He dumped me…I was desperate to get him back.'

'You're not making sense. What other thing? Get who back? Rick?'

'I never had anything to do with Rick.'

'Right,' I say slowly.

'I met Toby,' she says, 'at the beginning of 2016.'

'Hang on a minute. You met my father a year before you met me? That's not possible.' Her silence tells me it is.

'We were together for six months and then he dumped me. He said he had to think about his family. But I knew he didn't mean it. I knew that his marriage was empty and that his daughter was grown up. I knew that he was just trying to do the right thing, but that it wasn't the right thing at all, not for him. So I refused to let him go.'

'You refused to let him go?' I repeat after her, stupidly.

'I followed him from work one day and he came here. I

realised who you were straight away. And then I didn't know quite what I was going to do. I considered telling you about our relationship, but I didn't want to upset your father. When I saw you put up that ad in the supermarket, I knew I had a way forward.'

'You stalked my father? You stalked me too?'

'I followed Toby. Only once. I was upset. And I didn't stalk you – I just happened to see you in the supermarket.'

'That doesn't make sense. If you followed my father to my flat, you wouldn't even have known what I looked like.'

She shrugs. 'Look, you don't have to believe me. I'm just telling you what happened. After Toby came to dinner that time and then didn't tell you that he knew me…well, after that we got talking again. He came back to me.'

'You're telling me that for the last year you've been having an affair with my father, under my nose?'

'We never met here. We went to hotels.'

'Except for the week I was away at Netley Hall.'

'Right.' Why hadn't I quizzed Joe about that when he'd wanted to tell me? I don't know what to say to this person who I thought was my friend but who turns out to be a stranger. 'There's something else,' she says. 'You may as well know now. I'm not a barrister and I never have been.'

I stare at her. This is the last thing I expected. 'But you took me to Lincoln's Inn. To your work dinner. Last New Year.'

'I was a guest myself. I kind of…snuck you in.'

'So that woman, the one you didn't want me to talk to, the one you said had it in for you…'

'Sarah. Yeah, she'd have blown it. I was actually her guest. I met her at a choir we both go to. She felt sorry for me because I spun her a line about being single and wanting to meet some decent men for a change. She invited me to Lincoln's Inn and I saw it as my chance to convince you about my work.'

The thought of Katie singing her heart out in a choir jars with what I know of her, and I put the unlikely image to the back of my mind. 'She invited you to dinner out of pity, and you repaid her by using the chance to convince me that you really worked as a barrister. You took me to Lincoln's Inn as a set up, just so I'd think you had an important job. And you made me think that poor woman had some kind of personal vendetta against you. I blanked her for the rest of the evening.' I remember the well-spoken, elegant Sarah. Why did I take Katie's word against hers?

'But why did you pretend to be a barrister?' I ask. I'm truly baffled.

'You wouldn't have wanted me as a flatmate if you knew I was unemployed. And…I don't know…I liked the idea of having a proper career. Of being respected, looked up to.'

'You set out to fool me from the start.'

'I moved in with you for a reason,' she says crossly. 'I told you. It was a way for me to get back together with

Toby. I love him.'

I can't get my head around this. 'You love my dad?'

'We're properly together now. He's left Beth. I mean, your mother. That's why I'm here. He wanted me to talk with you, doesn't want you to hear about this from her.'

'And he was too much of a coward to tell me himself,' I say flatly.

'The thing is, Robyn, everything in your life has been handed to you on a plate. You have no idea what it's like to be me, to have to hustle to even make enough to eat.' I have to stop myself from laughing out loud. Katie has not only always had more than enough to eat, she also has designer clothes to wear, and she's been living in Kensington for the last year and half without doing a stroke of work to justify her existence. She sighs dramatically. 'Look, I didn't mean to upset you. We were friends. But I love Toby and he kept trying to leave me, saying he loved your mother…it started to make me crazy.'

'I know how you feel. You hid the missing child article because you wanted me to think I was going mad, or perhaps that I had psychic powers.'

'No. I didn't want you to think that. I don't even know why I hid it. I just wanted to see what would happen.'

I ignore her. 'Then you lied to me, telling me that you'd been with my boyfriend and that he was only after me for my money, so I split up from him.'

'I was upset, I was jealous. You had so much and I had nothing. I didn't mean to hurt you. I like being your friend.'

I hold her gaze. 'I think you did. You moved into my flat because you were stalking my father. Now you have broken up my parents' marriage and messed up my life. And you're saying that you like being my friend. You've never been my friend. And if you don't get out of here right now,' I'm warming to my theme, 'I won't be responsible for my actions.'

It's true. I think it's Katie who's scared of me now, because she stops trying to reason with me and simply turns tail.

'Okay,' she says over her shoulder, as she exits the flat. 'At least I can tell Toby I tried. Goodbye Robyn.' And this time she's really gone.

51

It's late afternoon. The flat darkens as I sit alone, thinking things through. I know who I need to speak to. I just don't know if he'll want to speak to me.

I pick up the phone. 'Rick, it's Robyn. I need to see you. I have to apologise.'

Remarkably, he arrives at the flat in less than an hour. We're seated in the living room, but on opposite sofas. The gulf between us seems too wide to bridge, but I'm going to try. 'I'm sorry,' I say. 'I know that Katie wasn't sleeping with you while I was away.' Our argument seems so long ago now.

He looks confused. 'I could have told you that. I didn't know you thought I was sleeping with her.'

'You didn't? But that's why we broke up. You didn't deny it.'

'I didn't know what you were accusing me of. I thought you'd found out I knew she was having an affair with your father.'

Now I'm confused. 'You knew about that?'

He looks uncomfortable. 'Joe told me. He tried to tell you too. I tried to encourage you to ask him about it, but for some reason you didn't seem to want to.'

'I thought it was you who had stayed at the flat with her when I was away. You didn't deny it.'

'You just went off on one. As I said, I thought it was about your dad. I told Katie I was going to tell you about that, and she said that if I did, she'd throw you out of the flat. I know how much you love that place. So I kept quiet.'

The flat. I'm going to have to tell him about that. But I stall for time. 'I didn't believe Katie at first,' I say, 'when she told me you stayed over while I was at Netley Hall. I knew it wasn't true. But then when I tried to talk to you about it the next day at lunch, you said sorry and that you should have told me yourself.'

'Like I said, I was apologising for something else. It was all a bit crazy that day. I guess we got crossed wires.'

'Well,' I repeat, 'I'm sorry. The thing is, Katie's moving in with my dad now. He's left my mum. According to her anyway. And there's something else. She's not a barrister. She never even had a job, all the time she lived with me.' He says nothing. 'Don't tell me you knew about that as well?'

'I knew that from the start. I'd seen her up in court ages ago. She got off lightly, it was a case that stuck in my mind. So as soon as you introduced me to her, that first morning after I stayed over, I knew she wasn't genuine.'

I think back. 'You couldn't stop staring at her. I thought you fancied her.'

He laughs. 'Far from it. I knew she was up to something, but I couldn't figure out what. So I went round to see her when you were away at Netley Hall. That's when Joe told me your father had been staying over. I said I knew about that and I knew she was lying about her job, but she just laughed. She said the two of you were friends and that you couldn't care less what she did for a living. And, as I told you, she said if I told you about her affair with your father, she'd chuck you out of the flat. She had me there.'

The flat again. 'You said you remembered Katie from court.'

'I used to report a lot of law cases. She had a memorable face. She'd got a job as a cleaner for an old lady and swindled her out of her savings.'

I'm shocked. 'Was she found guilty?'

'She got off almost scot-free. Spun some sob story and managed to convince the judge that butter would melt in her mouth. I mean, nobody could deny that she'd done it but she got no actual punishment, bar the actual criminal conviction.'

'If she never went to work, how do you think she earned enough to cover her rent?' I ask.

'I hate to tell you this, but I reckon your dad must have been bank-rolling her.'

It's not a pleasant thought, but it is the obvious answer. 'I feel so stupid. I should have worked it all out for myself. She took me for dinner at Lincoln's Inn and one of her supposed colleagues almost let the cat out of the bag, but I still didn't realise. And she never seemed to be working very hard. She told me the courts didn't open until ten so she never had to get up early. I never thought that might be a line she was feeding me. What time do the courts open, by the way?'

'About eight in the morning.' Rick laughs, but not unkindly. 'So why did you believe her? If you'd just stayed and talked to me that day, we could have straightened things out. Instead, you just went off in a strop and then wouldn't answer my calls or texts.'

'I don't know,' I say. 'I thought she was my friend. I'm sorry.'

It's my third apology and Rick finally accepts it. 'It's okay,' he says.

'And there's something else I need to tell you,' I say. I can't avoid it any longer. 'It's about the flat. It's mine. My grandparents left it to me. They left me the whole building in fact.'

Rick's shocked. 'The flat belongs to you? Katie could never have thrown you out? But…why did you lie about it?'

'I don't really know. I didn't mean to lie, it felt like… just a fib. I didn't know how I was going to end up feeling about you. And I suppose I didn't want you to like me just because I was rich.'

'Yeah, that might have influenced me.' We laugh. It seems trivial now, the lie that has caused me so much anguish over the last six months. We can put it all behind us now, I think happily. I wait for Rick to say something, to move over to where I am sitting and put his arms around me. But long minutes pass and when he finally gets up, he says only, 'Bye for now, then. Maybe see you back at the Globe soon?'

I nod, and he's gone. I missed my chance. Perhaps I should have made the first move, reached out to him, made it clear that I want to get back together. Or maybe he just wasn't interested, because it had sunk in how I'd lied to him about the flat for all that time. Maybe that couldn't be laughed off after all. Anyway, I haven't got time to think about that now. I get up from the sofa and make my way slowly into Katie's old bedroom, my new office.

52

Sitting in that room, surrounded by all my notes and files on the Jordan Taylor case, I think hard. I can see clearly now why my life has become such a mess. I've been sloppy. Rick was right – I'm not a good journalist. I don't do my research.

I should never have taken Katie at face value. Before she moved in, I should have insisted on getting references from the barristers' chambers where she said she was based. And then, when Joe told me she'd had an overnight visitor while I was at Netley Hall, I should have simply asked him who it was.

Then, before I went into Netley Hall, I should have tried to find out more about the college. If I had, I might have found that it was Jack who'd authorised the removal of all trace of the place from the internet and I might have figured out his connection with Laura too. I could have confronted him with the fact that he was sending me on a fabricated assignment to get publicity for his friend, and then I wouldn't have had to go at all.

At the very least, when I came back from my assignment, I should at least have looked into why there was no internet or mobile signal at Netley Hall. I never even bothered to try to find out what Laura and Danny paid for the place. I still don't know whether their claim to be paying a huge mortgage is true. It may be just background, but a good journalist wouldn't have let these things go.

Also, when Trudy appeared at my flat and insisted on me working with her, I didn't get around to looking on the microfiche to try to find the story I'd read, the one Trudy had said she couldn't find. I could have proved straight-away that I didn't have any supernatural powers. Looking back, I can see so many places where I veered off course. So many occasions when I vowed myself to look into this, or that, and then just didn't bother.

It's all been a journey though. I can't regret going to Netley Hall. If I hadn't gone there, I wouldn't have met Trudy. And at least Rick and I are back on speaking terms now. My life might have been turned upside down in the last six months but I have learned a lot along the way. I can sit here thinking of all the 'should haves' and 'could haves' in the world and they won't change anything. I need to move forward.

I've certainly learned that I'll have to up my game if I want to continue working as a journalist. Knowing how to write is just one part of the picture – I also need to be organised, disciplined, focused. And the first thing I'm going to do is find Jordan.

I think hard. I've been keeping up with all my social media accounts, checking and posting regularly, but there must be something else can I do. I wonder about Denise, my old school friend. The one who'd somehow found her lost bracelet in the park all those years ago. Maybe she would have some insight. How do I find her? I start with a call to my mother, who puts me in touch with Denise's mother, and eventually I get Denise herself on the phone. She sounds lovely, just as I remembered.

'Robyn!' she sounds really pleased to hear from me. 'I can't believe we haven't seen each other for so long. You do know I've tried to get in touch with you before?'

'I didn't.'

'Your flatmate told me she'd passed the messages on, that you would call me back. And then one day she acted all embarrassed, said you'd told her to ask me to stop calling, you'd told her that all people wanted from you was a place to stay when they came to London.'

'I never said that!'

'It didn't sound like something you'd say. But I had no other way of getting in touch except the phone and I didn't just want to turn up at the door after she'd spoken to me like that. I hoped you'd call me. And when you never did, I thought maybe she'd been telling the truth.'

Another mystery solved. Since Katie moved in, I'd gradually become isolated from all of my old friends. Yet I'd never suspected that she had a hand in it. I feel foolish all over again. I should have made more effort to stay in touch with people instead of waiting for them to call me.

I launch into the reason for my call. 'I'm writing a piece for the Globe,' I say. 'And I wanted to ask you about the spiritualist church. Are you still involved in that?'

'Oh no,' she laughs. 'I never really was, once I grew up and left home. Mum believed in it, though, until the end.'

'You don't go in for any of that spiritual stuff then?'

'Not really. I mean, I don't discount it completely, but I don't go to church. Not that you need to go to church, especially not these days. Most mediums are secular.'

'Are they?' This is interesting, it chimes with what Laura and Danny had said, but it's not what I called up about. 'I just wanted to ask you about something though,' I say. 'Do you remember that time when you lost your bracelet?'

'Oh yes,' she laughs. 'I found it in the park.'

'Well, how did you find it? I mean, how do you think it happened? Was there any paranormal power involved?'

She laughs again. 'There's no secret, Robyn. It wasn't magic or anything. I just really loved that bracelet and I wasn't going to give up on it. I just kept looking until I found it – and you helped me.'

'But you said it was the power of spirit.'

'Did I? Well, I was thirteen. I suppose I was trying to show off.' This time I join in with her laughter.

I promise not to leave it so long before I call her again and I hang up.

She kept looking until she found it. Right. So that's what I'll do. I'll just keep on looking. Because the reality is, nobody vanishes into thin air. There has to be some trace of Jordan Taylor somewhere, and I'm not giving up until I find it.

53

With a pang of guilt, my mind turns to my mother. I've been so tied up with my own drama that I hadn't even spoken to her properly when I called to get Denise's number. I just discovered that my father has left her and I didn't even remember to ask after her welfare.

I don't phone her again. Instead, I get the next train to Brighton. I go straight to the house, because my mother is almost always at home. But then, to my surprise, she's not. I walk down to the Grand, drink coffee and read the papers, then try again. She's back. 'I've been waiting up the road for you, for ages,' I say.

'You should have called.'

'It's just that you're usually here.'

'I went shopping,' she smiles. I sound sulky, proprietorial, and she, to my surprise, seems absolutely fine. Then I realise that she must not even know what's happened. My father hasn't told her. Or maybe Katie was lying and he hasn't left my mother at all.

'How's Dad?' I ask, trying to sound casual. She's picked some flowers from the garden and is busy arranging them in a vase.

She turns to me. 'It's okay, Robyn,' she says. 'I know

what's been going on. Your dad told me. He said if he didn't then this Katie woman was going to. But it wasn't a shock to me. We've been drifting apart for a long time. He's been staying away from home a lot and I think I sort of knew it wasn't for work. Marriages can limp along unhappily for years, but then when someone new comes along it acts as a catalyst.'

'I'm sorry.'

She shrugs. 'When it turned out that he was having an affair with your flatmate – that did come as a surprise.'

'To me too.'

She's making tea. The universal panacea. 'Your father said he didn't know that the girl had moved into your flat.'

'Katie,' I supply.

'Yes. He said that when you invited him to dinner he was really taken aback to see her there. But then Katie explained to him that she'd been just as surprised, that she had no idea he was your father.'

'She was lying. She's a bit of a bunny boiler, to be honest.' I don't go into details.

'Oh well. He said he wanted more excitement.' She seems completely unconcerned. I'm glad she's recovered her sense of humour but the wise-cracking seems a bit odd in the circumstances. In fact, she's remarkably cheerful for a woman whose marriage of twenty-five years has just been shattered.

'Has dad really moved out, Mum? Left you? Are you okay, really?'

'Of course, I'm okay. And your father didn't actually leave me. I told him to go.'

I change the subject. 'Mum, is it true that Dad bought me the job at the paper? He paid the owner to take me on?'

She sighs. 'I told him he should leave you to sort things out for yourself, that you would get the job on your own merit. But he didn't want to leave things to chance.'

'Why didn't you tell me?'

'It meant so much to you, that you'd won the place on that graduate scheme, against all that competition. I didn't want to spoil it for you. Anyway, I knew you would have got the job anyway, even if he hadn't interfered.'

'He thinks he can buy anyone and anything,' I say bitterly. 'I can't believe how deceitful the man has been.'

I expect my mother to join me in railing against him, but instead she surprises me again. 'He loves you Robyn,' she says gently. 'He's still your father.'

54

I stay overnight and the next morning, before I set off, I eat breakfast with my mother. 'It's been lovely to see you Robyn,' she says.

'I'll visit more often now you're on your own, Mum. I promise.'

She shakes her head. 'You really don't need to worry about me. I'm fine. In fact, I'm relishing my freedom.'

'You do look better.' I don't know why I didn't notice it before. She's had her hair done again, is wearing new clothes and looks generally brighter. 'What are you going to do with your new-found freedom, then?'

'I've enrolled on a course at Netley Hall. It starts next week.'

'Tell me you're joking,' I say, but one look at my mother's face tells me she's not.

'Don't you try to tell me what to do,' she says.

'I wouldn't dare.'

I call Trudy, and ask to meet her in Benny's. While I'm waiting for her to arrive, I think about my mother. She's made it clear that she intends to be in charge of her own life so there's no point in worrying about her, and in fact

I'm glad I don't need to. I'm not concerned about her drinking any more – I have a feeling that's not going to be a problem now that she's 'free', as she sees it. I wonder how she'll get on at Netley Hall though. I will definitely need to keep a check on that situation.

There's a new waiter at 'our' café and Trudy smiles at him as she orders our drinks. When he goes off to make them, she speaks quietly. 'When I was young, it was always women who worked behind bars or serving in restaurants. Now it seems to be mostly men who do these jobs.'

'I hadn't really noticed,' I admit.

'You haven't got the perspective of age,' she points out. 'Although you are remarkably wise for your years.'

I frown. 'I've been feeling pretty stupid recently.'

'Why?'

'There's something I want to ask you first. How did you get into my flat the first night we met? The second time?'

'Into your flat?'

'Through the downstairs door, I mean. Usually I have to buzz people up. I buzzed you up the first time, I thought you were Rick. But later, in the middle of the night, you just arrived at the door to my flat. So how did you get upstairs?' I ask Trudy.

'The doorman at the Gainsborough let me in. He had a key.'

'Joe?'

'Yes.'

Joe has a key to my building, and I didn't know. That's

creepy.

'Joe thinks you work for the police,' I say to Trudy.

'No great mystery there. Gino lets me keep a warrant card and I showed it to Joe, so he'd let me in. It's alright, Robyn, you don't need to worry about Joe. I already asked him why he had a key to the foyer. He told me the old lady downstairs gave it to him years ago, so he can pick up any parcels and put them into the building if she's out. I checked with her, and it's true.'

'Okay,' I say slowly. My sudden burst of paranoia is stilled. It's a relief to know I can trust Joe. I should have just asked him in the first place who Katie had to stay over, I think yet again. I'd have known then about her and my dad. But then, maybe Rick is right and I wasn't ready to know. It would have been so easy to ask Joe for details and for some reason I'd chosen not to.

Trudy's voice intrudes into my thoughts. 'Tell me, what is it you've been feeling stupid about?'

'You remember my ex-flatmate, Katie?' She nods. 'Well, she turned up the other day and told me she didn't sleep with Rick after all. She's been having an affair with my father.'

Her eyes widen. 'Is that better or worse?'

I can't help laughing. 'It's…different. The thing is, I've woken up to the fact that she was basically a snake in the grass all along and now I'm wondering whether she might possibly have been drugging me.' Trudy listens carefully as I tell her about my sleepless nights, the vivid dreams.

'That doesn't sound like fun,' she says finally. 'I had no

idea the case was affecting you so badly.'

I don't know what to say. 'I suppose it just crept up on me.'

She looks sympathetic and I stifle a sudden urge to cry. There's nothing like unsolicited sympathy to make a person start feeling sorry for themselves.

'How long ago did she leave the flat?' Trudy asks.

'Two weeks.'

'And are you still having these nightmares?'

'Yes.'

'Then it seems unlikely she's been drugging you. Any chemicals would be out of your bloodstream by now and you'd be back to normal again.' I suppose Trudy must be right, my state of mind can't be laid at Katie's door. That's just more paranoid fantasy. After all, how would she have administered the drugs? We've hardly spent any time together since I've been with Rick. 'Have you sorted things out with Rick yet?' Trudy asks.

I start. 'I was just thinking about him!' She smiles. 'We've talked,' I say. 'But he's not my boyfriend any more. Too much water under the bridge. We're friends again though, which is good. And something else has happened. I found out why my editor wouldn't print the piece about Netley Hall.'

'Why?'

'Because he's buddies with Laura. Basically, he sent me there to write a story on the place – a positive story – because she asked him to.'

Trudy is clearly struggling to understand. 'The whole

thing was a set up,' I say. 'I found out what was happening at the college – that Laura and Danny had collected a whole load of background information on their students, with the intention of conning them. But Jack ignored it. He made me write the story they wanted, a 'fun' account of the time I spent at Netley Hall, with an assurance that the directors' intentions were purely honourable.'

'Why would he do that?' asks Trudy.

'That's what I wondered. Apparently just because he and Laura are old friends, and she asked him for a favour.'

'Ways of the world…' Trudy muses.

'And it was Jack, apparently, who removed all negative reviews of Netley College from the net. Things had been going downhill financially for Danny and Laura for a while. They wanted some good publicity to try to turn things around.'

'I have to admit, I'm shocked. I'm in touch with Laura quite regularly and she didn't tell me any of that. But she's not a bad person. She believes in her work and she gets results.' I must look as sceptical as I feel. 'Anyway,' Trudy continues, 'it's not important now. I told you, as far as the Jordan is concerned, you're off the hook. I'm sorry to have ever involved you. I've taken this as far as it would go and now I have to accept you were right in the first place. You look shattered.' She seems genuinely contrite. 'I'm sorry Robyn,' she says again. 'Not everyone is cut out for this sort of work. Now you're free from it.

Go back to your job at the Globe or find something that suits you better. Relax and forget about all this.'

'The thing is,' I say slowly. 'In theory you're right, I'm free now. Nobody expects anything from me and that's how it should be. But forget about it all? As if it was that easy. I mean, this is what I've been hoping for but now it makes me feel kind of flat. There's no closure.' I realise I've echoed the word Trudy used recently herself, in relation to the Taylors.

'Sometimes there isn't,' she says now. 'We all want a happy ending but it doesn't always work out that way. Cases like Jordan's…well, there's nothing positive to say except that sometimes the publicity they conjure up makes parents keep their children closer, or deters other people from snatching them. Statistically, these cases are no more or less common than they've ever been – like all serious crimes. It's just that we hear more about them these days, through the media.'

'It's so sad.'

'It is sad, but it's not your job any more. Forget about it. You've got enough to deal with in your personal life.'

'I just feel bound, somehow, to keep looking for Jordan.'

'You're really not,' she says. 'None of us are. The case has been officially closed. Move on, Robyn.'

55

Now so many loose ends have been tied up, I expect my life to return to normal. It is certainly quiet. I spend a lot of time alone in the flat, secure with the new locks I've had fitted, or walking the streets of London, also on my own. At some point, I resolve, I'll go back to work at the Globe. Make Jack give me a proper job, reporting hard news. I do want to be a journalist, I realise, and I'll go about it properly this time. But I'm not ready yet.

As far as Trudy is concerned, I've taken her advice and moved on from Jordan's case. In reality though, I am still obsessed with it. My nights are disturbed by dreams that usually dissolve in the morning light. One day, though, I wake up drenched with sweat. I remember every moment of the dream and I realise it's familiar, it's the same one I've had many times before. A small blond child is lost in a hot country. I'm in a small house with a stone floor. There's a trap door in this floor, and although I can't see what's happening below, I sense a scene of such abject misery that I can't breathe. It is all so unbearable, so hopeless.

The lack of sleep each night now means that in the daytime hours I feel that my mind is unravelling.

However hard I try to follow a single thought through to its conclusion, my mind drifts off. I can't concentrate for long enough to read or even watch TV. And I know what the problem is. I won't rest until I have found out what happened to Jordan Taylor. I'm going to find that child, I decide, if I never do anything else in my life.

The trouble is, I am working on the case constantly and I still don't feel any closer to the truth. I hole up in what used to be Katie's bedroom with my computer. This room is still the centre of my investigation. I have worked my list of suspects down to just eleven people and for each of them I have folders stuffed with notes, from the police investigations and from the social media accounts I have found for them or their friends. I have befriended or followed every individual who has ever known any of my suspects and I spend hours on Facebook in particular checking to see whether any of them have embarked on anything that could be relevant – a move abroad, for example, or a change of work. I am constantly working on widening my network of contacts around them.

Weeks pass and the world outside the apartment is sweltering. Occasionally I watch the tourists wander below my windows, gawping at the London life that seems so glamourous to them but is so ordinary to those of us who dwell here.

I start to feel as though I will be stuck here forever, working methodically through this evidence, time and again. I don't even go out for walks anymore, and I get my groceries delivered to the door. I no longer bother trying to force myself to go to sleep at night. Instead I stay up later and later, trawling though Facebook, Twitter, Instagram…

I'm on the edge of exhaustion but whenever I feel ready to give up, I channel Denise and think about how she looked for that bracelet, how determined she was to find it, how single-mindedly convinced she was that things would happen the way she wanted. How she persisted in looking, although I nagged at her to give up and come home with me, get warm, have tea. She followed the force of her own conviction and it worked for her.

It's going to work for me too, I tell myself. It has to.

And then one day, it happens. After a session in which I have stayed up until well after midnight on social media, I see something. It could be irrelevant, but my instinct tells me otherwise. It's a picture posted by somebody called Janice Saunders, a friend of the hotelier Helen Watkins. Watkins' own Facebook account has tight security settings – she won't accept friend requests from anyone unless she knows them personally – so she's one of the people I track through their friends and acquaintances. The picture is of two boys, standing close together. The backdrop is thick woodland and when I zoom in I see that one of the boys has a frog gently cupped in his hands. His face is looking directly at the camera and he is smiling broadly. 'Live specimen for Biology. Who says home schooling doesn't work?' says the caption and I have to smile, because these kids really do look fulfilled. But why is the picture being sent to the hotelier, I wonder? She has no children herself. Perhaps these boys are her friend's children. But they look around the same age...

By the time I've picked up the phone to Trudy the photo has already disappeared from Janice Saunders' Facebook page. I scroll through her profile. She's had a Facebook account for quite a few years and from her posts she looks like a bit of a hippy. All four of her children are home-schooled.

'Trudy,' my voice is as shaky as the hand which holds the phone. 'It's Robyn.'

She sounds sleepy. 'Yes?'

'You have to come over, now.'

She's at my door in what seems like minutes. She must either live very close to me or have red-lighted it across town. I buzz her up.

'When you interview people, when you go back to see them, do you tell them you're coming?'

'Yes, we have to make sure they're going to be there.'

'Which means, if there was something they didn't want you to see, they'd have a chance to hide it?'

'I suppose.' Her tone is cautious.

I speak slowly and clearly, so the message will sink in. 'Helen Watkins,' I say. 'The woman who owned the Sea Horse Hotel. Where the Taylors stayed in Weymouth.'

'What about her?'

'I just found out that she has Jordan.'

In the few moments that the photo was on my computer screen, I'd taken another picture of it on my phone and it's this that I show to Trudy. The boy gazes out at us, holding his specimen, his eyes sparkling with fun. Around his face is a computer-generated box and the words below it on the screen are clear and joyous, 'Facial recognition match for Jordan Taylor.'

Trudy looks hard at me. 'Where did you get this?'

'Facebook.'

'Can you show me the page?'

'It was posted by Janice Saunders, a friend of Helen Watkins. But it's not on her page now, it was taken down almost as soon as it went up. I reckon Helen saw it and made her friend remove it.' Trudy seems to be frozen and so I speak loudly and urgently, trying to spur her into action. 'Can you find him?' I ask. 'Can you go and get Jordan, right now?'

She smiles grimly. 'Helen bloody Watkins,' she says, 'will never know what hit her.'

56

One month later, and Trudy's waiting for me in Benny's, our familiar meeting place. I know Jordan and his parents have been reunited, it's been in all the papers for the past few weeks and the furore is only just dying down. I'm excited to hear all the details from Trudy, but she's busy fiddling with her coffee spoon, stirring her drink vigorously although she doesn't take sugar. I figure she's got something to say so I let her speak first.

'So how did you do it?'

'Well, as you know, I'm not psychic.' She smiles. 'I was like a dog with a bone,' I say. 'I was never going to let go.'

'The universe gave in to your demands.' She says it straight-faced.

'You sound like Laura.' She doesn't smile this time. 'Okay,' I say, 'I realise that sometimes things happen, coincidences occur, and they seem so unlikely people are convinced these events must have had a helping hand. From spirit, if you believe in that stuff. But this really was pure legwork on my part. I just kept looking. When I went to Netley Hall Laura said the answers were all within me, and I was annoyed with her for not being more helpful.

But she was right, they were. I just needed to persevere, keep plugging away at the problem.'

'The Metropolitan Police Force investigated that case for ten years. And so did I.'

'I know. But I came into it with fresh eyes. And you guys didn't specifically focus on social media. That's where I made the breakthrough.' Trudy looks unconvinced and I change the subject. 'How's Jordan?'

'He's doing okay. Staying with foster carers while he gets his head around the situation.'

I'm surprised. 'It's been more than three weeks since he was found.'

'It's complicated. His parents are desperate to get him home, but he needs time to adjust. He's still in shock. He'd forgotten his early years and come to think that Helen Watkins was his real mother. He misses her. He says he loves her.'

'That must be awful for Lionel and Lucy to hear. How are they?' I think of the broken couple and their squalid home. I suppose at least the delay has given them time to get the place cleared up before Jordan moves back in.

'They're getting all the support they need,' says Trudy. 'The social workers and police liaison officers are dealing with everything. Jordan's parents are visiting him regularly, although he's insisting on being allowed to see Helen too. In fact, there's a chance that she won't even go down.'

'What do you mean?' I'm astounded.

'Jordan has been talking about it to Lionel and Lucy. He

says he doesn't want Helen punished. He says if she gets sent to prison he'll visit her every day. His parents are worried that they'll never re-establish a proper relationship with him if they insist on a prosecution.'

Helen. It sounds odd, hearing Trudy refer to Jordan's abductor by her first name. 'Surely it's not their choice,' I say.

'I know. Gino's furious at the suggestion that she might get off without any charges. But the Taylors are backing Jordan up, saying that Helen has suffered enough already from having him taken from her. They're saying they don't want her prosecuted.'

'Surely the police have the power to prosecute whether they want it or not?'

'In theory, they do. Gino's still saying he's going to throw the book at her. She's wasted millions of pounds of public money over the last ten years, shown up the Metropolitan Police, and nearly destroyed Jordan's parents. But Lionel and Lucy have a lot of power. Things seem to go the way they want, which in this case is likely to be the way Jordan wants.'

'So she becomes Aunty Helen and visits the family every Friday for tea and cake?'

Trudy grimaces. 'We'll see.'

'I've been wanting to ask you why Helen Watkins took Jordan in the first place.'

'God knows what makes people do these things. Maybe childlessness made her crazy. There's no excuse, obviously. All she says is that she'd clocked the boy the previous year, when the Taylors first stayed at her hotel and that she'd felt an affinity with him. He was an adorable baby, she said, she couldn't forget him. And when the Taylors booked in for another holiday, she thought it was some sort of sign.'

'So how did she do it?'

'She'd been playing with Jordan at the hotel. Established a rapport with him. They used to play hide-and-seek while his parents ate their dinner, it gave them a break for a few minutes. On the day of the abduction she turned up at the beach, nipped in incredibly fast while their backs were turned, and got him to hide inside the Punch and Judy tent in a break between shows. She stayed with him, kept him quiet, pretended it was all part of the hide-and-seek game. Then when everyone was distracted searching further down the beach, she slipped away with him.'

I feel a jolt of recognition. The Punch and Judy tent. I dreamed about that once. I shudder.

'How did they even get inside though? Surely it would have been closed and secured between performances?'

'You're right. Those old puppets are valuable. But we found the puppeteer, who's ancient now and retired, and he claims to have no memory of anything. According to Helen, it just happened to be left open.'

'Right. Also, you said the police were swarming all over the place for weeks. What did she do with Jordan while the investigation was happening?' I say to Trudy.

'He stayed with her mother. Apparently, she was in the

early stages of dementia and it was no trouble for Waktins to convince her that child was her own.'

'So Helen's mother helped to hide Jordan until the initial fuss died down? From when she first took him from the beach, for – how long?'

'A month or so.'

'But if the mother had dementia, how did she manage to care for the boy? How did she do it without being detected when the whole country was looking for him?'

Trudy shrugs. 'We'll never know exactly. She's still alive but she's in the last stages of the disease now. And Watkins isn't very forthcoming. She doesn't seem to think the details matter.'

'But then what?' I say. 'I mean, how did Helen keep Jordan's identity hidden for the last ten years? It seems impossible in the circumstances.'

'She home-schooled him. Grew his hair long, which changed his appearance a fair bit. Over the years he came into contact with only a limited number of other people, many of them with alternative lifestyles who were home-schooling their own children. She'd moved away from Weymouth, to Walkford, and everybody she met there simply assumed that Jordan was her son. Of course, she also changed his name. She must have kept him at home for quite a while until he forgot what he used to be called.'

'Would he really forget his name entirely?'

'Anybody would. It's unusual to retain any memories laid down before the age of four.'

'What did she call him?'

'Sonny. Quite clever really. Probably started off using it as a nickname, until he'd forgotten his real one.'

'Is Jordan using his own name again now?'

'No. Maybe that will happen in time. As I said, he's finding it hard to adjust. He's nearly a teenager, remember. It's a difficult age for any child, and this kid has had an awful lot to deal with. He's been upset recently anyway, because Helen was planning a move abroad. She'd managed to get hold of a fake passport for him. He kicked off, didn't want to leave the country and lose all his friends. She only signed up on Facebook a few months ago, so that he could keep in touch with them.'

'We reached him just in time.'

'Yes. And only because you happened to see that photo at that exact moment. Apparently, Helen was up late and saw it get posted too. She went berserk when she saw it. Phoned the woman who'd posted and made her take it down straight away. If you hadn't seen that picture in the few minutes it was online, Helen and Jordan would be abroad by now. We might never have found them.'

'What would have happened if Jordan had got poorly?' I wonder aloud. 'Helen wouldn't have been able to register him with a doctor if she didn't have his birth certificate or national insurance number. She had no proof, really, that he existed.'

'There are plenty of people who live under the radar. Think about the thousands upon thousands of people who have entered the country illegally. They don't visit doctors, I suppose, or if they're desperate, they're pointed to healthcare workers who are aware of their situations and who sympathise.'

My mind is frantically working its way around the subject. 'How did Helen manage financially?'

'She had the money from selling her hotel. She lived quite frugally. And her new friends in Walkford thought she was a single parent who'd been abused and was avoiding her partner. She said she feared for her life and Jordan's because her ex-husband was so violent. They all felt sorry for her, helped her a bit with money and second-hand clothes for Jordan – and kept her existence quiet. Now, have you got any more questions?'

I shake my head.

'Then I want to ask you something,' Trudy says. 'How do you feel about carrying on working with me one day a week? As an investigative consultant? Paid by the Met, at the usual rate?'

The usual rate. An arm and a leg, in other words. 'I really don't think Gino will agree to that,' I tell Trudy.

'He already has.' I stare at her. 'I can square it with your boss, if you want,' she offers.

'Jack wouldn't mind me continuing to moonlight. In fact, he already suggested it,' I say. 'I must admit, I'm tempted. Especially now you're finally not under any illusions as to how I helped solve the case.' In fact, I'm aware that, if I do ever work with Trudy again, she'll probably still hope that some sort of magic is going to happen. It seems to be the way she's wired to think. 'But

surely you can find a better way to spend police money?'
I say. 'There must be better qualified people, if you really
want somebody to help you with your investigations.'

'Maybe. I want to work with you though. And Gino has
agreed. I do have to tell you though, Robyn, not every
case has an outcome like this. Remember the child, Pippa,
who we found under the bed at her family home in
Croydon?'

'Yes.'

'She'd been hurt. And she was only being hidden until
that man – a person she was taught to call 'uncle' but who
was just a sleazy family friend – could move her on
somewhere else. We busted a whole ring of paedophiles
when we arrested him. There are some truly evil people
out there. And some of them are extremely dangerous.'

'That makes me want to help you more, not less.'

'I appreciate that. But do you think you could handle
it?'

I consider this. 'I'm not entirely sure. I thought I was
starting to lose my mind at one point, you know.
Remember the day we went to Weymouth? I was so sleep
deprived I started to think that maybe, if I was in the place
where Jordan disappeared, I'd get some sort of hunch
about what had happened to him. I tried the same thing in
the Taylor's house that day, do you remember?'

'You thought you might be gifted after all?'

I laugh. 'I really think I was going a bit mad. But the
fact is, Trudy, there's a rational answer to everything,
although we might not always be able to work out what it

is. I dreamed about a Punch and Judy tent, you know, the night we got back from Weymouth.'

Her eyes widen. 'You did?'

'Yes. And for a second, when you told me Helen had hidden Jordan in there, I thought perhaps there might be some other-worldly influence at play. But then, I've had so many dreams and nightmares in the last few months. Night after night, I dreamed about a child hidden somewhere abroad, under a flagstone floor, and that didn't turn out to be true. Which means there's no reason for me to assume there's anything in the Punch and Judy dream. It was just another coincidence. Even my mother was wittering on about puppets at one point, and there's no way I'm going to read anything into that. It's just too easy to make non-existent connections about all sorts of things, with the benefit of hindsight.'

'You really think Laura and people like her are all just putting on an act?'

'Not exactly. I think some of them, Laura included, genuinely believe that they have supernatural powers. But there could be other explanations for why they seem to have special insight. For example, they've been traumatised in some way and so they've learned to be extra watchful, because they're still unconsciously looking for signs of danger. What I'm saying is that their instincts are more highly developed than those of the average person, and because of this they pick up on subtle signals in language and behaviour and manage to convince others, and sometimes even themselves, that they have mystical powers.'

What I don't say is that I also suspect there might be a connection between emotional distress and supposed paranormal abilities. I can't help wondering how many people first discover these abilities when they are in crisis, as Justin did. Although you don't have to be mentally ill to hear voices, of course. The bereaved, apparently, often hear the voices of their late beloved, which probably explains why Charlotte thought she could talk to her deceased grandmother. Voice hearing could explain Hilary's experience too, although I have to admit that story is a striking one. If it's even true. 'There's always an explanation,' I say again.

'You really don't think there was any other influence at play when you found Jordan? You just happened to be on the computer at that exact moment when Janice Saunders posted that picture of him? Against all the odds?'

'I was stalking social media night and day,' I say. 'I know what you mean, though. It feels a little like a miracle. It was unexpected, wonderful that I was there at the right time. But it really was just persistence and luck that led me to that photo.'

'You might not have a psychic gift, but that doesn't mean nobody else does.'

I don't reply. After all, I'd said the same thing myself to Laura, when I was desperate enough to ask her to use her powers to find Jordan. And before that I'd stood in the boy's room, at his parents' house, hoping for some super-natural intervention. So I suppose I finally have to admit that I can't possibly be sure that nobody in the world has psychic powers, or that there is no element of 'spirit' at play, ever. But I do know for a fact that it was sheer doggedness on my part that solved this case. I definitely did not have a helping hand from the spirit world. I suspect that Trudy thinks differently but I let it go. She has her beliefs and I have mine, and if we're going to work together in the future, we'll just have to agree to disagree on the subject.

Back at home, there's something I need to do. Someone I want to see. It won't be easy, because I'll have to swallow my pride. I remember, though, how quickly Rick came over to the flat the last time I called him, and the thought gives me courage.

I pick up my mobile and as I press the buttons my stupid stomach feels as though it's on a rollercoaster ride all over again. But when I hear Rick's voice saying, 'Hello Doris,' I laugh properly for the first time in what feels like years.